I0785414

# Redeeming Brodie

## J. Carol Nemeth

# DEDICATION

While this story isn't predominantly about NASCAR, it does contain a certain element about NASCAR within it. Due to that I would like to dedicate this book to the two NASCAR lovers in my life. The first is my husband, Mark. We've been watching NASCAR together since we've been married coming up on 40 years. His favorite driver was Rusty Wallace until Rusty retired. He's been to a few races and even took me to one, but I soon found I'd prefer to watch from the comfort of the family room as it rained the whole weekend. My husband is my rock and my support, and he's always got my back. Even amidst my several health issues, he's always there for me. No matter what.

The second person I want to dedicate this story to is my younger brother, James "Jim" Pruitt. He's always been a big NASCAR person, too. His favorite driver was Bill Elliott, until he retired. Jim has gone to many a race at his favorite Martinsville Speedway.

These two special men are more than NASCAR. They are hard workers and providers, and I'm thankful they are in my life. However, when we were young, I'm not sure that was my sentiment about my little brother, but I sure don't feel that way now. Even though I'm older, I call him my Big Bro because he's a lot taller than me. He was an immense help during the years when my parents were struggling with dementia and Alzheimer's. It was a rough time, but with his help, my sister and I got through it. She was their primary care giver, and I'm thankful for all she did as well.

I'm thankful for Mark and Jim. May God bless them both.

# ACKNOWLEDGMENTS

First and foremost, I want to thank my Lord and Savior Jesus Christ. Without Him, there would be no book, and there would be no me to write this book. My father, James Pruitt, led me to Christ when I was six years old. I don't totally remember what it was that made me realize I needed Him, but it was likely a sermon at church or a discussion with my father. He used to talk with us a lot about the Lord and emphasized our need for Him.

The Lord has been so good to me. Although it was many years before He allowed me to publish my first book, He has since allowed me to publish fifteenth. No matter what I face daily, no matter how hard the battle, He's always with me. I love these verses: Psalm 113:2 & 3 "2. Blessed be the name of the Lord From this time forth and for evermore. 3. From the rising of the sun unto the going down of the same The Lord's name is to be praised." Far too often we get wrapped up in the happenings of the day and forget to thank God for His goodness and mercy to us. But, Hallelujah! He's still there, waiting for us to call on Him and praise His name.

I want to thank my publisher, Cynthia Hickey. She's amazing. She comes up with the beautiful book covers that reflect my stories, formats the books and prepares them for selling, and supports us authors. That names just a few things, and the list goes on. Above all else, she's a friend. Thanks for all you do for us, Cynthia. You're the best.

A big thank you to my editor, Sherry Boomershine. She takes my words and makes them sparkle. She's one smart lady, and I don't know what I'd do without her. Thank you, Sherry. You've mentioned how much you enjoy my books, and I want you to know—the feeling is mutual, my friend.

And then there's Janice Bittner, my beta reader who is such a blessing to me. Janice finds the plot holes and inconsistencies in the story, even after my multiple reviews. She spots the tiniest things I've missed. Thanks, Janice.

Although we didn't travel for this book, my husband, Mark, is always ready with the RV to head out on a research-seeking mission. Whether we're hitting the highway or not, he's my steadfast support. Thanks, sweetheart, for always having my back. I love you more!

June 4<sup>th</sup> 1945
The Mountains of East Tennessee

# Prologue

"Thanks for the ride, Mr. Howard." Brodie Sawyer glanced over at the old timer sitting in the driver's seat. When the rickety pickup truck hit a rut in the dirt road, Brodie turned to stare out the front windscreen into the darkness. The vehicle had seen better days; that was for sure. A spring in the seat poked Brodie where he felt it most. Shifting toward the door, he watched as the raindrops dwindled between the creaky windshield wipers. "It would've been a long walk from the train station. Especially in this rain."

Mr. Howard cackled. "Yup. Would've been for sure. Not much of a welcome home, seeing as how you've been off in the shooting war and all. Me and the missus, well, we got us one of those new-fangled radios for Christmas. We listened when President Truman announced the war was over. Woohee, but that was good news." He shook his head as he sobered. "Not ever'body was so lucky. The Overmans over on Huckleman Holler, well, their son ain't comin' home. Real sad thing, that is."

Brodie clapped the old man on the shoulder as he recalled the faces of many of his own buddies who wouldn't be coming home. He swallowed hard at the emotions that washed through him.

Mr. Howard reached over and turned off the windshield wipers. "Looka' there. The rain's stopped."

"And just in time." Brodie's heart squeezed when a mountain cabin came into view. A couple of the windows were lit up bringing a grin to his face. Had they gotten his telegram saying he was coming home? He'd sent it a week ago, but news from outside these mountains sometimes took a while to reach its destination.

"They expectin' ya?" Mr. Howard halted the old truck on the road below the cabin. Brodie would walk the rest of the way up the drive. Ma and Pa didn't own a vehicle. They still drove everywhere in an old hay wagon, and the rutted driveway to the cabin wasn't easy for vehicles.

Brodie opened the truck door and stepped out. He grabbed his duffle bag that had sat between his feet on the trip from the railway station. Tossing it over his shoulder, he tipped his officer's cap back on his head. "I have no idea. I sent a telegram, but you know how that goes."

"Indeedy, I do." The old man gave him a gap-toothed grin and a wave. "Give your Ma and Pa my best."

"I'll do that. Thanks again, Mr. Howard." Brodie slammed the truck door and tossed a mini salute. Turning, he headed toward his childhood home. More than his ma and pa lived inside. The love of his life awaited his return there, and he couldn't wait to hold her in his arms again.

When he reached the house, he climbed the wooden steps and crossed the plank boards of the porch. How many times in his youth had he crossed this porch returning from hunting in the woods or from a school event?

Never had it meant so much to come home as it did now. He'd seen so many things over the last few years. Mostly unpleasant things. Death, pain, suffering. Everything war brought, he'd seen. As a captain in the Army, he'd led men through it all. He'd led them on missions where too many had died and the too few that had lived had become discouraged that they would lose the war. In the end, they'd accomplished their mission. They had…. He had…

He swallowed. Hard. Glancing down at his uniform to the award hanging there, he rubbed gentle fingers across its shiny surface. The Purple Heart. It was a reminder of all he and his men had endured. His leg ached—the wound still fresh and healing. Maybe one day he wouldn't hurt anymore. Maybe one day the memories would go away… Maybe.

Brodie swallowed the lump in his throat and shook his head. He lowered his duffle to the porch floor. No. It was over. He had to let it go. They did their job. No, not everyone came home. But he had. He was here. Now. And his family waited inside. Drawing in a shuddering breath, he released it slowly and lifted his hand to knock, but…didn't.

"Lord, thank you for bringing me home. I know I've said that before, and I will again. Probably over and over again. I need You," he whispered. "I need to leave the war behind and get on with my life. My family's inside. I want to move on. I need to move on. Help me."

He drew in a deep breath then released it in a rush. Lifting his fist, he knocked on the door. *Breathe in and breathe out. They're going to be as happy to see me as I am them.*

As Brodie tried to control his excited breathing, the wooden door flung open and his father stood there, his shoulders a bit stooped, a carved pipe in his hand.

"Hey, Pop." Brodie felt the grin on his lips widen as astonishment etched his father's face.

"B…Brodie?" The simple word that left George Sawyer's mouth came out weak. His features crumpled, and tears gathered in his eyes. "Son? Is it truly you?"

"It's me, Pop." Brodie stepped inside and gathered his father in a hug. "It's so good to see you."

"I've missed you, son. I've prayed you'd come home to us." George squeezed Brodie for all he was worth, then stepped back, holding him at arm's length. "Let me get a good look at you. Why didn't you tell us you were coming home?"

Brodie chuckled. "I did. A week ago. I'm not surprised you didn't get my telegram, though. You know how it is around here."

"Yup." George clapped Brodie's shoulder. "Well, it's good to have you home, son. When we heard the war was over, we prayed and prayed you'd come home." His brows lifted then he grinned. "I supposed we should tell the women folk, huh?"

"Where's Ma and my bride?" Brodie glanced around the living room of the cabin. "Are they in the kitchen?"

"Nope. They're in the back putting the little one to sleep."

Brodie had started toward the kitchen then halted. "Little one?"

Georgie gave a laugh then shouted, "Ma! Shelby! I think you'd best come out here. Now!"

Within seconds Brodie's mother charged through the doorway followed by the love of his life holding a baby.

"What in tarnation are you bellowing about, George Sawyer?" The older woman halted nearly causing the younger one to plow right into her. Etta Sawyer's eyes grew as large as saucers. "Brodie?" Her voice was faint through trembling lips.

"What is going…." His bride backed up to prevent the baby from smashing into his mother's back. Shelby peered around Ma, her mouth dropping open.

Brodie warmed at the sight of her. "Shelby." His smile widened as his young wife pushed past his mother.

"Brodie." She flew into the arms awaiting her. "Oh, Brodie. I've missed you so much."

Brodie laid his lips on Shelby's, and suddenly his world was right again. When he released her, he gave his mother a hug then eyed the child in Shelby's arms. "Who is this doll baby? When was she born? What's her name? How did you not tell me about her? Where…?"

Shelby laid a finger on Brodie's lips. "But I did, my love. I sent you letters telling you everything. Remember when I went to Washington, D.C. early last year to see you when you were there for training?"

Brodie waggled his brows, eliciting warm color in Shelby's cheeks. "How could I forget? The memory of that weekend got me through a lot of tough days afterward."

A gentle smile curved her lips. "I wrote you letters before she was born, then I wrote letters afterward telling you everything. Can't believe you never got them."

Brodie chuckled. "Think I did. Three days ago. They gave me a packet of papers just before I shipped out for home, but I was in a big hurry to send out my telegram and do the paperwork to travel that I never looked to see what they were. I'm pretty sure your letters must be in with the papers. Then on the train, I was so exhausted I slept most of the trip. Let's read them together, what do you say?"

"That sounds like a fine idea." Etta reached for the baby. "Why don't I take care of this sweetheart while the two of you get reacquainted."

"I'm not going to say no, Ma. I'll simply say thank you." Shelby dropped a kiss on the baby's cheek before Ma took her to the back of the cabin.

No sooner had Brodie brought in his duffle bag from the porch and closed the cabin door than a knock sounded.

George took a puff from his pipe and strode toward the door. "Wonder who that could be." He opened it to find the sheriff standing there, his hands on his hips, his brow drawn, and lips compressed. A young deputy stood behind him.

"Sheriff Baker?" George's hand still held the doorknob. "What can I do for ya?"

"George." The sheriff nodded as he removed his hat, his eyes scanning the room. They landed on Brodie. "When did you get home?" Without an invitation to enter, the Sheriff stepped inside and approached Brodie.

"About fifteen minutes ago. What's going on, sir?" Brodie crossed his arms over his chest. He still wore his uniform jacket.

"I'm lookin' for that brother of yorn, son. Have you seen him since you got home?"

"Bufford? No, I haven't, but like I said, I just got here. Why are you looking for him?"

The sheriff glanced at George and Shelby then back at Brodie. "There was a robbery this evening. Miller's Pharmacy in Oliver Springs. Another at the Cattoochie gas station outside o' town."

"Just hold on a minute, Sheriff—" George waved his pipe in the air, "—what makes you think Bufford had anything to do with it?"

The sheriff turned toward George and released a heavy sigh. "I'm sorry, George. Two witnesses saw him and two o' his buddies as they drove away."

"What were they driving?" Brodie removed his jacket and tossed it over the back of the armchair nearest him.

"Griff Jenkins' old Studebaker. All three o' them were inside as they sped out o' town." Sheriff Baker swiped a hand through his graying hair. "Brodie, I'm short on deputies. I could use you."

Brodie's heart sank. "You've got to be kidding. I just got home. Isn't there somebody else you can deputize?"

"Not without wastin' time, son. Besides, Bufford's likely to listen better if you're there. I've called for backup, but it'll take time for them to arrive. Come on, raise your hand. Let's get this done so y'all can get back home to Shelby." He tipped his head in the young woman's direction. "Sorry, Shelby."

Tears forming in his wife's eyes, she gave a slight nod, her chin up. "I understand."

Brodie swallowed the lump in his throat as he raised his hand. *Lord, please let this be over quickly so I can get back to my wife.*

Within minutes Brodie sat in the backseat of the sheriff's car while Deputy Harding sat in front with Sheriff Baker.

"Sorry to drag you away on your first night home, son," the sheriff called over his shoulder as they bumped along the dirt roads. "Hopefully we can find these boys and take 'em in quick like."

Brodie stared out the front windscreen. Rain began to drizzle again. *Great. Just another thing to add to an evening gone south.*

The sheriff's voice interrupted Brodie's thoughts. "It's best to try Griff Jenkins' place first since it was his vehicle that was spotted." They parked a short distance from Griff's house and headed into the woods out back where it was rumored Griff ran a moonshine still. Rumor had it that he and his friend Harper Kent ran their moonshine liquor across state lines into Georgia and North Carolina. Brodie's dad had written him a letter about it early in the war. The boys had been conscripted to serve just like most young men had, but apparently, they'd picked up their old illegal activity once they'd returned home. It sure hadn't taken them long. Running moonshine was profitable, for sure. Honky-tonks and bars all across the South and Mid-west paid for whatever they could get their hands on. Illegal or not, Brodie wasn't happy they'd gotten Bufford involved.

Brodie followed Deputy Harding through the woods, the young lawman holding his revolver in his hand. Sheriff Baker had split off to the east. Brodie sure hoped they knew where they were going. Although he'd been to Griff's place a few times, he hadn't spent any time out in these woods. Not at night and certainly not looking for a still.

When Brodie's eyes adjusted to the darkness, he spotted a dim glow ahead. "Is that it?" he whispered.

"Most likely." Harding slipped over the soggy forest floor.

"By the way, what did they steal from Miller's

Pharmacy?"

Harding cast a glance over his shoulder. "A boat load of alcohol."

"Figures." Brodie couldn't prevent the tension that tightened his gut.

They edged toward the lit area where three figures were working around a still. Brodie's heart sank when he spotted his twenty-year-old brother, Bufford, filling glass jars from a wooden bucket with a tin ladle. Brodie clamped his lips tight to prevent calling out his brother's name. He needed to allow the law to deal with this.

"Halt right there, all o' ya! Don't make a move. You're all under arrest for the illegal production of moonshine. And I'll be checking that Studebaker o' yorn, Griff Jenkins. I suspect you're transportin' it across state lines." Sheriff Baker stepped out of the woods, his revolver trained on the two men working at the still. "Griff Jenkins and Harper Kent, raise your hands. You, too, Bufford. Go on, raise 'em high."

Before Brodie knew what was happening, gunshots rang out. The sheriff fired then Deputy Harding fired. There was so much firing going on Brodie ducked for cover then sprinted to Bufford and dragged him to the ground. An all-out gunfight raged around them. Brodie glanced up as the firing ceased. Griff and Harper were nowhere to be seen, but a vehicle engine fired up and raced away at break-neck speed.

Sheriff Baker lay still on the ground. Deputy Harding leaned against a tree holding his shoulder, blood seeping between his fingers over the wound

Brodie pulled Bufford into a sitting position. "Are you okay? Are you hurt?"

Bufford shook his head, avoiding Brodie's eyes. "No, I'm fine."

"Stay put. I'm going to check on the Sheriff."

Bufford leaned against the leg of the table where he'd been working. He wrapped his arms around his knees, fear stamped on his features.

Brodie moved to the sheriff's side. The man's eyes were wide open, but it didn't look like he was breathing. A red bloom spread over his chest where he'd taken a shot to the heart. Brodie checked his pulse, and sadness filled him. This man had simply wanted justice and in return received death. His gun lay in his limp fingers.

"He's dead, ain't he?" Harding dropped his head against the tree, his face pale against the darkness of the woods.

Brodie nodded. Glancing down, he spotted a second gun lying beside the sheriff. "This must be Griff's gun." He reached for it.

"Don't pick it—"

But the deputy's warning came too late. Brodie picked it up. Suddenly, a group of state troopers surged onto the scene, and chaos broke loose with shouting and grabbing and shoving. Brodie and Bufford were arrested.

"But I didn't kill him," Brodie protested as he was led away, his hands cuffed behind him. "I'm out here because Sheriff Baker deputized me. That wasn't my gun. Ask Deputy Harding. He'll tell you."

"Sorry, Buddy. Harding's passed out." The state trooper grasped Brodie's arm and shoved him into a squad car. "He's on his way to the hospital. Looks like you and the kid are going to jail. Could be murder in the first degree for you."

Early October 1970

# Chapter One

**Skylar Simpson stood** at the dining room window staring out at the October Wyoming view. She had work to do, but she couldn't get enough of the amazing autumn colors spread across the mountain range in the distance. Having lived in Wyoming her whole life made no difference in her appreciation of its beauty. Skylar never tired of it or took it for granted. She released a sigh. Work called. She couldn't stand here all day.

Turning from the view, Skylar strode to the dining table where she'd set up her manual typewriter, notebook, and the notes her boss, Editor Megan Howard, had given her for the article she was working on. Retrieving her pen, she glanced over the notes and attempted to form a thought. Her eyes strayed again to the window. *Nope. Gotta work. My deadline is looming.*

After several more attempts with no success, Skylar dropped her pen and closed the drapes to keep the temptation of the view at bay. Once again, she settled at the table and began working. Without the distraction, she quickly got down to business on the article for the *Casper Gazette.*

She was busy typing away when something creaked on the wooden floor behind her. Before she could react, a finger slid across her neck moving her hair to the side, and a soft kiss touched her skin.

Skylar drew in a sharp breath as goosebumps danced up and down her spine. She turned to find her boyfriend, Matt Scott, grinning over her shoulder.

"Hard at work or hardly working?" He dropped onto the chair beside her.

"I was until a *big* distraction came along." She scrunched her nose at him. "Actually, I was distracted by the view earlier."

"Is that why the drapes are drawn?" A brow lifted on Matt's handsome face.

"Yup." Skylar twisted her pen between her fingers. "That autumn view is almost as distracting as a certain man I know."

"Is that so?" Matt's other brow lifted. "Well, I have an idea. Why not come out riding with that 'certain man' and get your fill of the view? The fresh air will do you good. Then you can get back to work."

Skylar waved a finger at him. "Oh no, no, no. You are not good for me, mister. I have a deadline. Your sister's coming this afternoon and is expecting this article to be finished. It's supposed to run in the *Gazette* the day after tomorrow. I can't let you or anything else distract me. Remember the drapes?" She pointed a finger at the window.

Matt grasped the finger and twined his fingers with hers. "I get it. Megan's a slave driver. What can I say? She's only my half-sister."

Skylar smiled. "You're lucky to have her. And Kate."

"Yes. And Kate." Matt sobered, his eyes on their clasped hands. "Kate is special. I'm so glad she and Gabe got together. My twin and my best friend. The perfect match."

Skylar placed her other hand on Matt's arm. "It *was* a beautiful wedding. I'd never been to Ohio before, but I'm sure they'll be happy there."

"Yeah, and Kate's bakery is flourishing. We have the advantage of Gabe's legal expertise, and now he's checking into reciprocity in Ohio before possibly having to take the bar Exam in that state. Hopefully, he won't have to take it and can practice law in Ohio and Wyoming."

"I hope so. Then Kate will have the advantage of his legal expertise too." Skylar heaved a sigh. "Imagine. A handsome husband and a built-in lawyer."

"The best of both worlds, I suppose." Matt shrugged then slid a hand onto Skylar's cheek. "Now, if I leave you alone to finish your article, will you go riding with me later? Your favorite mare, Sheba, needs to be exercised. I can't ride all the horses on this ranch, you know."

Skylar laughed. "Sure. I'm almost finished with this article, but then I need to review it to ensure it's polished before I hand it over to Megan. I'll ride with you after."

Matt leaned in and placed a kiss on Skylar's lips. No quick peck this one, but a long kiss that melted her heart and indicated just how he felt about her. He lifted his head, his eyes dark and intense. "Don't take too long, sweetheart. That's to let you know I'm waiting. For you."

He stood and strode from the room, leaving Skylar with her heart pounding and her breathing ragged. If it was hard to concentrate before, well…. She released a sigh. She'd known Megan's brother for a few years, but he'd been engaged to another woman. That was until he'd journeyed to Germany in the spring with his newly found twin sister, Kate Cigler, to discover secrets concerning their biological mother, Elena Cigler.

Skylar journeyed with them. They'd found Elena's secrets all right, and Skylar and Matt had hit it off, necessitating him breaking up with his fiancée, who was unhappy indeed.

Skylar shook her head. Enough of the past. She had an article to finish. Buckling down to the job, Skylar shoved thoughts of Matt aside. Drawing in a deep breath, she picked up where she'd left off and continued typing.

~

Skylar had just finished the article and placed it in the folio she'd hand to Megan when she arrived later that afternoon. She packed up her typewriter and was putting her notebook and paperwork in her satchel when the front door of the ranch house opened then closed. Hmm. Who in the world could that be? Nobody around the ranch used the front door, and anyone coming to visit wouldn't just walk right in. Leaving her things, Skylar strode into the living room to see who was there.

Gina Harris wore the same smirky smile on her beautiful face as she always did. Tossing her blond hair over her shoulder, she paused beside an armchair and leaned a shapely hip against it. "Well, well, well. You're just the person I came to see."

Skylar crossed her arms over her chest and leaned her shoulder against the large beam upright that stood in the middle of the room. She crossed an ankle over the other one. "Is that so? I can't imagine why."

"No?" Gina's brows lifted as she pursed her lips. "Funny how a journalist can have access to so much information but be completely in the dark about her own family history." She lifted a shoulder in a shrug. "Or are you? Can you truly be so blind? Or are you simply inept?"

Skylar felt her blood pressure notch up. She narrowed her eyes at the woman. "There's not a doubt in my mind that you don't like me, Gina, but is there a reason you've come to insult me?"

"Insult you?" Gina placed a hand over her heart, an innocent expression masking her features. "*Moi*? Now why would I do that?"

"Indeed. Why?"

Gina clasped her hands in front of her, maintaining the innocent demeanor. "I've only come to inform you of what you may or may not be aware of, dear."

Skylar's internal warning meter pegged in the red. What was Gina up to? Knowing this woman, it had to be no good. Skylar lifted her chin and remained silent. She wouldn't give her the satisfaction of responding.

A slight smile lifted the corners of Gina's red lips as she stared down her nose at Skylar. "Well, you seem to have a dreadful lack of curiosity, don't you? No matter. I'll tell you anyway." She gave a carefree shrug belying her malevolent smile. "You see, I picked up some information concerning your family. Your father, to be precise. You see—" she paused, her chin dropping and her eyes gleaming, "—it would appear, he was a naughty boy back in the day."

Skylar's heart froze. What could this nasty woman be talking about? Skylar's father had served in WWII and been awarded the Purple Heart for wounds received during that conflict. Her father, Capt. Brodie Simpson, had come home after being treated for wounds he'd garnered by saving the lives of several of his men during a mission behind enemy lines. Skylar's father was a hero. Anger filled her heart. Where did Gina come off saying he was a 'naughty boy' in his past?

"You have your facts mixed up." Skylar straightened and took a few steps toward Gina. "My father was a war hero."

"Perhaps, but that doesn't mean he didn't come home to commit a crime." Gina reached into her blazer pocket and withdrew a nail file then smoothed the edges of her long, red-lacquered talons.

"A crime? What are you talking about? My father wasn't a criminal."

Gina lifted her eyes to meet Skylar's. "Really? Then you never heard that he was a murderer?" Her tone was matter-of-fact, as if she was imparting some trivial bit of information.

Skylar's breath caught. A murderer? Not Dad. What game was Gina playing? She had to be making this up. "My father was no murderer. What are you doing, Gina? Why are you saying this? Because Matt broke up with you, you want to make my life miserable? Or his?"

Gina dropped the file back into her pocket, straightened from the chair, and strolled slowly toward Skylar. A crooked smile twisted her lips, and her eyes narrowed. "Both, perhaps, but I'll use the truth to do it." Reaching into her other jacket pocket, she withdrew a yellowed slip of paper. "I overheard a conversation the other day between two gentlemen in Gillette. One was my father and the other a business associate of his. They were reminiscing about the old days, if you will. Your father's name came up. They didn't talk about him for long, but the business associate mentioned he'd met your father back east. Before your family moved to Wyoming."

Skylar's breath caught.

"Ah, now I have your attention, don't I?"

Skylar had lived in Wyoming so long she'd forgotten her family had moved from the east. Her mother had mentioned family lived there once, but they'd lost touch with them long ago. Most were likely long passed by now.

"I got in touch with Dad's business associate," Gina droned on. "He told me your father ran away from back east because he killed a man." She held the paper out between two slim fingers. "Here's the proof."

Skylar's eyes darted from her smirking face to the paper. Was it a newspaper article? Her heart pounded. This couldn't be happening.

"Go on. Take it." Gina held the paper out further toward Skylar. "You know you want to read it. It's your family history, after all. Since your dad is long gone, it's not going to hurt him."

Skylar lifted her eyes back to Gina's. "No, but you'll do everything in your power to hurt me and my family."

Gina shrugged. "I'm sure Matt will find it most interesting."

Skylar sucked in a ragged breath and took the paper—a folded article from a Tennessee newspaper dated June 1945. It stated that a man named Capt. Brodie Sawyer had been arrested for the murder of Sheriff Baker. Skylar shoved the paper back at Gina. "This isn't my father. It's a coincidence that his name is Brodie. You know our name is Simpson."

"Tsk, tsk, tsk. My goodness, Skylar. Haven't you been listening? Your father killed the good sheriff then he ran away to Wyoming with your family. He likely escaped jail. Doesn't it make sense that he would change the family name?" The self-satisfied smirk on Gina's face galled Skylar.

*Lord, I could use Your wisdom and discernment here.* Skylar lifted her chin. "You're simply jealous that Matt dumped you, Gina, and this is your way to get even. Perhaps you should have a talk with him."

"Perhaps, but the person you should talk to is your mother." Gina turned and sauntered toward the exit. "She'll have a lot of explaining to do since your dad's not around to do it. When she does and you find out the truth about him, you can tell Matt yourself. Then he might not be so happy to have the daughter of a murderer for a girlfriend." She turned at the doorway to the foyer. "I'll be waiting in the wings when he realizes that." She tossed a wave with her fingers. "Toodle-oo."

~

Matt removed the halter from Cochise and closed the stable door. He gave the Arabian one last stroke down his muzzle then headed to the tack room to stow the halter away. He was getting antsy. He'd worked with Cochise to while away the last few hours until he could ride with Skylar. It was time to see if she was finished with that article she was working on. The journalist side of her had won out, and she'd forgotten their date to ride. Closing the barn door, he strode across the yard toward the ranch house.

"Hey, Matt. Hold up."

Matt turned at the sound of his dad's voice. Mark Scott strode toward him from where he'd just stepped out of his pickup truck.

"Hey, Dad. Where have you been?" Matt shoved his cowboy hat back on his head and propped his hands on his hips.

"I was over at Frank Hickham's ranch. He's willing to loan us a bull for breeding. We'll give him a descent percentage of the newborn herd."

"Sounds like a good swap."

They headed toward the ranch house. "I thought so. Frank's easy to work with. So, what have you been up to this morning?"

Matt told him. "I'm anxious to go on a ride with Skylar. It would do her good to get out and get some fresh air."

Mark clapped his son on the back. "Wouldn't hurt you to spend some time with that young lady either. Have I told you how much I'm glad you and Skylar got together? She's a great gal, son."

Matt laughed. "Only a time or two, or a dozen." He sobered. "I know, Dad. I was on the wrong track with Gina, but then I didn't know the Lord back then."

Their boots clicked on the patio paving stones as they approached the sliding glass doors into the house. "I know. Me either." A grimace crossed his dad's features. Then he smiled. "Knowing the Lord has made a huge difference in both of our lives." He reached for the door handle and slid it back. "Come on. Let's see what that gal of yours is up to."

Matt removed his hat and hurried through the house to the dining room where he'd left Skylar that morning. The room was empty, and her typewriter was gone. No sign she'd ever been there. He strode through to the living room thinking she'd finished up and might be waiting there. With the cooler fall air outside, she loved reading by the fire when she wasn't working.

His dad followed him into the living room. "I bet she's

in the kitchen with Mrs. Holcomb. It's after lunchtime. Did you eat lunch? I grabbed a bite with Frank."

"I ate with the boys at the bunkhouse. Harvey had a good meal cooked for the ranch hands, and I didn't want to disturb Skylar by coming back in." Matt hurried back through the dining room in the direction of the kitchen. There amongst the industrial-sized appliances stood the housekeeper/cook, Mrs. Holcomb, already preparing the evening meal. She was alone.

"This isn't good." Matt leaned a hip against the huge island in the middle of the room, his dad stopping nearby.

"No, sir, it sure isn't." Mrs. Holcomb turned from the sink where she was washing vegetables. She dried her hands on a dishtowel then tossed it over her shoulder.

"Skylar was working on an article in the dining room this morning, and she promised to go riding with me this afternoon after she finished it." Matt lifted a shoulder and shook his head. "I can't find her anywhere. Her things are gone." He paused. "Wait a minute. What did you say, Mrs. H.? You know something about Skylar?"

The housekeeper crossed her arms over her chest and nodded. "I'm afraid I do. She's gone."

"Gone?" The word shot from Matt. He straightened. "What do you mean, she's gone? Where'd she go?"

Mrs. Holcomb's brows lifted. "Said she was going home. Needed to see her mother."

"I don't understand." Confusion etched Matt's features.

His dad held up a hand. "Martha, can you explain what's going on?"

"Indeed, I can." The housekeeper huffed out an indignant breath. "*That* woman showed up and said some terrible things. I heard it all. They didn't know it, but I was listening. Yes, I know eavesdropping isn't right, but in this case, it's probably a good thing I did. If I hadn't, you wouldn't know what happened to Miss Skylar, right?"

"Martha, we don't think any worse of you because you

eavesdropped. Certainly not in this case. Now—" His father drew in a deep breath and placed a hand on his son's shoulder, "—please tell us who 'that' woman was and what she said."

Mrs. Holcomb nodded. "Why, yes, of course. It was that Gina woman. Your old flame, Mr. Matt. She came by here to talk with Miss Skylar. That woman had no good up her sleeve." Mrs. Holcomb huffed and shook her head. "I still can't believe—"

"Mrs. H., what did she say?" Matt patted the housekeeper's shoulder. "We need to know."

"Yes, sir. She called Miss Skylar's father a murderer. Had some kind of paper and said it proved it. She said Miss Skylar's father ran away from back east and brought his family to Wyoming. She told her, Miss Skylar, that is, that you wouldn't want her anymore because she was the daughter of a murderer. That Gina woman said she'd be waiting in the wings when you realized it."

Matt saw red. Was this a scheme of some kind on Gina's part to get him back? Had she made the whole thing up? It certainly seemed farfetched. Was there any truth to the story? He didn't care what Skylar's father had done. Her father could be Jack-the-Ripper for all Matt cared. It wouldn't change how he felt about Skylar. He intended to marry her and had planned to ask her soon. Matt turned toward his dad. "I have to go after her. She must be confused and afraid. No telling exactly what Gina told her. I want to see for myself what that article said."

A furrow dug between his dad's brows then he smiled. "I'd be surprised if you didn't. Go, son. She's worth fighting for. I knew Brodie Simpson, and he was a good man. I didn't know him in the war, but I did know him in Gillette. He was an honest business man, and I did a lot of business with him until his death. Get to the bottom of this. If you need anything, and I mean anything, call me."

A lump formed in Matt's throat. He'd seen firsthand,

time and again, the generosity of his father. Most recently he saw it displayed when he'd helped save Matt's twin sister's bakery. "I will."

He glanced at the housekeeper. "Mrs. H., did Skylar finish her article? Did she leave it for Megan?"

"Indeed, she did." She pointed at the small table and chairs arranged by the window in the corner. A black folio lay on the table. "She left it there for Miss Megan when she comes later this afternoon."

"She didn't miss a beat, did she?" Matt shook his head. "Even in her distress, she made sure Megan had what she needed."

"That's our Skylar." Dad clapped him on the back. "Son, now that you know Megan's taken care of, you should go pack for a few days. You don't know what's ahead."

"Yeah, I'll do that." Matt started to leave the room but instead grabbed his dad in a hug. "Love you, Dad. I'll stay in touch."

He returned Matt's hug then held him at arm's length, the emotion evident in his father's eyes. "Don't worry. If Gina shows up, we won't tell her where you went."

Matt chuckled. "Thanks." He turned toward Mrs. Holcomb, but before he could say anything, she did.

"Don't worry, Mr. Matt. She'll get nothing from me."

Matt gave her a quick hug. "Thanks, Mrs. H., and thanks for eavesdropping. You have my permission to do it any time Gina comes around."

# Chapter Two

Skylar dropped her overnight bag, typewriter, and satchel on the floor beside the couch in the living room, planning to put them in her room later. She had to find Mom who was most likely in the kitchen where she spent most of her time baking and cooking. It was far too soon for her youngest sister, Becka, to be home from school yet. Her other two sisters, Holly and Charlotte, or Charlie, were away at college.

"Mom?" Skylar called as she wove her way through the house. "I'm home. Mom? I need to talk to you." Skylar stepped into the yellow and white kitchen that hadn't seen an upgrade since the house was built. Dad had wanted to, but money had always been tight. Then he'd gotten sick and passed before he could make any changes. Mom never complained though.

"Mom?"

She wasn't in the kitchen. Skylar hurried to the back door that led to the backyard. Perhaps she was hanging out clothes. Slipping outside, she spotted her sweet mother doing just that. A wicker laundry basket at her feet, Mom clipped sheets to the clothesline as a soft breeze lifted them, causing a gentle snap to the fabric. They would smell so clean and crisp from the fall air once they were placed on the beds. Skylar's heart sank. Too bad she wouldn't be around to smell them.

"Mom?"

Shelby Simpson turned at the sound of her daughter's voice, a bright smile transforming her face. "Sky? Honey, you're home earlier than I expected. Was Megan happy with her article?" She clipped the last clothespin into place and bent to retrieve the clothes basket. She strode across the yard to meet Skylar who skipped down the back steps and rushed toward her mother. Mom gave her a hug. "I know it's only been two days since you drove out to the ranch, but it seems a lot longer. I miss you when you're gone."

Skylar wrapped an arm around her mother's waist and leaned her head against her mother's graying brown hair as they turned back toward the house. Was it possible to have the sweetest mother in the world? "I missed you, too, Mom. I finished the article and left it for Megan, but I left before she arrived to pick it up."

They stepped into the kitchen, and Mom stowed the laundry basket in the little space where the old-fashioned electric wringer washing machine stood. Another outdated item Dad had wanted to upgrade but never seemed to afford to. Skylar was saving to do just that as a surprise for her mother. She just wasn't sure when that would happen. Now, it would have to wait a bit longer.

"Oh? Why was that? Didn't you want to see Megan? She was coming from Casper, wasn't she? Or will you see her here in Gillette?" Mom walked to the fridge and took out a bowl to begin lunch preparations.

"No, I…I won't see her this time." Skylar inhaled a deep breath and released it all at once. "Mom, I have something I need to discuss with you. Something I need to know."

Her mother turned toward her, leaning her hip against the counter and crossing her arms over her chest. "Your tone sounds serious. What is it?"

"It is serious. Someone handed this to me today." She tugged the newspaper article from her jacket pocket and handed it to her mother, then she removed her jacket and hung it by the back door. "This person said Dad was a…a murderer."

Mom gasped as her hand flew to her breast. "Sky! Your father was no murderer. You must know that." She opened the folded piece of newspaper. "What is this?"

"Read it." Skylar pulled out a chair at the kitchen table and dropped onto it. "I need you to tell me what happened."

Her mother's forehead wrinkled. She pulled a pair of reading glasses from her apron pocket and slipped them on. After several moments, her head began to shake back and forth as if in denial. Folding the paper again, she closed her eyes for several moments before laying the paper on the counter. She shoved a lock of her hair back then put her hands into the pockets of her floral apron. "I can't believe this. I just can't. After all this time…."

Skylar stood and approached her mother. "What do you mean? 'After all this time.' What does that mean?" She placed an arm around the older woman's shoulders.

Shelby clamped her lips tightly together, her eyes skimming her daughter's face. Drawing in a ragged breath, she swallowed hard, then shook her head. "I…I don't know all the details, Sky. All I know is something terrible happened the night your father returned home from the war. After he was deputized by Sheriff Baker to go find your father's brother, Bufford, they went to Griff Jenkin's place and found Bufford there along with Griff and Harper Kent. They were moonshiners. A shootout ensued, the sheriff was killed and his deputy was shot and injured. Your father and Bufford were arrested for the murder of the sheriff.

"A couple days later, your father came home and told me we had to pack up and leave right away. He said we'd never be able to go back." Mom pulled her hands from her pockets and twisted her fingers together. "We moved out here to Wyoming where your father thought nobody would know us or find us." She studied down at her fingers. "You were just a tiny thing back then. Not even a year old. Our last name wasn't Simpson back then. It was Sawyer." She met Skylar's gaze. "Your father changed it to Simpson when we moved here. His father, your grandfather, took us in his wagon into Oliver Springs where your father bought a used car. Then we drove out here to Wyoming. He got a job at one of the local grocery stores. It wasn't long before he was managing that store. Then he decided to strike out and start a store of his own. Next thing you know, he had two. But then, you know the rest of the story."

Skylar gently squeezed her mother's shoulder. "Yes, I do, but I didn't know any of the early history." She leaned her head against her mother's. "You know I have to go find out what happened, don't you? I have to go prove Dad wasn't a murderer. I have to find out why he felt the need to leave Tennessee in such a hurry."

Mom whipped around to face Skylar. "No, you don't." She snatched the newspaper article from the counter. "This means nothing, Sky."

"Yes, it does. Gina, Matt's ex-girlfriend is the one who gave it to me. She's threatened to tell Matt all about it, and you and I both know what kind of spin she'll put on that tale." Skylar took her mother's hands within her own. "Mom, I love Matt, and he's worth fighting for, but until I figure out what happened in 1945 and lay this issue to rest, Gina will always hold this over our family's heads.

"She's simply that spiteful. I saw how mean she was when Matt's sister, Kate, came to Scott Ranch for the first time. Gina wouldn't even acknowledge that Kate was Matt's sister, no matter how much they looked like twins. Sadly, Gina is a hateful person. I've tried praying for her, and of course, I'll continue to. It's going to take the Lord to make a change in her life. But I will fight for Matt, and I'll fight to protect our family. I don't want her vengefulness to make things hard for you or the girls."

A sigh escaped Shelby's lips. She placed a tender hand

along her daughter's cheek. A soft smile eased the tension on her features. "I know, sweetheart. That's a fine young man you've fallen in love with. As you say, he's worth fighting for. And our family is worth fighting for. I would love to go back east with you, but with Becka in school, I can't. I'm not as worried about Holly and Charlotte right now."

"I know, Mom. Holly and Charlie need to concentrate on their studies. Holly will graduate in the Spring and Charlie's a sophomore. They'll be fine." Skylar squeezed her mother's hands. "Do you know of any family who might still be living back east?"

Shelby shook her head. "Your father said we had to cut all ties when we moved out here. My parents and grandparents had already passed before we left. You and I were living with Brodie's parents when he came home from the war, but I have no idea if they're still living or not. I don't know what happened with his brother, Bufford, after he was arrested. Last I knew he was still in prison."

Skylar wrapped her arms around her mother. "It'll be okay. I'll pack a bag and head to the airport as soon as I can get a flight. Don't worry about me. You know Who will be with me. He always is."

"I know, darling. The good Lord will go with you wherever you go. I'll pray for you constantly. I love you more than you can ever know."

Skylar held her mother at arm's length and smiled. "Oh, I have a pretty good idea. I love you too."

Her mother cocked a brow at her. "I know you do, but until you've been a mother, you have no idea what a mother's love is. I won't rest until you're home safely."

~

Skylar's plane landed in Chicago where she had a few hours' layover. She found a coffee shop to while away some time and watched passengers scurry along the concourse on their way to and from their planes. O'Hare International

Airport certainly was a busy place. Skylar and the others who had flown to Germany in the spring had flown through Chicago. She'd been amazed then at the masses of people who passed through.

She sipped her coffee and nibbled on a pastry. It failed to meet the quality or taste of the ones made in Kate's bakery in Ohio. Her friend had brought some samples on the trip to Germany and spoiled them all for any other pastries.

Skylar released a heavy sigh. Oh, how she missed her friend. What she wouldn't give for a long talk with her right about now. Had Kate and Gabe returned from their honeymoon in Greece? A smile lifted the corners of Skylar's lips before she took another sip of her coffee. Gabe had wanted nothing but the best for his bride. The young lawyer had moved from Wyoming to Ohio to live with her in her home, for goodness sake. He'd travel back to Wyoming when they needed legal advice at the ranch if a phone call wouldn't suffice.

Skylar's smile faded when Matt's grinning face appeared in her mind's eye. How much did he truly care for her? Would he believe the story Gina would tell him? Had she already told him about Skylar's dad, and what kind of spin would she put on her story? It wouldn't be good, that was for sure. When Gina finished with him, Matt wouldn't have any feelings left for Skylar. She wished she could've stayed and denied everything to him, but without proof, how could she?

Skylar shoved the unfinished pastry away and sipped the tepid coffee. Suddenly sour in her mouth, she gathered the cup and the pastry and tossed them in the nearest trash can. Picking up her small suitcase, she slung the strap of her purse on her shoulder and meandered down the concourse. With time remaining until her flight, she checked out a couple of shops then slowly headed toward her gate.

"Skylar Simpson? Is that you?"

A familiar voice drew her attention to the gate seating

area on her right. Shock filled Skylar as none other than her friend, Kate, ran toward her and gathered her in her arms.

"Kate?" Skylar hugged her friend then held her at arm's length. "What are you doing here?"

A wide smile lifted Kate Flanagan's lips. "Why, I'm here with Gabe." She turned and pointed at the young man standing by their carry-on luggage. "We're returning to Ohio from our honeymoon. Come on."

Kate tugged Skylar toward her husband.

"Skylar?" Gabe's smile grew when he saw her. "What are you doing here?" He wrapped her in a hug then released her, his eyes filled with concern. "Is everything okay?"

Skylar sighed. "No, not really."

Kate slid an arm around Skylar's waist. "What's wrong? Are you traveling alone? Do you have time to sit and tell us about it? Our flight doesn't leave for over an hour."

Skylar nodded. "I still have time until my flight departs."

"Here, sit down." Gabe made room for her before they all sat. "What's happened?"

Skylar told them all that Gina had told her. She withdrew the newspaper article from her purse and handed it to Gabe. "I left before I saw Matt and hurried home to talk with my mom. She couldn't tell me much. I'm flying back east to discover for myself what happened and try and clear my father's name. I don't believe he was a murderer. There has to be more to the story than what that article indicates."

Gabe lifted his eyes from the newspaper clipping to hers. "It is vague. Simply because he was arrested doesn't make him a murderer. He could have been cleared and released. Perhaps he found it best to take his family and leave town for a good reason. Without him around to tell you, there's not much to go on, especially if your mom doesn't know anything."

"Exactly why I have to go back to Tennessee and try to find out for myself." Skylar accepted the clipping Gabe held out to her. She folded it and returned it to her purse. "I don't even know if I have relatives still living back there."

Kate laid a gentle hand on Skylar's arm. "I'm so sorry. Gina can be…difficult. If she doesn't get her way, then she makes things burdensome for those around her. She wasn't happy when Matt broke up with her and started dating you." Her lips turned up at the corners. "Were things still going well with Matt before this happened?"

Skylar nodded, warmth invading her face. "Oh yes. Most definitely."

Gabe chuckled. "Then that's likely why Gina decided to stir up trouble. Has she seen you two together?"

"I would think so." Skylar lifted a shoulder and smiled. "It's not like we've hidden our relationship. We've been going to church together as well as to several public events in Gillette. There were the rodeos this summer and the cattle auctions. Gina certainly saw us there. Matt isn't shy about holding hands or…well…you know…."

A sly smile slid across Gabe's lips. "Kissing? Who, Matt? A red-blooded male? Now why would he do that?"

Skylar rolled her eyes, ignoring his comment. "Anyway, I think that should answer your question."

Kate laughed. "I believe it does. I have to say I'm proud of that brother of mine. For one thing, he's going to church, and for another, he seems to pay an awful lot of attention to you. Good for him." She chuckled. "And you."

"I think so." Skylar's brows lifted then gathered in a frown. "Unless he believes what Gina tells him."

"I've known Matt Scott for a long time." Gabe crossed his ankles in front of him and leaned back in his seat. "He has more sense than that."

Kate nodded. "Even though I haven't known Matt that long, I believe he does too. And, Sky, that's where trust in a relationship comes in. Of course, you can't speak for him right now because you left before you two talked about this. You're simply going to have to trust him until you do. If you can't now, how will you trust him later when your relationship becomes more serious?"

Skylar stared at her fingers as she twisted them in her lap. How indeed? Did she trust Matt to still care for her no matter what? Her heart constricted. To tell the truth, she wasn't sure. Or perhaps she was uncertain of Gina's ability to wheedle her way back into Matt's good graces. Especially in Skylar's absence. The woman was far more beautiful and charismatic than Skylar was. Had that been Gina's plan all along?

Finger's snapping in front of Skylar's face drew her back to the conversation. "Where did you go, my friend?" Concern etched Kate's brow.

Skylar shoved her hair behind her ear. "Sorry. I was thinking about the trust issue."

"And?" Kate cocked a delicate brow.

"What if Gina manages to spin the story in such a way that Matt believes it? She'll go after him while I'm gone. You know she will. That's the point of this whole debacle."

Kate pressed Skylar's hand within her own. "Dear Skylar. Gina can try to do her worst. You don't think for a minute that brother of mine will sit back and do nothing, do you?"

Gabe huffed. "Of course not. I'm sure he's already making a plan."

"A plan?" Skylar's gaze ping-ponged between them.

"Yep. He'll figure out some way to help you." Kate patted Skylar's hand.

"So-o-o, I should…?

"Go on your way. Do what you planned to do." Gabe lifted the palm of his hand. "There's no way of knowing Matt's plans. Only God knows that. Hopefully Matt is seeking the Lord's will in all this just as you are. We'll be praying for both of you."

"And Gina." Kate tossed in. "She certainly needs prayer."

"Can we pray with you now?" Gabe asked, leaning forward, his hands clasped between his knees.

"Please." Tears formed behind Skylar's eyelids as she bowed her head. *Thank you, Lord, for allowing me to run into my friends here in the airport. I needed this, and You knew that. My goodness, what a blessing. What an encouragement.*

"Dear heavenly Father, we pray for our dear friend, Skylar." Gabe's deep voice was soft as his words lifted toward heaven. "She's in quite a quandary—put there by someone who doesn't know You, yet we know that even in this, You are in control. Please keep her safe as she travels back east. Guide her every step of the way. Protect her as she seeks the truth about her father, and may she find that truth if it's Your will. We also pray for Matt. Work in his heart that he will seek and find the truth. Give him discernment when it comes to Gina and her words to him. Give Matt wisdom in what You would have him to do in this situation. Guide and direct in the relationship between Skylar and Matt, and bring all things to pass according to Your will. We love You, Father. May all things be done for Your honor and glory. Amen."

Skylar lifted tear-filled eyes. "What would I do without you two? You're the best, you know that?"

Kate removed a tissue from her purse and handed it to her friend. "You're not so bad a friend yourself. I wish we could go with you to Tennessee, but there's a bakery in Ohio we need to get back to. My great-aunts and great-uncle need some relief from working hard while we've been gone."

Skylar slipped an arm around Kate's shoulders. "I appreciate that, but I'll be fine. You go home and take care of your business. Eat some of those delicious pastries for me."

Kate laughed and wrapped Skylar in a hug. "We'll keep praying," she whispered. "I love you, dear friend. God's got this, and He'll be with you every step of the way."

Skylar eased out of the hug and gave Kate a watery smile. "I know. I love you too."

After Gabe gave Skylar a hug, he stepped back and looked her in the eye. "If for any reason you need legal advice, call me. No hesitation. Just call."

Skylar gave a nod. "I will. Thank you."

Gathering her suitcase, she turned to head down the concourse but gave a final wave to her friends before making her way toward her gate. *Thanks again, Lord, for the precious few minutes spent with dear friends in this busy airport. What an unexpected blessing. But that's just like You, isn't it? 'Surprise! Here's your blessing, Sky.' And right when I needed one. What a great God You are.*

# Chapter Three

**With his duffle** bag in hand, Matt headed to his pickup truck to toss it inside. Then he strode toward the ranch office near the barn where his dad spent much of his time poring over the business ledgers. A smile lifted a corner of Matt's lips. Mark Scott kept this ranch running seamlessly. There wasn't anything that happened here that Dad didn't know about, and that included all thirty ranch hands. Dad might be fairly strict when it came to rules, but he was fair, and the men loved working for him.

Matt grabbed the doorknob and yanked it open. He was heading down the short hallway to an office when he heard men's voices. Matt stopped at the open doorway and spotted Clayton Vázquez, the ranch foreman, standing beside his dad's desk, his arms folded over his chest, his cowboy hat held in one hand.

Dad frowned and shook his head. "Take several of the boys and go find those cattle, Clayton. Get the others to mend that fence. We can't afford to lose any more cattle. If you think it was a hundred head or so, that's significant. Let's get this taken care of as soon as possible."

"Yes, sir, Mr. Scott. I've already got twenty of the boys out attempting to round 'em up now. I'll put the rest on the fence." Clayton turned to spot Matt in the doorway. "Hey, Mr. Matt. Want to go round up some cattle?" A grin lifted a corner of his mouth.

Matt shook his head. "I'm afraid I can't go along this time, Clayton. I have to go round up my girlfriend."

One of Clayton's brows lifted. "Say what? Miss Skylar? Where'd she go, *mi amigo*?"

Matt sighed. "She took some bad advice and left town. I...I need to go find her."

"Oh, sorry to hear that." Clayton's lips twisted. "She's a nice lady for you, Mr. Matt. Go bring her home."

Matt chuckled. "I'll do that."

Clayton clapped his cowboy hat against Mark's back. "Okay, boss, we'll take care of the cattle and the fences. I'll report back to you later."

"Right, Clayton. Keep on 'em." Matt's Dad leaned back in his office chair, which released a squeak.

Clayton donned his cowboy hat then slapped Matt on the shoulder. "Safe travels, *mi amigo*. Bring your lady home soon."

"I will. You bring those cows home soon as well," Matt's voice followed the foreman down the hallway.

"You bet we will," Clayton called from the exit just before the door slammed behind him.

Matt met his father's eyes as he moved to the edge of the desk and sat on the corner.

"You ready to go?" His dad clasped his fingers across his stomach.

"Yeah." Matt gave a brief nod. "My bag's in the truck."

"You know if you need anything while you're away, all you have to do is call, right?"

Matt smiled. "Understood. I appreciate that, but I should be all right."

His mouth pursed as he blinked several times. Were those tears gathering in his eyes?

"Don't worry about me, Dad."

He waved a dismissive hand. "Who's worried about you? I'm concerned about Skylar."

Matt chuckled. "Sure. I'll take care of her when I catch up to her at her mom's house."

"Then you'd better get a move on." When they stood, his dad grabbed him in a hug. "Be careful, son. I don't know what path the Lord's got laid out ahead of you, but take care of yourself."

"I might be home by dark, Dad." Matt laughed and returned his father's hug.

"Something tells me that won't happen. Be safe. I'm praying for you."

"I'll do my best."

Matt strode across the barnyard toward his truck. As he opened the door, he heard his name called from the direction of the house.

"Hello, Matt." He turned to find Gina strolling toward him, her blonde hair lifting in the cool afternoon breeze.

Matt slammed the truck door and walked toward Gina. A surge of anger welled up inside that he hadn't felt in…well, he couldn't remember feeling anger like this in a long time. "What are *you* doing here? Haven't you done enough damage for one day?"

"What? Me? What do you mean?" Gina halted a couple of steps from Matt. She lifted a shoulder and blinked, shoving her hands into her rear jean's pockets.

"You know exactly what I mean." Matt propped hands on his jean-clad hips. "That cockamamie story you spouted to Skylar this morning sent her flying out of here. That's what you intended, wasn't it? You wanted her gone. Now you're here to tattle, right? You want to tell me the same sordid tale."

Gina's chin lifted and her lips pouted. "It may be sordid, but it's the truth, Matty. Skylar's father was a murderer, whether you want to hear it or not." She slipped closer to him, her hand resting on his arm. "There was a newspaper article. You can't argue with facts." Her voice wheedled softly, "Besides that, a business associate of my father's knew Skylar's dad from back east. He knew the history, and he told my dad Skylar's father had killed a man. I heard it with my own ears."

Matt shook Gina's hand from his arm. "Don't touch me. I don't want to hear anything you have to say." He whipped around to return to his truck.

"It's the truth, Matt." Gina followed close behind. "You can't run from the truth."

Matt jerked the truck door open and turned back to face the irate woman. Somehow, she wasn't as beautiful as he once thought. "We'll see. One thing I can do is run from you."

He climbed into the pickup and slammed the door closed. Starting the engine, he jammed it into gear. In a swirl of dust, Matt sped down the long, dirt driveway toward the road to Gillette, putting as much distance as possible between him and the woman he once thought he loved. As soon as he hit the pavement, he drove as fast as he could to find the woman he now loved more than life.

~

At first Skylar thought the road from Knoxville to Oliver Springs had seen better days, then she changed her mind. It likely had always been a bad road. Pitted with potholes and missing pavement, she swerved the rental car and shook her head in disgust. Everyone talked about how bad the roads in Wyoming were due to long, harsh winters. They had nothing on this road.

Without warning, a deer stepped out in front of her headlights and stopped in the middle of the road, forcing Skylar to slam on her brakes. Fortunately, there were no cars behind her. There hadn't been for miles. With eyes blinking, the doe stared at her, unmoving.

"Really?" Skylar beeped her horn. "Aren't you supposed to be afraid of cars? Move along, Mama. I've got places to go."

Another smaller deer stepped from the foliage along the

roadside and joined the first. White spots decorated her back.

"So that's why you're not moving, huh? You're waiting on your baby. Had her in the spring, did you? She's a cutie."

The deer and her fawn stepped gingerly across the road and bounded into the trees.

"Bye. Next time wait until there are no cars coming." Skylar put the rental into motion. "Then you won't give a driver a heart attack." She was talking to wildlife that paid not one whit to her. A wave of exhaustion washed over Skylar. It seemed days ago since she'd stared at the amazing autumn mountain view from the window at Scott Ranch. Was that just early this morning? Was it also just this morning that Gina had come into the ranch house living room and accused Skylar's father of murder? Skylar had managed to catch flights to Chicago then Knoxville, Tennessee, much quicker than she'd expected. Now, as dusk fell, the day caught up with Skylar.

A few moments later, Skylar passed a sign that read Oliver Springs, Population 3405. With her head on a swivel, Skylar drove past Victorian homes on the outskirts of town, many still standing tall and proud. Lights began to turn on as dark descended. A few people strolled along the sidewalks in the autumn evening under the streetlights. Young couples held hands as they ambled down the street. Parents pushed strollers, their older children scampering around them. Skylar couldn't blame them. The autumn air would be delightful for an evening stroll, and with winter soon to follow, it would be a shame to miss this.

She crossed a railroad track where most of the buildings were two- and three-story red brick. On the right she spotted the Oliver Springs Drug Co. sitting next to Reaves Café, their neon signs brightly lit. Right on time Skylar's stomach emitted a growl. Glancing at her watch she realized it was an hour past suppertime. No wonder she was hungry. With no idea where her destination was, she needed to find a place to stay for the night. Perhaps Reaves Café would be a good place to grab a meal, ask some questions, and find a good place to spend the night.

Turning the car onto a side street, Skylar headed back to the little café. She parked in front, grabbed her purse and headed for the door. An older man exited as she reached it, and he held the door for her.

"Thank you." She gave him a bright smile.

"My pleasure." He tipped his hat and waited for Skylar to enter before moving along. How nice. Not too many men these days held doors for women anymore. Being 1970, and the feminist movement had women frowning on men's chivalrous behavior. Skylar sighed. She wasn't one of them. Give her a gentleman any day. Like Matt. He knew how to treat a lady. Her heart clinched. Oh, how she missed him. She'd only been gone a day, and she wanted him close by.

Skylar shoved thoughts of Matt away and approached the cashier's counter. A thin, older lady with wire-framed glasses glanced up and flashed a bright smile. "Hello there. You lookin' for somethin' good to eat?"

"Yes, ma'am."

"Then, dearie, you've come to the right place." She grabbed a menu from the stack on the counter. "Follow me."

The woman led Skylar to a booth along the wall and placed the menu on the table. Once Skylar slid into the booth, the woman placed napkin-rolled silverware beside the menu. "Our waitress, Ruthann, will be right with you. Enjoy your meal."

"Before you go, is there a place you can recommend for me to spend the night? I'm…not from here." Skylar clasped her hands on the table.

The woman grinned and gave her a wink. "I picked up on that already. Oliver Springs is a small town. It's easy to see when somebody new drops by." She screwed up her brow and leaned on the table. "Well, let me think. There's Martha Hildebrand's B&B over on Walker Avenue. Then Joe and Darcie Peters have a little cottage they let out behind their house on Hen Valley Road." Her face brightened and she held out her hand. "By the way, my name's Helen. Helen Carter. What's your name?"

"Skylar Simpson." Skylar shook Helen's hand as she watched for a reaction to her name but received none.

"Welcome to these parts, Skylar. Can I call you Skylar, or do you want me to call you Miss Simpson?"

"Skylar is fine."

"You staying long in Oliver Springs?"

"I'm not sure yet, but for now the B&B would be fine, if they have a room."

"Sure. Why don't I give Martha a call and find out while you order up somethin' to eat?"

Skylar wasn't at all sure she wanted the whole town knowing her business, and somehow, she had a feeling that's exactly what was about to happen. Could she prevent it? She didn't think so.

"I don't want to put you to any trouble. If you give me Mrs. Hildebrand's phone number and the address, I'm sure I can find out."

Helen waved a hand. "Won't be no trouble a'tall. I'd be happy to help out. I'll go get Ruthann to take your drink order while you take a look at the menu. Take your time."

Once the woman headed toward the back of the restaurant, mixed feelings invaded Skylar. She wanted help from the locals, but just how much help did she want? In small towns, word spread fast. She was a stranger in this town, and everyone would want to know what she was doing here. How would it affect her search for the truth? Would it help or make things difficult?

"What can I get for you?" A young girl with a long brown ponytail who looked to be about sixteen stopped beside Skylar's table with an order pad and pencil in her hands. Her words were soft, and she barely met Skylar's eyes.

"I'll have a glass of water with ice, please. Thank you."

Skylar opened her menu. "I haven't looked at the menu yet, so I'll need a few minutes. Any specials this evening?"

Ruthann listed a few items then rushed away to get the water.

Being a waitress was not a good fit for this girl. She needed something less public, or she needed some help working with people.

Skylar glanced over the menu and settled on a bowl of homemade ham and potato soup and a side salad. It didn't take long for Ruthann to bring it out.

Before the girl could escape, Skylar asked, "Are you still in high school, Ruthann? If so, what grade are you in?"

The girl visibly swallowed, looking like she wanted to be anywhere but here. "Yes, ma'am. Eleventh. I graduate next year."

"That's great. What are your favorite subjects?" Skylar wanted to get this girl to talk.

"Music." Ruthann twisted her hands together. "I play the piano. I take lessons at school."

"Wonderful. Do you play for any school bands or music groups?"

"Yes, ma'am. I play for the chorus groups." Ruthann's eyes danced around, mostly staring at the floor. "I have to go. Need to check on my other tables."

"Of course you do. Thanks for telling me about yourself. I wish you the best with your music."

"Thank you. Enjoy your food." Ruthann waved a stilted hand toward the table then hurried away.

Skylar lowered her head in prayer. *Abba Father, thank You for protecting me through my travels today and for bringing me here safely. Thank You for this food. Bless it to my body that I may serve You as You want me to. Help me find the right place to sleep tonight that will be safe and restful. And guide my steps to find the truth about Dad. Please protect Matt. I love him and want him to know the truth too. And please protect my family at home. I love You,*

*Abba. Amen.*

When her soup arrived, she ate her fill, but her tiredness grew.

Toward the end of her meal, Helen returned and sat across from her. "Well, dearie, I called Martha, and she has plenty of room for you. She'd love for you to come. Her prices are fair, too, if you're concerned about that." Helen listed the price, and Skylar also thought it was fair. Helen stood. "Take your time. There's no rush. I'll write down the address and give it to you when you pay at the register."

Skylar laid her spoon beside the nearly empty bowl of soup. "Thank you, Helen. I appreciate your help, and I'm sure I'll rest easy tonight."

"Oh, I'm sure you will. Martha's place is on a nice quiet street in a great part of town." She strode toward the front of the restaurant, leaving Skylar to finish her meal.

When she'd finished eating, Skylar gathered her purse and approached the cash register.

"I hope everything was to your satisfaction, dearie." Helen rang up the check and waited for Skylar to hand over the money.

"It truly was. After the long trip today, I found myself famished." Skylar slipped her wallet back into her purse.

The cash register dinged as the drawer popped open, and Helen placed the money into the correct slots. "I'm glad we could feed you somethin' good." She slammed the drawer shut and picked up a slip of paper, handing it to Skylar. "Here you go. This is Martha's address. I drew you a little map. It's just a few blocks over. Shouldn't be hard to find."

Skylar accepted the paper. "Thank you for all your help. Perhaps I'll see you again soon."

"Maybe so. Stop in anytime. Take care now."

With a smile, Skylar hurried out to her rental and followed the map to the address Helen had given her. Martha Hildebrand's B&B was a two-story, white Victorian home. Several of the windows were lit as well as a carriage post lamp beside the sidewalk. A bright light beside the door illuminated the wide half-wrap-around porch. Skylar chuckled. With all the lights lit up, Martha obviously didn't want her to miss the house. It made for a nice welcome. Skylar parked in the wide driveway, grabbed her suitcase, and approached the front door then rang the bell.

The door opened immediately, and a plump older woman stood there, a wide smile on her face. She wore a dark purple plaid skirt and a lavender high-collared blouse with a dark purple sweater over it. Although surely in her late-sixties, her teased soft-brown hair held not one gray hair. "You must be Miss Simpson. Please do come in. I'm Martha Hildebrand."

She opened the door wider and ushered Skylar into a round entryway. "Helen told me you've traveled far today. Y'all must be exhausted. I'll take you straight to your room where you can settle in and rest. Please follow me." The woman's soft, almost genteel southern accent warmed her heart.

"Thank you." Skylar followed the woman to a circular staircase along the edge of the entryway. She spotted a parlor through a wide arch. "You have a beautiful home."

The older woman tittered. "Why thank you. It was my late husband's family home. Unfortunately, taxes are so high on these old homes that I was forced to open it up as a B&B. But it's so conducive to that, you know." Her feet were silent on the plush carpet treads of the stairs. "And I do so enjoy meeting new people."

At the top of the stairs, Mrs. Hildebrand led Skylar along a short hallway to a room along the back of the house. She opened the door and flipped on the light, then she stepped back and allowed Skylar to enter first.

"This is one of my favorite rooms in the house. Isn't it simply lovely?" Mrs. Hildebrand clasped her hands in front of her.

Skylar lowered her suitcase to the suitcase stand against

the wall and turned to glance around the room. It was indeed lovely. The lamps beside the bed gave off a subdued light. The walls were sage green while the carpet was cream. The drapes and the bedspread on the four-poster bed had a pleasant printed floral pattern in greens and soft reds on a cream background. Throw pillows on the bed matched in dark solid green and red. Two dark green chairs sat by the window with a small table in-between. A solid oak mantel sat above the lit gas fireplace that emitted soft warmth. What a welcoming room in these Smoky Mountains on an October evening.

"How beautiful, Mrs. Hildebrand. Thank you for allowing me to stay in here."

"Oh, no, my dear. Thank you for choosing to stay in my home. And please, call me Martha. Mrs. Hildebrand sounds so…formal."

Skylar tilted her head. "Then Martha it is."

The older woman turned toward the open doorway. "Breakfast is between six and nine. If you have a preference, please tell me. If not, simply show up, and I'll make sure you're served a full hot breakfast."

"Thank you. I look forward to it."

Martha reached for the doorknob. "Oh, I almost forgot. There's a bathroom through that doorway. Rest well, my dear. Good night."

"Good night."

Skylar turned the lock on the door and prepared for bed. The bathroom held all the modern conveniences. After her travels, a shower was in order. In a short time, she climbed under the covers of the four-poster and sank into the cloud of the soft mattress. Heavenly day. *Thanks, Lord. What a nice place You led me to. A good meal. A great mattress in a delightful room. I don't know what tomorrow holds, but I know You'll be there. I love You. Good nig….*

Skylar failed to finish her prayer as exhaustion overtook her, and she drifted asleep.

~

"Mrs. Simpson, where is Skylar?" Matt sat at the kitchen table in Skylar's mother's kitchen. "She told me she'd go riding with me this afternoon, then the next thing I know, she's gone. Gina came in and told her a story about Skylar's dad." Matt leaned back in his chair, one leg propped on the other knee. "What can you tell me?"

Shelby Simpson poured iced tea into two glasses then returned the pitcher to the refrigerator. She brought both glasses to the table and placed one in front of Matt and the other in front of the chair next to Matt's, then she sat down. "Skylar came in late this morning quiet upset. She had a newspaper article that Gina had given her. It was from a newspaper back in Tennessee in 1945 that said my husband, Brodie, was arrested for murder."

Shelby released a heavy sigh and shook her head. "My husband was no murderer. Yes, he was arrested long ago in Tennessee, but he never killed anyone. I don't know what Gina is up to, but it can't be good. My husband would never talk about those days, but he did tell me once that he did not killed Sheriff Baker. It was right after the murder happened. He was arrested then released. He came home and told me we were moving. Brodie decided Wyoming was a good place to move and start over."

"Did you read the article? Was there anything in it I should know?"

"You're going after Skylar, aren't you?" Shelby laid a hand on Matt's arm.

"Yes, ma'am, I am. As soon as you tell me where she went." Matt straightened. "I can't leave her to go off on her own. Who knows what she may run into? If your husband was accused of murder and he moved your family away, we don't know if they ever caught the real murderer. Is it possible? Absolutely, but we don't know that. *I* need to know that."

Shelby's hand flew to her mouth. "Oh, my word. I never

thought of that. Matt, there are a couple of things you need to know. Skylar flew to Tennessee. She went back to Oliver Springs where we used to live in the mountains near there, but I don't know if any of our relatives are still living. It's been twenty-five years. We lost all contact with family. And—" Shelby paused, "my husband, Brodie, changed our last name to Simpson. When we lived in Tennessee it was…Sawyer. You might want to write some of these names down." She grabbed a notepad and pencil from the counter below the wall phone and handed them to Matt. "I have some other names to give you, but as I said, they may not still be living."

"It's okay. I'll write them down anyway." Matt jotted down the names of Brodie's parents. He could always ask about them if he couldn't find Skylar. But he had to catch up to her. He *would* catch up to her. *Lord, help me. Guide me. And keep Skylar safe.*

# Chapter Four

Skylar took a seat at a small table beside a window in the dining room. Mrs. Hildebrand…Martha…had arranged a few small tables around the perimeter of the room and one six-seater in the middle. It was a good thing this old house was built big back in Victorian days. It made it conducive for a beautiful B&B. Small, cream-colored tablecloths topped autumn floral cloths on each table, and little vases with live fall flowers sat in the middle. Deep rust-colored drapes adorned the windows that matched the autumn feel of the room.

"Good morning, my dear." Martha breezed in from a door at the back of the dining room, a frilly, fall apron tied around her ample waist. Her cheeks bloomed pink as she hurried over with a carafe in her hand. "I hope you had a blissful rest last night."

"I did, thank you." Skylar sent her a broad smile. "As wonderful as that mattress was, I still hope that's coffee you're carrying."

"Of course, it is. What better way to start the day?" Martha paused beside the table and flipped over the coffee cup already arranged on a saucer on the table. "As you can see, there's a little pitcher of creamer waiting for you as well as sugar in the little bowl, should you like to doctor your coffee." She poured the steaming dark brew into the cup.

"The menu is right there. I make a few different choices, so take a look. I'll be out in a few minutes to take your order."

"Am I your only customer at the moment?" Skylar glanced around.

Martha grinned and raised her eyebrows. "Well, no. There's a honeymoon couple here, but—" she glanced over her shoulder and lowered her voice as she leaned closer. "I don't expect them to come up for air anytime soon."

Skylar chuckled and picked up the menu. "I suppose not."

After Skylar finished eating, she sat enjoying her coffee. She watched the fall leaves drifting to the ground outside the window. What would the day bring? Martha returned to clear the dishes away.

"That was delicious. Thank you." Skylar glanced up as Martha picked up her plate.

The woman preened. "No, thank you. I love cooking for my guests. Since my husband is no longer with me, it gives me pleasure to prepare meals for others."

"After you take those to the kitchen, would you come back and sit with me for a few minutes? I'd like to ask you some questions about the area." Skylar set her cup on the saucer. "I'm obviously new here, and I'm looking for a family. If you've been here any length of time, as it seems you have, perhaps you know them."

Martha tilted her head. "I've lived in this area since I was a child." Her cheeks pinked again. "I won't tell you how long that's been, but believe me, it's been a long time." She held the plate against her side. "I'll be happy to sit and answer whatever questions I can. Be right back."

Moments later, Martha lowered into the chair opposite Skylar, a cup of coffee in front of her and a fresh cup for Skylar. "Now, ask away. I'll do my best to answer."

Skylar sipped her fresh brew then set the cup down, her hands wrapped around the cup. "I'm from Wyoming, but I've been told my family came from here. I've come to find out about my family's past and see if any of my relatives are still living."

"Wyoming? Oh my. That's an awfully long way for a young lady to travel alone." Concern etched the older woman's features. "May I ask if you flew or drove all that way?"

Skylar smiled. "I flew then rented a car and drove from Knoxville."

Martha placed a hand over her heart. "Well, I suppose that's not as terrifying. Pardon me, but I'm old-fashioned. I don't hold with how these modern young women are so fancy-free and uncaring these days. They simply go off and—"

Skylar placed a hand over Martha's. "It's all right; however, as I said, I'm on sort of a mission to find my family. My father's family name was Sawyer. Do you know any Sawyers in this area?"

"Sawyer?" Martha's gaze moved to the ceiling as her features screwed up in thought. "Hmm. Sawyer." Then she nodded slowly. "Yes, there was a Reverend and Mrs. George Sawyer that used to live over on Honeysuckle Hollow. You know, now that I think of it, I haven't heard of them in years. I was a young mother back then raising my sons. My husband and I had two sons, you know. They live over in Knoxville now with their families. I usually see them on holidays and special occasions like birthdays. I stay so busy with the B&B, and of course, they're busy with their jobs and school."

"I see." Skylar wished Martha would hurry along, once she'd mentioned the names of her grandparents. Those were the names her mother had given her and the name of the place where they lived. Were they still living, and did they still live on Honeysuckle Hollow? Excitement filled her at the thought that her grandparents were still known here. Well, they *had* been known here. It was a start.

"Can you tell me how to get to Honeysuckle Hollow?"

Skylar placed her hands in her lap and knotted the cloth napkin between her fingers.

"Oh yes. That's easy enough. However, when you get there, finding where they live may not be. The hollow is deep and long. Lots of folks live back in there." Martha took a sip of her coffee then returned the cup to the saucer. "There used to be a little country store out there with a post office. I don't know if it's still there or not, but if so, perhaps they can help you find your relatives. If not, you could stop at someone's house. Just be careful. Sometimes folks up in the hollows are a bit suspicious, and…well, just be careful."

Skylar wasn't sure she liked the sound of that. She hoped the country store was still open. "Thank you. Your help has been invaluable. I'm not sure what the outcome of my search will be, so I may or may not be back this evening. I won't know until I show up."

Martha smiled. "If you show up, the room is still yours. If you don't, I'll know you found your folks, and they welcomed you with open arms. I'll be praying the second happens."

Skylar patted the woman's hand. "I appreciate that prayer. Now, I need to pay my bill and be on my way. I want to find that country store and begin my search."

~

Matt was unable to find a flight out of Gillette until the following morning. Frustrated, he spent the night at Mrs. Simpson's house then caught the first flight to Casper then onto Chicago. He put his pickup truck into long-term parking at Gillette. He didn't want to drag any of the ranch hands away when they were attempting to wrangle the lost cattle back to the ranch and fix the broken fence. It would cost a pretty penny, but he didn't care. His priority was Skylar.

She already had a full day on him, and he only had a little information from Mrs. Simpson to guide him. No, that wasn't all. He had his new-found faith as well. He'd come to Christ on his trip to Germany in the spring, and he was learning to lean on Him. *That's right, Lord. I may have only a little information, but You know everything about this situation. You know the whole story about Skylar's dad. Please guide and protect Skylar as she's got a jump on me, and guide me as I go after her. Help us both find the truth.*

Once he finally reached Knoxville, Matt walked past the rental cars and chose a pickup truck. If he had to have a rental, it would be what he was used to driving. He drove out of the lot and headed northwest toward Oliver Springs, the little town Mrs. Simpson told him was closest to where they used to live.

He was used to bad roads, but these were terrible. Later that afternoon when he reached the little town, he drove around to get the lay of the land. The industry here was coal. It appeared to be a fairly busy place, so he pulled into a little café to grab a bite and ask some questions.

He glanced up at the sign over the door: Reaves Café. A local hangout, no doubt. If Skylar had come into town, word had likely spread and everyone would know. It didn't take long in a small town like this. Grabbing the handle of the glass door, Matt yanked it open then stepped inside. It was between lunch and supper, and only a couple patrons sat in the booths.

"Hello, handsome. Lookin' for somethin' good to eat?" A thin, older woman smiled from behind a cashier's counter. "We've got a great menu."

Matt couldn't help but return her smile as he stepped closer. "I'm certainly hungry. Haven't eaten since early this morning."

"Then follow me. I have a great table for you." The woman led him to a booth along the wall. "Have a seat, and one of our waitresses will be right with you."

"Thank you." Matt opened the menu and perused it. Before long a waitress appeared and took his order. "Can you ask the lady behind the cash register if she's got a few minutes?"

"Sure thing."

Right away the older woman appeared. "My name's Helen. What can I do for ya?"

"Nice to meet you, Helen. I'm Matt. I just got into town, and I'm wondering if you've seen a young lady that might've come through yesterday or today. Her name's Skylar Simpson. She's my girlfriend, and I'm trying to catch up with her."

Helen's eyes narrowed, and her fists planted on her hips. "Yeah? Why?"

Red flags went up in Matt's mind. Uh oh. This woman thought he was after Skylar for bad reasons. "No, really. I'm trying to find her to help her. I think she may be in danger and not from me. Please, have you seen her?"

Helen slipped onto the bench across from Matt. "Honest to goodness? You aren't after her to hurt her?"

"No, ma'am. Honest. I would never hurt Skylar." Matt released a heavy sigh. "I'm in love with her. I'm trying to find her to protect her."

Helen seemed to be searching Matt's features with a thoroughness that made him want to squirm, but he had nothing to hide. He returned her gaze without blinking.

Satisfied, she nodded, "All righty then. Yeah, she came in here. She asked if I knew of a good place to stay for the night. Didn't say anythin' else about nothin'. Just wanted a place to stay."

"Can you tell me where you sent her?"

"Sure, I can. I called Martha Hildebrand and made the arrangements myself. Your Skylar said it wasn't necessary. Said she could do it herself, but I said twern't no trouble a'tall. Anyway, I'll write down the address for you and draw you a map. Martha's place ain't too far from here. Easy peasy to find, it is. Finish up your meal, and I'll have it ready for you when you pay."

"Thanks, Helen."

"No problem." She started to climb from the bench then

turned back to Matt, her eyes once again narrowed. "You pinky-swear you're not after her to hurt her? That gal's a good'n. I ain't about to send no lowlife after her."

Matt leaned forward and stared Martha in the eye. He held up his hand, pinky extended. "Helen, someone back home in Wyoming told Skylar something awful that sent her back east searching for information. I don't know what's true and what's not, but I aim to find out. Unfortunately, that information may have put her life at risk. I need to find her. Now look me in the eye and tell me I'm lying."

Helen once again searched Matt's features. "I'm a pretty good judge o' folks. I believe you." She entwined her pinky with his. "I'll get that map drawn up." She surged from the seat and headed for the cashier's desk.

Matt shook his head and chuckled. After he finished eating, he left a tip for the waitress then headed toward the cashier's desk and handed the check to Helen. "That was delicious just like you said it would be."

"We have a great short-order cook back there. He's been cookin' here for nigh on thirty years. Had a long time to perfect the menu, don't you think?" Helen cackled.

"I suppose so." Matt grinned. "If I'm in the area for any length of time, I might drop back in."

"You do that. Try somethin' different." She winked at him. "Go find that young lady o' yours. Keep her safe. She's a sweetheart." Helen handed him the slip of paper with Martha Hildebrand's address and the map on it.

"Yes, ma'am. She certainly is."

"If I keep sendin' people Martha's way, I'm gonna have to print up maps to hand out." She cackled again.

Matt waved as he headed to the door. "I appreciate all your help. Take care."

"You too, handsome."

~

Skylar followed Martha's directions to Honeysuckle Hollow without any trouble. The roads, however, were no better than any others she'd driven on. In fact, they were worse. Potholed pavement gave way to sort-of-graveled dirt to just-plain dirt. Skylar was fine with that. There were dirt roads in Wyoming too. It wasn't long before she found the little country store Martha had mentioned. It was more like a convenience store with two gas pumps out front. And, glory be, a bright-red neon sign indicated it was open.

Skylar turned in and parked in front of the store. Glancing to the left, she spotted an old building that looked like it may have been the original store way back in the day. It was small with a faded and cracked wooden door, the glass window inset broken out. A torn screen door half hung off its hinges. A couple broken windows sat on either side of the door. Vegetation had long ago taken over what man had abandoned. An old, rusty Mae West gas pump sat out front under an overhang. Parts of it were missing. The newer convenience store must have replaced the old country store long ago. Those old gas pumps hadn't been used in decades.

Turning off the car engine, Skylar climbed out and locked the car. Then she glanced around her, though she wasn't sure why. She was the only customer and doubted theft was a big problem in this area. But then, the car was a rental.

She strode inside to find a man who looked to be in his late sixties sitting on a high stool behind the counter. He glanced up from the newspaper he was reading. Staring at Skylar over the top rim of his glasses, he gave a brief nod.

"Morning. What can I do fer ya?"

"Good morning." Skylar gave him a bright smile. "I'm trying to locate some family that I've been told live up on Honeysuckle Hollow. My family name is Sawyer. Do you know any Sawyers up here?"

The man folded the newspaper and laid it on the counter. "Well, now, that depends on why you're lookin' fer 'em." He scratched his stubble-lined cheek. "You come fur in your search?"

"Yes, sir, I flew from Wyoming to find my family." Skylar lifted her chin. "And my reasons are my own. Do you know of the Sawyers, sir, or not?"

A grin lifted one side of the man's mouth. "I like your spunk, girly. You come a long way to find your family, so, yeah, I know of some Sawyers out here in the holler. You keep going right out o' here, then take a left on White Oak. Follow that for about ten minutes till you come to Deerlick Lane. Take that. It's the last cabin on the road." He took a notepad and a pencil and tossed them toward Skylar. "Here you go. In case your memory's as bad as mine."

Skylar took them then asked the man to repeat the directions. "Thank you. I appreciate your help more than you know."

He waved a hand. "No problem. Sorry fer giving ya a hard time. We don't cotton to strangers in these parts, but if you got family out here, you ain't a stranger."

Skylar smiled. "Thank you. I appreciate your welcome. I think."

"Sure nuff." He picked up his newspaper as she headed out the door.

Martha had warned her the people in the hollow were a bit suspicious, but they also seemed to be welcoming. At least to family. Skylar shook her head in wonder as she started her car and backed out. She turned it in the direction the storekeeper had indicated, then she followed his other directions. Her heart clinched. It wouldn't be long before she would find out if the Sawyers he'd told her about were, indeed, *her* Sawyers.

As Skylar made her way further into the hollow, the potholes and ruts were ever present. After making the last turn, she followed the road until she came to the last cabin as directed. Stopping the car, she paused at the end of the driveway. She wasn't sure she'd make it up that deep-rutted path with the rental. The yard should have been a welcoming sight, had it been taken care of recently, but it looked like the grass hadn't been cut in a couple of months. Was anyone still living here?

Considering this was the end of the road, Skylar slipped the gearshift into park and turned off the engine. She stepped out of the car, closed the door, and walked up the driveway. Caution made her keep her head on a swivel. She had no idea if a guard dog would come racing out at any minute. Glancing at the house, she spotted the movement of a curtain. That was a good thing, wasn't it? She hastened toward the front porch, her heartbeat picking up. She had no idea who she was going to meet.

When she was halfway from the car to the porch, the front door swung open and someone stepped out onto the porch.

"Hold it right there. Not a step closer."

Skylar halted at the sight of an old woman holding a shotgun aimed right at her. Skylar held her hands in the air. "Please don't shoot. I'm not here to hurt you. I…I'm looking for my family, and I was told they might live here."

The woman wore a long-sleeved, blue plaid shirt tucked into worn blue jeans. Her gray hair was pulled back in a braid that hung over her shoulder. "I don't have any family. You need to go away. Now."

Skylar swallowed hard and tried again. "My father was Brodie Sawyer. My name is Skyler."

With a jerk, the woman took a step back, the barrel of the shotgun slowly lowering. She stared long and hard at Skylar. "Where did you come from?" Her voice was barely more than a whisper.

"I flew from Wyoming to Knoxville then drove to Oliver Springs. The townsfolk said there were still Sawyers out here. My mother's name is Shelby. She told me our family lived on Honeysuckle Hollow before we moved to Wyoming. I was just a baby when we moved away."

A myriad of emotions crowded for a place on the woman's features. Skylar read anger, sorrow, fear, and something akin to happiness. Uncertainty added to the other emotions and settled there as she stood the shotgun at her side. "You've got a lot of the right answers to questions I haven't asked yet." She sighed heavily. "Suppose I should ask you to come in and talk." She stood still a few moments longer. "You can put your hands down." A slight smile lifted the corners of her mouth.

Skylar swallowed and drew in a deep breath of relief as she lowered her hands. At least she wouldn't be shot. At the moment. She met the woman's eyes squarely. "I'll be happy to answer whatever questions you have, and I have a lot of my own."

The woman gave a slight nod. "I bet you do." She turned toward the house then waved a hand. "Come on in. It's high time you met your grandma."

~

Shortly after leaving Reaves Café, Matt parked in front of Martha Hildebrand's B&B. He was impressed with the exterior of the Victorian home. He'd bet his prized horse that Skylar had been too. One just didn't see homes like this in Wyoming. He rang the doorbell and within seconds the door swung wide. An older, pudgy woman wearing a skirt, a sweater and pearls greeted Matt. Her smile was a mile wide. Unless he missed his guess, Matt was certain that Helen Carter had made a phone call.

"Welcome, Mr. Matt. Please, do come in. As you already know, I'm Martha Hildebrand." She swung the door wider and ushered Matt into the foyer with a sweeping hand. "I've been expecting you."

"Have you?" Matt removed his cowboy hat and held it between his hands. "But I just—"

She waved a dismissive hand. "Helen called and told me you were on your way."

"Of course she did." He wasn't surprised the helpful cashier had stooped to meddling. "Well, thank you for allowing me to stop by."

"Oh, it's no trouble at all, young man." She turned to walk away. "Please, come with me."

Matt hadn't planned to stay long. He only wanted to ask where she'd sent Skylar. "Ma'am—"

"This way, please." Mrs. Hildebrand disappeared through a wide arch leaving Matt to follow if he wanted his questions answered. She led him into a beautiful parlor that looked as if it had been furnished in Victorian days. Mrs. Hildebrand turned to him and indicated an overstuffed armchair. "Please have a seat. We can talk in here more comfortably."

"Oh, but I can't stay long."

"I understand, but I prefer talking while sitting." His hostess sat on the overstuffed sofa and waited for Matt to sit in the armchair. She reached for a silver carafe that stood on the coffee table accompanied by China coffee cups and saucers and a silver creamer and sugar bowl. "How do you prefer your coffee?"

"Oh, that's no…" Matt stared at the woman and saw how much she delighted in entertaining. "Thank you. I'll take mine black, please."

"Certainly." A satisfied expression settled on her rounded features. She handed him the delicate cup.

Matt was used to drinking from heavy mugs not delicate China. He accepted the cup and saucer and felt like he was all thumbs. He drew a deep breath and released it slowly, forcing himself to slow down when all he wanted to do was extract information from her and find Skylar. He took a drink. "This is delicious."

"Why, thank you. I have a wonderful distributor. They have the best coffee I've found to date. I often get compliments from my guests."

"I can see why. Do you have a lot of guests who come through, ma'am?" He winced. Small talk wasn't one of Matt's best qualities.

"I do indeed." Mrs. Hildebrand told Matt all about the

B&B and how it became one.

*Lord, help me.* Matt sighed inwardly. *I suppose there's a reason You're slowing me down? Maybe this little old lady simply needs some company? Hmm. She had Skylar's company, and she said she has a lot of folks come through. So, why me, Lord?*

He drank more coffee and attempted to pay attention. When Mrs. Hildebrand paused to delicately sip her own coffee, Matt stepped in. "Helen mentioned she'd sent my girlfriend, Skylar, to stay here last night. I don't suppose she's still here, is she?"

"That's right. Helen did mention that you're Skylar's boyfriend. And, no, she's not here right now. You probably know she's looking for her family. I sent her up Honeysuckle Hollow to the Sawyer family that lives there. She left this morning." Mrs. Hildebrand glanced at her wristwatch. "That was hours and hours ago. I told her if she couldn't find them to come back and stay here tonight. If she found them, then I would know not to expect her. I suppose it's still too early to know that yet."

Matt drew in a heavy breath and released it slowly. He was beginning to feel like he was on the proverbial goose chase, only replace the goose with Skylar.

"Would you like to hang around and wait to see if Skylar returns for the night?" Mrs. Hildebrand asked, lifting her cup for another sip. When she set it back down, she added, "It's going to get dark before you can get up into the hollow. The little country store will surely be closed before you get up there. Most likely no one will be around to tell you where to go, and you can easily get lost on those roads in the hollow."

Matt hesitated.

"You can always stay here tonight and begin after breakfast in the morning." Mrs. Hildebrand lifted her cup for another drink.

As anxious as he was to find Skylar, the woman's words of wisdom grew wiser and wiser to Matt. He stood and strode over to the window where he slid back the drape and stared out. The sun sat at the top of the mountains. He glanced at his wristwatch. It was close to five o'clock. Mrs. Hildebrand was right. The country store would be closed, and without their directions, he would have no idea where to search. If Skylar hadn't yet returned, she'd likely found her family. Or worse. She'd found trouble. His stomach knotted. *Lord, what should I do?*

He stared at the place where the sun had rested on the mountaintop just moments ago. It had slipped behind the top and left a glow that cast a silhouette of the mountains. A sense of peace settled over Matt. He'd leave Skylar in the Lord's hands to protect because, goodness knows, Matt couldn't protect her. *She's Your child, Lord. Wherever she is, she's in Your hands. More solid than that mountain is Your love and Your protection for both of us. Now help me to leave her in Your hands.*

Matt turned back to the B&B proprietress who sipped her coffee. "I'll take a room for the night, Mrs. Hildebrand, if you have one. I don't know if you're a woman of faith or not, but I just had a conversation with the Father. He told me to leave Skylar in His hands. I'll start looking for her in the morning after breakfast."

A gentle smile curved Mrs. Hildebrand's lips. "I am a woman of faith, Mr. Matt. My faith has seen me through many a trial over the years. Whatever you and Skylar are dealing with, your faith will see you through as well." She set her cup on the coffee table. "And please, call me Martha."

# Chapter Five

"I have coffee left over from this morning still on the stove if you'd like some." The old woman leaned the shotgun in the corner next to an oak table. The living room of the cabin was bigger than Skylar had anticipated. An oak rocking chair, a love seat, and an overstuffed armchair were arranged comfortably around a woodstove that emitted a warmth that eased the chill from the October air. An old upright piano sat against the end wall. Loads of what Skylar assumed were family pictures hung on the walls as well as a couple of amateur oil paintings. A large oval rag rug lay centered on the patinaed wood floor.

"Have a seat wherever you'll be comfortable." The woman waved toward the arrangement of furniture. She reached into a wood box near the woodstove and removed two pieces, adding them to the stove. The flames leaped brighter as she closed the squeaky door.

She turned back to Skylar who'd sat in the armchair. "Did you want some of that coffee?"

"I don't care for any, thank you."

"Suit yourself." The woman sat in the rocking chair and began a slow rock. "So, you're looking for family, you said."

"Yes, ma'am. You mentioned my grandmother?"

A grin crossed the woman's face, and she nodded. "That would be me, child. I'm Etta Sawyer, your grandma and your daddy's mother."

A small gasp escaped Skylar. "You are?"

A wry expression etched Etta's features. "Am I that disappointing?"

Skylar smiled. "Not at all. It's just the way you said it earlier led me to believe my grandmother might be someone other than you."

The wry expression morphed to sheepishness. "Suppose so. I've been told I can be persnickety."

"If that's a sample, I'd say so." Skylar laughed then sobered. "Why did you meet me with a shotgun? Is it that dangerous up here? Do you have many unwelcome visitors?"

Etta scowled. "Not really. I just prefer to be left alone."

"I see. But when you heard who I was, you decided to allow me in?"

Etta's thin shoulders rose in a shrug. "I haven't heard my son's name in many a year." Her eyes roamed over the floor and once again emotions chased across her features. "I've missed my Brodie and your mama and you." Her eyes flew to Skylar's. "You were just a baby when you lived here. Once y'all left, I never heard anything from your daddy except once. Brodie sent me a Mother's Day card one year, then I didn't hear anything ever again." She leaned forward. "How is he? How is my Brodie?"

Skylar slowly shook her head. "He died several years ago. Lung cancer. He'd always been a heavy smoker. Mom said he started as a teenager."

"Yes, he did." Etta nodded then shook her head. "Oh, my poor Brodie. Always the good son. He went off and served his country and fought in the war. Brodie was a wonderful husband. I have no idea what kind of father he was. He moved y'all away before I could ever find out."

Skylar stood and walked over to kneel at Etta's feet. She took the old woman's hand in hers. "Rest assured that Brodie Sawyer was a wonderful father as well as a wonderful husband. He worked hard to provide for his family, Mrs. Sawyer."

The old woman chuckled and slid a hand along Skylar's cheek. "I'm your grandma, child. You don't have to call me Mrs. Sawyer. Please, call me Grandma."

"If you're sure…."

"Of course, I'm sure." She paused and stared at her new-found granddaughter. "You have your daddy's eyes. The same color blue." Grandma Etta patted her cheek then placed her hand on top of Skylar's. "I knew as soon as you said his name and I got a good look at you. The color of your hair is the same as your mama's. It's the same golden brown. Your mama's a beautiful woman, and so are you. Is she…?"

"Yes, she's still with us and doing well. I have three sisters. Holly and Charlotte are both in college. Charlotte's nickname is Charlie. The youngest is Becka. She's in the eighth grade."

"My goodness. I have three granddaughters I didn't even know about." Grandma Etta placed a knuckle over her lips.

"It's okay. Hopefully you'll get to meet them before long."

"That would be nice, wouldn't it?" Grandma Etta swiped dampness from her eyes. "I'd love to see your mama again too."

"We'll see if we can make that happen." Skylar squeezed the old woman's hand. "What about Grandpa Sawyer? Will he be back soon?" Skylar glanced toward the door.

Grandma Etta shook her head. "I'm afraid not, child. My George passed away about seven years ago. Had a heart attack while he was chopping wood out back." Her eyes stared as if seeing into the past. "I found him lying on the ground, his eyes wide open while he held his chest. But he was…he was gone. I couldn't do anything for him. The good Lord had already called him home."

Skylar's eyes brimmed for the man she'd never met. She squeezed her grandma's hand. "I'm so sorry. You must miss him so much. I'm sorry I never got to meet him. What was he like?"

A tender smile curved Grandma Etta's lips. She met Skylar's eyes. "George was the kindest, most generous man I ever knew. He had a good sense of humor too. He was a preacher, you know. He knew the Bible front to back and back to front. That man loved the Lord. He preached in a little church here in the hollow, and Sunday mornings found the pews full.

"After George passed, some young preacher came from the city and tried to make a go of it, but for some reason, it didn't work out. Folks didn't take to him, I suppose. The people in these parts are kind of funny like that. They're suspicious of outsiders, you know. I had hoped the Lord would raise up a local man to take the pulpit, but it didn't happen. That young man didn't last but a few months before he hightailed it back to the city. The church closed up, and, well, we don't have a good church up here to go to anymore. Some of us get together and have a Bible study every week taking turns in different homes. For the time being, it's the best we can do. It's kind of far to drive into town."

"It is kind of far, but wouldn't it be worth it if you found a good church to attend? I saw a few you could try out."

Skepticism planted itself on Grandma Etta's features. "Maybe."

Skylar decided not to push the issue. "Grandma Etta, where is Grandpa George buried?"

Grandma Etta rested her head against the back of the rocker, her foot setting a gentle pace. "He's buried in the old graveyard at the little church where he used to preach."

"I'd like to see his gravesite sometime. Would you show it to me?" Skyler kept her voice soft.

"I'd love to, sweetie. Think he'd be proud for you to see his church too."

"I'd like that." Skylar drew in a deep breath before delving into her purpose for coming to Tennessee. "Grandma Etta," she smiled and paused, "I have some questions for you. You see, I never knew I had family back here because I wasn't told until just before I came. But a young woman in Wyoming handed me a newspaper article from 1945 that accused Dad of murder. This young woman had her own reasons for doing this. I have a boyfriend named Matt who is an amazing young man, but she used to date him, and she wants him back. I suppose she thought that by stirring up trouble with my boyfriend, she could get him to dump me and come back to her. That's why I'm here. I need to find out the truth about my dad in order to protect our relationship."

"Hmm. Sounds like a real vixen to me." Grandma harrumphed. "I don't like the sound of it either. What did your young man have to say about it all?"

"I didn't have a chance to ask him because I left town in a hurry after I talked to my mom. She gave me our real family name and where we used to live. You see, when Dad moved us to Wyoming, he changed our name to Simpson. Now I know why."

Grandma Etta sighed and gave a nod. "What you don't know is that although his name was cleared, he knew the murderer was still out there, and he didn't want to be connected with anything that had to do with that night. Brodie thought it was best to hightail it out of Dodge."

Skylar waited for her to continue. "Whoa, I didn't think about that."

"Yep." Grandma Etta stroked Skylar's hair away from her face. "Brodie thought it best to get away from here and go somewhere no one would know your family. I didn't realize he'd changed the family name, but it was a smart thing to do, I suppose."

"I need to know the whole truth about what happened back then."

"I just told you the truth, child." Grandma Etta leaned back and began to rock faster.

Skylar lifted her chin. "I need to know everything, Grandma Etta. If someone in Wyoming is accusing my father of murder, and she's spreading that untruth, I have to be able to prove it's untrue."

Grandma Etta stopped rocking. "Why do you think your father moved his family to Wyoming? It's dangerous to go asking too many questions." She started rocking again.

Skylar climbed to her feet. "I'm sorry, but I'm going to ask the questions with or without your help. You know the truth, don't you? You can make it easier and safer by helping me. Please?"

Grandma Etta stopped rocking. "Why didn't your mama—?"

"Apparently, Dad didn't tell her everything. Maybe he did so to keep her safe. The only thing he told her was that he didn't do it."

Grandma Etta heaved a heavy sigh and stared long and hard at her new-found granddaughter. "Fine. I'll help you. But only as far as I can to keep you safe. And no, I don't know the whole truth. I still don't know who killed Sheriff Baker that night in 1945."

Skylar bent and laid a kiss on the old woman's cheek. "Thank you. Your help means more than you can ever imagine."

"Hmph. Maybe so, but our searching may put us in a pickle. We may find ourselves in more trouble than we can find answers for."

~

"Take a left up here." Grandma pointed a short distance down the road.

Skylar slowed the car and turned where her grandmother indicated. They'd left Grandma Etta's house and headed northwest into the mountains. It was a beautiful, clear fall day with a slight breeze to stir the colorful leaves on the trees. A few leaves drifted on the breeze as they wound their way along the curvy mountain roads. It was gorgeous here in east Tennessee and about as far removed in scenery as you could get from Wyoming's landscape. Skylar was used to the wide-open ranges. Yes, they had mountains, but they were craggier. Wyoming had its fair share of fall colors, to be sure—just not as saturated as here in Tennessee.

"You sure you won't tell me where we're headed?" Skylar turned the steering wheel to take a sharp curve and head up an incline.

Grandma Etta chuckled then turned back to stare out the front windshield. "I think I'll simply surprise you."

"Are we going to see a person?"

"You just won't let it rest, will you? Yes, there's a person involved in our…visit."

Skylar cast a sideways glance at the woman but remained silent. After a few more turns the road ended in a valley surrounded by mountains that were in full autumn bloom. In the middle stood what looked to be a prison. A prison? What…?

"Is that what I think it is?" Skylar halted the car in the middle of the road well back from the gates to this bleak-looking fortress.

"Yep." The older woman nodded and turned to Skylar, a sly grin on her features. "You wanted to learn some things, so this is where you're going to start."

"At a…prison?" Skylar's voice rose several notches. "But…who—"

"Your uncle Bufford. Your daddy's younger brother. He's been here for…well, he's been here a couple times actually. But that's not my story to tell." She waved her hand toward the prison. "Drive on. You're headed for Bushy Mountain State Penitentiary."

Skylar put the car in motion. "Are you sure he'll talk to us?"

Grandma shrugged. "I'm not sure if Bufford will be

open to talking to you, but it's about time for my weekly visit. I can't make any promises, but it's worth a try. Since I don't have a phone, I couldn't call ahead to ask."

As they approached the front gates, Skylar rolled down her window and allowed her grandmother to do the talking. Apparently, the guard knew her.

"Hello, Miss Etta. You here to see Bufford?"

"Sure am, Paul. This is my granddaughter, Skylar Simpson. She's in town, and she's never met Bufford. Skylar's my oldest son's daughter. You know the office has me on their roster. It's all right if I bring my granddaughter, isn't it?"

The uniformed guard gave a brief nod. "Give me a minute to make a call, but I'm sure everything will be fine." He eyed Skylar then turned into his kiosk to make the call. After a few moments he returned. "Everything's fine, Miss Etta. They said bring Miss Simpson on in. They'll sign her in when you get inside." He tipped his hat. "Enjoy your visit with Bufford. Have yourselves a nice day."

"Thank you, Paul. Take care." Grandma Etta waved and cast him a wide smile while Skylar waited for the gate to open then drove through.

"Park over there, dear." Grandma Etta pointed toward the small guest parking lot. "You should leave your purse in the car, except for your driver's license. It's easier that way, believe me. They'll search it if you take it in."

They entered the building and checked in with the young guard at the entrance. He wasn't as friendly as the guard at the gate. Skylar could understand him not trusting her, but didn't he know Grandma Etta? Perhaps he was new to the prison.

"Over here, ladies. Put your arms up and don't move." His referral to them as "ladies" didn't match the tone of his voice. He almost sounded like they were inmates.

Grandma Etta turned on him. "Excuse me, young man, but I am *not* one of your inmates. I don't like the tone of your voice, and neither my granddaughter or I deserve that tone. We are not here to break anyone out; we are here to visit only. Change your tone or I'll have a visit with the warden. I've been visiting this prison since 1945, and I'm not about to start being treated like an inmate. Do you understand me?" By the time Etta Sawyer finished speaking, she stood toe-to-toe and nearly nose-to-nose with the guard but for being five inches shorter.

The guard swallowed hard. "Yes, ma'am."

"I'd apologize if I was you, Harvey." A guffaw came from behind them. "That's Etta Sawyer, and I'm here to tell ya, she don't take guff off'n nobody."

Three pair of eyes turned to find another uniformed guard striding toward them. A wiry man about fifty-five chuckled again. "How ya doin', Miss Etta? Don't pay no mind to this idiot. He ain't been here long. I can bet he'll remember y'all the next time ya come, though. What do ya say?"

Grandma Etta's head tilted to the side. "I'd bet on it, Chuck." She eyed the young guard with a narrowed glance. "I'll let it go this time since he didn't know me, but there won't be an excuse the next time. Got it, young fellow?"

"Oh yes, ma'am. I'll surely remember you the next time." The young guard stood at attention.

She grinned at him. "I'm certain you will."

The older guard's eyes moved to Skylar. "Now who's this?"

Grandma Etta's arm slipped around Skylar's waist. "This is my granddaughter. She's visiting from Wyoming."

He nodded. "She looks like you. You here to see Bufford?"

"That we are."

"Well, let me take you to the visitation room, and I'll have him brought out." He turned to open another gate.

"But wait a minute. I haven't wanded them yet." The young guard held up the metal detecting device. "What if they—?"

"This is Etta Sawyer, junior." The older guard propped his hands on his hips. "Miss Etta said she's been comin' here since 1945. If she wanted to break her son out of prison, she'd have done that a long time ago."

"But what about her granddaughter?" The young guard grew insistent.

Skylar turned a smile on him. "I've never met my uncle, nor have I ever been in this prison. How would I have a plan to break him out?"

The young guard's shoulders sagged, and he released a heavy sigh.

"It's okay, sonny." Grandma Etta patted his arm. "I'm sure somebody will come along today, and you can wand them. How about that?"

The wry expression on the young guard's face almost had Skylar laughing out loud, but she forced it down.

"This way, ladies. Follow me."

The guard led Skylar and Grandma Etta to a room with thick bulletproof glass dividing the prisoners from the visitors. He told them to take the seats in front of the window and to wait for Bufford Sawyer to be led in. A phone hung on the wall of the little cubicle where they sat. Within minutes, a man was led in from a door in the room behind the glass. He approached their cubicle and sat down. Bufford picked up the receiver on a phone on his side of the glass, and Grandma Etta took the receiver from their phone and put it to her ear. She held it so Skylar could hear as she leaned in. The man eyed Skylar with a mix of suspicion and curiosity.

"Hey, Mama. How are you?" Bufford asked in a deep voice.

"I'm doing just fine, son. How are you doing? You know you're my main concern when I come here."

A tiny lift of one corner of his mouth softened his expression. "I know that. I'm fine. Just whiling away my time till the day I get out."

"I know that's not true. They keep y'all working hard, don't they?" Grandma Etta put her hand on the glass, and he placed his up to match it.

He nodded, and a grimace crossed his face. "At least it makes the time go by." He paused. "Who is this?" He tilted his head toward Skylar.

"This is Skylar Simpson, your brother's oldest daughter and your niece."

"Simpson?" Bufford's brows puckered in the middle. "Did you marry a Simpson, gal?"

*Oh, boy. Here we go.* "No, sir. Daddy changed our name when we moved to Wyoming. He thought it would be safer that way."

Bufford nodded slowly. "Well, he's probably right." He sighed then rubbed his forehead. "How is your daddy? What's he up to these days?"

"Daddy died several years ago. He got sick then passed soon after." Skylar held the gaze of the man behind the glass. Those eyes were so like Daddy's. Uncle Bufford's features were similar to Daddy's, too, only thinner and harder somehow. Was that what came from years in prison? Gray streaked his brown hair and dotted the stubble on his narrow chin. He wore horn-rimmed glasses. Muscles bulged beneath his prison-blue chambray shirt. Scars marked his cheeks and forehead. From prison fights?

Skylar couldn't begin to imagine what life could be like here. Grandma said she'd been visiting Uncle Bufford since 1945. That was a long time to be in prison. How much longer would he be here, and why was he here? Did it have anything to do with the murder her father had been accused of?

"I'm sorry to hear Brodie's passed on." Uncle Bufford shook his head. "He was a child of God, though. I'm sure he's doin' just fine."

Skylar smiled and leaned into the phone receiver. "I'm not worried about my dad. As you say, he's doing just fine.

Are you a believer, Uncle Bufford?"

A gentle smile curved his lips. "I am, gal. It took me a lot o' years to realize what a rotten scoundrel I am and just how much I needed Jesus, but yeah, I'm more than a believer. I put my trust in Him. Perhaps you've heard the sayin', 'Satan believes in God, but he sure ain't a Christian.'" He chuckled. "You gotta do more than believe, gal. You gotta put your trust in Him."

"Yes, sir. That's right. I'm so happy you trust in Him." Skylar's heart sang at the news that Uncle Bufford loved the Lord. That was icing on the cake. Now would he answer some of her other questions? "Uncle, I have some questions for you. About that night a long time ago."

"Listen to her, Bufford. Hear her out," Grandma Etta urged.

Bufford's eyes ping-ponged between the women on the other side of the glass then settled on Skylar. His lips straightened into a compressed line. "Go on."

Skylar took a fortifying breath then continued. "Someone in Wyoming handed me a newspaper clipping from 1945 and accused my dad of murder. The woman has an ulterior motive. She's trying to drive a wedge between my boyfriend and me. He used to date her, and she wants him back. I'm determined that won't happen. I know my father. He's no murderer, and my mother told me so. She said that Dad told her once that he never killed anyone. Please tell me that's true. What exactly happened that night in 1945?"

Bufford leaned back in his chair and crossed an arm over his chest, propping the elbow of the arm holding the receiver. "Won't your boyfriend simply trust you, gal? Why stir up the past? What's done is done. Your daddy ain't around no more to worry with it."

"No, he isn't—" Skylar shook her head, "but my mother and my three sisters are. This woman who is telling this tale comes from a wealthy family. She'll do everything in her power to destroy my family in our town. The woman has no scruples about doing her worst. I need the truth not only to defend my father's name but also to protect my family and my relationship with my boyfriend. Please, tell me what happened. Send me to talk to whoever I need to talk to. I flew all the way from Wyoming to search out the truth."

Bufford glanced at the clock on the wall. "My time's almost up, so there ain't enough to tell you all that happened that night." He sighed. "They only allow two visitations a week. Come back Saturday, and I'll tell you more. In the meantime—"

A guard strolled by and poked Bufford in the shoulder with his billy club. "One minute warning, Bufford. Hang up the phone." He moved on to the next inmate to give the same warning.

Bufford gripped the phone and leaned forward. "In the meantime, go down to Calhoun, Georgia, and look up Eli Harding. He was a deputy back in 1945 and was there that night. He left town right after that—kind of like Brodie did. You might be able to get him to talk to you. Tell him I sent you."

"Time's up, Bufford. Hang up the phone." The guard poked Bufford in the back, harder this time.

"See you Saturday." Bufford hung up the phone, stood, and tossed them a wave as the guard pushed him toward the door where another guard led him away, the door slamming behind them.

Grandma Etta hung up the receiver and turned toward Skylar. "Well, that's that. We'd better go."

Skylar drew in a frustrated breath and stood to follow her grandmother back the way they'd come to exit the building. She'd learned next to nothing, but she did have a name to follow up with and the promise of another visit to Uncle Bufford. If the next visit was as short as this one, and that was likely, then there would be hardly any time for him to tell her much. It could take several visits to glean any information. Perhaps the visit to the former deputy would be more fruitful. *Please make it so, Lord, or this search could take forever.*

# Chapter Six

After a stop at the little country store for directions as Martha had suggested, Matt traveled until he arrived at his destination. The cabin that sat back at the end of the road had a quaint appeal. Matt would dearly love to relax in one of those rockers on the porch for a while, but his mission was to find Skylar. The yard looked like it needed a Brush Hog mower taken to it. The grass hadn't been mowed in a month of Sundays. Could he have landed at the wrong address? He glanced around. There were no vehicles in sight. Not even a rental, which he'd expected to find if Skylar were here.

Matt drove the pickup truck up the driveway and parked in front of the house. He climbed out and strode up the steps to knock on the front door. It sure was quiet out here with only the last fall crickets and birds singing. He knocked again and waited for a few more moments. When it was confirmed that no one was home, Matt turned to stride down the steps when an old pickup truck hauling a trailer carrying a…well, look at that. A Brush Hog. Someone had come to cut the tall grass, it seemed.

Matt waited at the top of the porch steps while the truck parked behind his. A man who looked to be in his late fifties climbed out and paused behind the open truck door. He rested a double-barrel shotgun in the open window frame of the door, then tilted a faded wool hunting cap back on his head and leaned forward. "Hold it right there, young fella." The man closed one eye and aimed down the shotgun barrel with the other one. "Don't move."

Matt raised his hands in the air, his heart skipping several beats. "Now wait a minute, sir. Don't shoot. I'm here looking for someone, but I knocked on the door twice, and no one seems to be home."

"Uh-huh. Sure, ya are." A wad of tobacco shot out of the side of the man's mouth. Other than that, he didn't flinch a muscle. "I 'spect yor here to rob the place, but I'll give ya the benefit o' the doubt. Who y'all lookin' fer?"

"Can I put my hands down and come out there to talk man-to-man?" Sweat trickled down Matt's back even with the autumn chill in the air.

"Keep 'em up, boy. We can talk man-to-man right where ya are. Now, who are ya, and who are y'all lookin' fer?"

A frustrated huff of air blew from Matt. "My name's Matt Scott, and I've just arrived from Wyoming. I'm looking for Etta Sawyer and my girlfriend, Skylar Simpson, Etta's granddaughter. Do you know Etta?"

The man's other eye popped open, and he raised his head a few inches but didn't lower the shotgun. "O' course, I know Henrietta. She's my oldest sister, but she ain't got no granddaughter named Skylar Simpson."

"Then do you know her son, Brodie Sawyer?"

The snide expression that marred the man's face shifted. A mixture of doubt, curiosity, and disbelief fought for a place on his features. "Brodie ain't been around these parts in nigh on twenty-five years, boy."

"No, he hasn't. His daughter's here to visit her grandmother, and I'm looking for both of them. Skylar arrived before me, and she doesn't know I came."

"Surprisin' her, huh?" A slight grin lifted a corner of the man's mouth. "It's always good to keep the womenfolk a guessin'. Still and all, I never heard the Simpson name."

"Sir, can I put my arms down?" Matt wiggled his fingers. "My fingers are going to sleep."

The man narrowed his eyes. "Go on. Put 'em down, but don't try nothin'. I still got ya covered."

Matt lowered his arms and let them hang at his sides. "So I see. As for the Simpson name, your nephew, Brodie, changed his name when he moved his family to Wyoming."

"Yeah, it ain't surprisin' after all he went through back here in'45." The man gave a brief nod. "Don't blame him. How is Brodie?"

"He passed away a few years ago after his illness."

"That's a shame. He always was a good man. Didn't deserve what they put him through."

Matt crossed his arms over his chest. "You don't think he committed murder?"

"What do you know about it?" The man's brow lowered. Where he'd seemed to relax, he now bristled like a porcupine.

"Not much, I can tell you that—" Matt shook his head, "—but I did read the article from 1945 that stated Brodie was arrested for murder. Skylar wants to prove he didn't do it."

"O' course, he didn't do it." The man straightened and withdrew the shotgun from the window. He tossed it onto the seat inside the truck and slammed the door. "My nephew was a decorated Army captain and a man o' God. There was no way he would'a killed somebody in cold blood. If'n your gal needs a character witness, I'll be glad to tell her a thing or two."

Matt nearly chuckled but rammed it down deep. This man, Skylar's great-uncle, meant what he said, and although there wouldn't be a trial where a character witness was needed, she would be happy to hear good words spoken about her father. "I'm sure Skylar will be glad to hear whatever you're willing to tell her about her father." Matt waited on the porch as the older man strode across the yard and approached the steps. He wasn't about to move. The man may have left his shotgun in the truck, but there was no telling what he may have up his sleeve.

"Boy, I think I'm beginning to take to ya." He stopped at the base of the steps and met Matt's eyes. "Ya say you're from Wyomin'?"

"Yes, sir." Matt shifted his stance but left his arms across his chest, keeping his eyes on the other man.

"I can tell from that hat o' yorn, you must be one o' them cowboys. You ride and break horses?"

"Yes, sir."

"Y'all are polite to your elders, that's fer sure." The man nodded in approval.

After several moments, he waved a hand toward Matt. "Come on. I want to show ya something."

~

Skylar followed Grandma Etta through the old cemetery until they reached a granite headstone near the base of a weeping willow tree. Skylar spotted the etchings of George Sawyer's name along with his birth and death dates.

It had only been seven years since her grandfather had passed away, yet bright green moss had already made its appearance on the granite stone. Fortunately, it didn't obstruct the important information. Grandma Etta's name and birthdate were already on the stone waiting for the day she would join her husband. Skylar hoped that day wouldn't come too soon. She longed to know this woman she hadn't even known existed.

She slipped her hand into her grandmother's then hoped she hadn't presumed too much. After all, she didn't know her yet. She was pleased when Grandma Etta gave Skylar's hand a squeeze.

"That's my George's grave." The older woman's voice wavered slightly. "It was the worst day of my life when I had to bury him. The next worst was the day my Brody took his family and moved to Wyoming." She sniffed, gave Skylar's hand another squeeze, and dropped her hand. "Come on. I'll show you the church, then we'll head home."

Out here in the country it seemed they didn't see fit to lock the church, so they walked right on in. It was a typical white clapboard country church with a steeple. Grandma Etta told Skylar the steeple held a bell, but it hadn't been rung in many years. Inside the sanctuary, a layer of dust covered everything. The old patinaed oak pews and pulpit, the tiny choir section, the communion table. Even their footsteps left prints on the creaky oak floorboards.

Skylar sneezed.

"Bless you. It looks the same as it did after the young fellow came to preach a few times then left. Sadly, there's only dust left now." Grandma Etta shook her head. "This church was built in the early 1800s. It's a perfectly good church but has no preacher."

A chill ran through Skylar as she slowly turned around in the middle of the aisle. "It is sad. I'm glad that at least some of you are meeting to study the Bible. It's something at least."

"True." Grandma Etta jammed her hands into her coat pockets. "Perhaps the Lord will send someone back here one day. We can always hope and pray."

Skylar slipped an arm through her grandmother's. "Thanks for bringing me to see where Grandpa George preached. It's a beautiful little church."

"Yes, it is." Grandma Etta turned to give it one last look then headed for the door. "Come on. Let's go home."

As Skylar approached Grandma Etta's cabin, she stopped the car suddenly at the sight of two pickup trucks in the driveway, one with an empty trailer on the back. "Were you expecting company?"

"I was expecting my brother, Jimmy, to come over and mow my yard. Not sure who's here with the other pickup." Grandma Etta tapped her chin. "I suppose there's only one way to find out, child."

Skylar chuckled and drove on, parking along the end of

the driveway. Climbing out, they strode up the yard where an older man at the side yard raked the cut tall grass into piles.

"Jimmy, it's going to take you a while to rake up all this grass," Grandma Etta called as she approached him. "I'll get another rake and give you a hand. Whose truck is that?" She tossed a thumb over her shoulder.

Her younger brother shrugged and kept on raking. "Some young feller who stopped by. Said he'd give me a hand. He's out back runnin' the Brush Hog."

"Huh. Wonder who that could be." Grandma Etta cast a curious glance at Skylar. "Jimmy, this is my granddaughter, Skylar. She's Brodie's oldest. You might remember her from when she was just a little baby before Brodie took his family west."

Jimmy paused in raking and eyed Skylar, a smile lifting the corners of his mouth. "I sure 'nuff remember. You was just a bitty little thing." He held out a hand. "I won't give ya a hug right now. I'm all sweaty from workin'. I'll owe ya one."

"It's good to meet you." Skylar smiled and shook his outstretched hand. "Can I call you Uncle Jimmy?"

"Y'all better. I'm your great-uncle, but Uncle Jimmy will do fine. I'm sorry to hear 'bout your dad's passin' and all."

Skylar stared at him. How could he have heard about her father's death?

"How did you hear Brodie died, Jimmy?" Grandma Etta propped a hand on her hip.

A dear-in-the-headlights expression etched itself on Jimmy's features. He scratched his chin and chuckled. "Hmm. Not sure where I heard that. Well, I better get back to work. Talk with y'all later." Jimmy turned his back on them and commenced to raking.

Grandma Etta frowned. "Jimmy?"

No answer.

Grandma Etta tilted her head for Skylar to follow, and they walked toward the back of the house. Some of the grass was still knee-deep. Skylar watched her step as the sound of the Brush Hog grew louder. She spotted a man on the seat of the machine as it rode away from them through some trees, and he made her think of Matt. Her heart ached with how much she missed him. She'd only been gone a couple of days, yet not being with him was excruciating. No telling how long it would be until she saw him again. She swallowed hard in an attempt to force the emotions down. Whoever this stranger was, she didn't want to meet him with her heart on her sleeve.

Skylar and Grandma Etta crossed the backyard and waited while the man on the mower turned the machine around and came back toward them out of the shadow of the trees. Skylar spent a few minutes glancing around. The yard looked different with shorter grass. It would be nice to sit out here in the chairs by the firepit once the yard was cleaned up. Why was the yard allowed to get into such a state to begin with? Did Grandma Etta ever sit out here in the evenings when it was nice? Would Skylar if she lived way out here alone?

When the mower approached, Skylar turned and spotted the man sitting in the seat. She stared for a moment, then she gasped. Matt? Was it really him? But…but how? Why…?

Her feet took off before her brain engaged, and she ran to meet the mower. Matt halted the Brush Hog and turned off the engine. He jumped off and gathered Skylar in his arms, swinging her around and around.

"Matt. Why are you h—" Before she could finish her sentence, Matt planted his lips on hers. He didn't release them as he lowered her to her feet and kept his arms wrapped around her waist and back. Skylar's heart raced where moments ago it had felt the pain of separation from the man she loved. She didn't know anything except that Matt was here. Now. Holding her close.

After several moments, someone cleared their throat, and she stepped back.

Matt shoved his hat back and gave her a brilliant smile. "Miss me?"

Skylar slid a finger down his stubbly cheek. "How could you tell?"

He cocked a brow. "Ask me later."

Someone cleared their throat again. "Hello. I'm still here."

Skylar turned to find Grandma Etta with her hands planted on her hips, a wry smile on her lips.

"Sorry, Grandma Etta. I suppose you can tell this is my boyfriend."

"Well, I should hope so. If not, you've got a lot of explaining to do." Grandma Etta approached Matt with her hand outstretched. "It seems you've knocked all manners out of my granddaughter's mind, so I'll introduce myself. I'm Henrietta Sawyer, young man. You may call me Grandma Etta just as Skylar does."

Matt shook the older woman's hand. "Thank you. I'm Matt Scott. It's a pleasure to meet you, Grandma Etta."

"This is quite a surprise, to say the least." Grandma Etta jammed her hands into her jacket pockets. "What are you doing here?"

"Two reasons, ma'am." Matt glanced at Skylar. "I don't believe anything Gina had to say to me. She can try all she likes, but I'm not going back to her. I've found a godly woman that I'm in love with, and there's nothing she has to say that will change my mind. Skylar, I talked with your mom before I left Gillette. She gave me some information to help me find you. She also told me what your dad said about not having killed anyone. I believe what he told her. However, having said that, I'm concerned that because you're on this quest to prove him innocent, you may be in danger. If the murderer is still out there, you may have put a target on yourself."

A sharp intake of breath had both of them turning toward Grandma Etta. "Oh, my goodness. I never thought of that, child. You need to stop this search right now."

Skylar shook her head. "I can't do that, Grandma Etta. Dad's record will never truly be cleared if the murderer is still out there."

"You don't have to do this, Sky." Matt turned her toward him. "You don't have to prove anything. I believe your dad was innocent."

Skylar reached and clasped his hands within hers. "I appreciate your trust, but Gina will never leave our family alone unless we have solid proof. She'll never stop pursuing you and trying to drag my family down." She paused. "Matt, we have a lead to talk with the deputy who was there that night. Let's see what he has to say."

Matt exchanged a glance with Grandma Etta.

"It can't hurt to see what he has to say." She shrugged. "We were going to go down in the morning. He's in northern Georgia about two and a half hours from here. If you're okay with it, we'll leave about eight o'clock."

~

Grandma Etta invited Jimmy to stay for supper. A widower, Jimmy was more than delighted to stay and eat a meal prepared by his sister and enjoy family company than eat by himself. After supper, Jimmy built a fire in the stone pit out back, and they all sat around in the wooden Adirondack chairs Grandpa Sawyer had built years ago. Jimmy and Matt spent some time repairing them while Skylar helped Grandma Etta prepare the meal.

"I sure do love this time of year." Grandma Etta tugged a wool blanket around her as she stared into the flames dancing in the firepit.

Jimmy tossed on another log sending sparks into the night sky. He drew in a deep lung-full of air and released it slowly. "Yup. Just somethin' about the cool, crisp fall air, ain't it?"

From their two-person Adirondack chair, Skylar leaned closer to Matt. He tucked a wool blanket around them. Her fleece coat was warm, but the feel of his arm around her warmed her heart. Having him here in Tennessee sent her heart skipping with joy. She gazed into the star-speckled, inky sky. *Thanks for sending him, Lord. My heart is overjoyed to have Matt by my side.*

Jimmy began telling Skylar about her dad and the memories he had of his nephew. She was thankful for the stories he told and the perspective he gave on her dad's younger life. Grandma Etta threw in a few from Brodie's childhood as well. It was in the middle of one of these stories that a young woman strolled up out of the darkness. She looked familiar to Skylar, but she couldn't place her at first.

Grandma Etta turned and stared at the young woman who halted beside her chair. "Ruthann? Is that you? What are you doing here, child? It's kind of late to be driving out on these roads at night."

"Ya betcha, gal." Jimmy tossed in. "There's bears out here, not to mention all the deer on the roads. Ya never know what'll come out from the woods at night."

The young woman smiled as she gave Grandma Etta a hug then straightened. "I know that, but I'm careful when I drive. Besides, it was the only time I could come after work. At least I didn't have to close up the restaurant tonight, so I had time to run out here."

Grandma Etta peered up at her. "Well, it's good to see you, sweetie. It's been a long while."

Ruthann met Skylar's eyes, and she smiled before returning her gaze to Grandma Etta's. Restaurant? Was this the young waitress who had waited on Skylar the night she'd arrived in town?

"It has been. Between work and school, I stay busy. Mama wanted me to bring this to you." She held out a large brown paper bag. "There's a lot of mending in it. She wants to know if you can fix these things. There's no rush; just whenever you can get to it."

"Sure, I can." Grandma Etta smiled and pointed to the ground beside her chair. "I'll be happy to fix them for her. Just set it right here."

Ruthann set the bag beside the chair. "Well, I'd better go."

"Won't you sit for a little while?"

"I have to get up early, and I have a long drive back. Mama or I will pick them up in a couple of weeks, if that's okay."

"That'd be just fine."

"It was good seeing y'all."

"Love you, sweetie. Tell your mama I said hello."

"I'll do that." Ruthann gave Etta another big hug then waved to the others.

"Give my regards as well." Jimmy called after her.

"I'll tell her." Ruthann's voice faded into the darkness.

Skylar pointed after her. "I remember her from the night I arrived in town. I ate at Reaves Café, and she was my waitress."

"That's right." Grandma Etta laughed. "She's your cousin."

"What?" Skylar sat up, dislodging the blanket.

Jimmy stood to stir the fire and chuckled. "Yep. She's Bufford's youngest."

"I don't understand. Hasn't he been in prison since 1945?" Skylar leaned back against Matt again, drawing the blanket under her chin. "Ruthann told me that night that she's in high school. If I remember correctly, she told me she's in the eleventh grade. Am I right?"

"You are," Grandma Etta said.

"Then how could Bufford have a daughter in high school if he's been in prison since 1945?"

"You're quick on the uptake." Grandma Etta dropped her gaze to the flames as if she was remembering the past. "Bufford did indeed go to prison that night in 1945. He was there the night Sheriff Baker was shot and killed." She shook her head, sadness settling on her weary features. "As you know, your daddy served in the Army and came home a hero. Bufford…well, he wanted to emulate his older brother and serve his country, but he has a clubfoot and walks kind of awkward. The Army drafted him all right, but they took one look at him walking in the door and stamped 4-F on his draft card and sent him home. That was a discouraging blow for him. I understand they can fix a clubfoot these days, but he's been in prison, so there's been no opportunity for that."

Grandma Etta paused and tugged her blanket under her chin. "Bufford was always a smart boy in school. He had high grades, but he got teased a lot. There were two fellows who came home from the war and started moonshining out back of one of their properties. They got Bufford involved. He did a lot of the dirty work for them. They were several years older than him. Bufford had married a young girl about sixteen years old. He'd gotten her pregnant before they married, and her daddy made him marry her before a preacher at the end of a shotgun. Turns out they had a pretty good marriage for the two years before he went to prison. Moonshining paid him nicely. He did the work at the still while the other two fellows drove the shine out of state to the honkytonks. Unfortunately for Bufford, it all came to a head that night in 1945."

"What happened? How was Dad involved?" Skylar shifted beneath Matt's arm.

Grandma Etta took a deep breath and plunged on. "Sheriff Baker and Deputy Harding, the one Bufford told you we should go see, came by our house looking for Bufford. There was a robbery, and Bufford and his two buddies had been seen by witnesses. The sheriff deputized Brodie, and off they went to find them. On your daddy's first night home from the Army too."

"Grandma Etta," Matt piped in, "what does this all have to do with Ruthann being Bufford's youngest child?"

The older woman turned her gaze on him. "I'm getting to that. Just hang on. It's a long and not-so-pretty story. Believe me, Bufford has lived a sordid life."

Matt sighed and lifted a hand. "Sorry. Please continue."

"Now where was I?" Grandma Etta thought for a moment. "Oh yes. Off they went. The next thing I know, I get a call from Brodie at the state police station in Knoxville. He'd been arrested for the murder of Sheriff Baker. Bufford had also been arrested for robbery and moonshining, but his two cohorts had skipped the county. They eventually were apprehended and arrested for armed robbery as well as moonshining and transporting moonshine across state lines. However, that night there was a ruckus that took place in which the sheriff was shot and killed. Deputy Harding was also shot as Bufford's buddies ran. Harding passed out eventually, but I have no idea when. That's something we need to find out because I don't know what *he* knows about that night."

"What about Dad? Do you know why he was released?" Skylar stared at her grandmother.

"Not a clue except that he was found innocent."

"You mean he was released, then came home and we moved west?"

"Yep, all in about two days' time. I have no idea why or how. He never said. Just packed y'all up and headed to Wyoming. He didn't even tell your grandpa and me where." Grandma Etta shook her head as she stared into the fire. "We lost all contact with Brodie and your family. It was downright disheartening."

"I'm so sorry." Skylar tossed off the blanket and stood, then crossed over to her grandmother and leaned over to wrap her arms around her. "I wish I could go back and change the past, but I can't. There's so much I would change. It seems that night destroyed so many lives."

Grandma Etta lifted Skylar away then swiped at her own eyes. "It did indeed." She patted Skylar's cheek. "Now, go back and sit down. My story isn't finished. Or rather, Bufford's story isn't finished."

Skylar returned to sit beside Matt who drew her close once again. Bufford's life had touched so many others and not in good ways. She was happy that he had surrendered his life to Christ. At least something positive had come from his years of disorder and destruction.

Grandma waited for her brother as he tossed another log onto the fire. "After being in prison for about nine years, Bufford was up for parole. The parole board approved it, and he walked out of Bushy Mountain State Pen. Soon after, he decided he'd had enough of Tennessee, and he violated his parole. He took his wife, Casey, and headed west to visit his brother, Brodie, and your family. For a man who'd always been so smart, that was a dumb move. His parole officer put out a warrant for his arrest, and they caught him in Nebraska. He's serving another twenty years for crossing four state lines. He went through Kentucky, Illinois, and Missouri before they caught him in Nebraska.

"Now, you're wondering where Ruthann comes into this story. I'm sure I don't need to tell you about the birds and the bees. Somewhere along the highway before the cops caught him, Bufford and Casey, well, they got pregnant, and the rest is history, as they say. Ruthann was born nine months later, but Bufford was back in prison. She lives with her mama in Oak Ridge. Casey is the sweetest woman you could ever meet, especially considering all she's had to put up with my Bufford. She's actually the one who led him to the Lord."

"That's wonderful. At least when he eventually gets out, he has a good woman to come home to." Skylar smiled. "Hopefully Uncle Bufford's story will end happily someday."

"Bufford's got another child, a boy, ya know." Jimmy leaned forward and held his hands toward the fire. "Smart as a whip. Well, he's not a boy no more. He's all grow'd up, and he's a doctor in Knoxville. They had him before Bufford went to prison the first time in 1945."

"Really?" Matt chimed in. "That's great."

"He has two smart and talented children." Grandma Etta stood and folded the blanket she'd had wrapped around her. "Bufford may have ruined his own life and several others, but he and Casey did all they could to encourage their children to make something of themselves. I'm proud of both of them."

"What do you do, Skylar?" Jimmy stood to stir the fire.

"I'm a reporter for a magazine back in Wyoming. The *Casper Gazette*." She and Matt stood as well. Matt took the blanket from Skylar and folded it. "I work for Matt's sister who is the editor of the magazine. She's an amazing woman."

"I dare say, so is her brother." Grandma Etta cast a smile toward Matt, who ducked his head as he slipped the blanket over his arm.

Skylar slipped her arm through Matt's other one. "Yes, without a doubt, and I'm thrilled he's here."

"Well, I'm happy he's here too. You're a lot happier since he arrived." Grandma Etta patted Skylar's arm. "It's time we head to bed though. Tomorrow's another day, and we have a trip to Georgia ahead of us."

"I'm headin' home." Jimmy grabbed a bucket of water sitting behind one of the chairs. "Y'all head on inside, and I'll douse this fire."

"Good night, Jimmy. Safe travels home, and thanks again for taking care of my yard. Next time don't wait so long," Grandma Etta chided with a chuckle.

"Don't worry. I'll be around next week. The growin' season's 'bout over, thank goodness. Won't be long. Good night."

"Good night." Skylar and Matt called in unison then strolled hand in hand toward the back door. A sense of peace washed over Skylar as they entered the cabin. This was her dad's childhood home, and she'd met family she never knew existed. They'd welcomed her with open arms. The man she loved had followed her to Tennessee because he loved her and was concerned for her safety. He didn't care what Gina had told him. He cared about her. Skylar Simpson.

The memory of his kiss when he drew her into his arms after jumping off the mower returned to her mind when she slipped into bed later that night. Yeah, Matt Scott loved *her*. He'd said so. She felt safe in his arms. And the concern he felt for her safety? Was she truly in danger? Was there still a murderer on the loose? Had there been since 1945? She didn't know about that.

It had seemed Grandma Etta's story was long and detailed, but so much information was missing. Skylar's grandmother had no idea if the murderer was ever caught. One would think in a place where everyone knew everyone else, if the murderer was caught, that news would have been known for miles around. In order to clear her dad's name, Skylar would have to see this search through.

*Thanks for sending Matt, Father. Wow. Another wonderful surprise and blessing. His help will be invaluable in this search I'm on, but we need Your direction. Concerning this visit to Deputy Harding tomorrow, if it's Your will, help him give us pertinent information. Then show us where to go from there. Please guide our steps, Father.*

# Chapter Seven

It was nearly a two-and-half-hour drive to Calhoun, Georgia, where retired deputy Eli Harding lived. Matt drove his pickup with Skylar sitting in the middle between him and Grandma Etta. They found lots to talk about as they navigated the winding roads between Oliver Springs and Calhoun, mostly life in Wyoming and Tennessee.

"I was raised in the hollow not two miles from the cabin," Grandma Etta explained, "but I left when I was sixteen to go away to college to teaching school. When I returned, I taught in a little one-room school house until I married your grandpa. I taught a few more years until the boys came along, then I stayed home to raise them. Your Grandpa George, as I told you before, was a preacher. We had services at the schoolhouse, at least until too many folks started coming, then we had to build a church." She chuckled. "That wasn't a bad problem."

"Is that why your vernacular is more proper than your brother's?" Skylar hastened to add, "I mean no disrespect to him."

Grandma Etta patted Skylar's hand on her knee. "No need to apologize, child. Mine wasn't so proper when I went away to school. Yes, I learned to speak properly while at college. I had a wonderful teacher who took the time to work with me. She was beyond patient, and I worked hard to learn to change the way I spoke. I must admit I was teased rather harshly by the other students when I first arrived. Suppose that motivated me to change." She chuckled. "I also wanted to make a difference in my students' lives. Some students I helped, and others looked at me like I had a green face and horns on my head."

"I'm sorry." Skylar squeezed Grandma Etta's hand.

"Don't be. We make changes in this life where we can. That's all that's expected of us. God gives us the tools, and we do what He asks. If someone is helped, so be it. It's the same with His Word. We share it by spreading the gospel and telling others about Him, then letting them make their own decisions. No one can force them to choose Him. We have to simply plant the seed of His Word and let Him do the rest."

"That's so true," Matt chimed in. "My sister had been after me for years to accept Christ, but I kept putting her off—or rather, putting Christ off. Then back in the spring, I finally accepted Him. At the same time my dad did."

Skylar patted his arm. "It was awesome."

"Yeah, it was." He cast a glance at her before turning his gaze back to the road. Then he pointed at a sign along the roadside. "Hey, we're here. We're in Calhoun."

"Good." Grandma Etta shifted in her seat. "My butt's getting numb. I was about to tell you to stop and let me stretch my legs."

Skylar shook her head and laughed. "Grandma Etta, you may speak better English, but you don't hold back."

"I'm too old to worry about it anymore, child." She side-eyed Skylar. "Did that offend you?"

Skylar wrapped an arm around her grandma. "No, not at all."

Grandma Etta leaned into her. "Good. You'll get used to me before long."

"So where do we begin?" Matt's eyes scanned the road as they entered the little Georgian town. "Not much here.

Look. We'll be out of town in about thirty seconds."

Skylar pointed at a service station on the next corner. "I'm sure he comes in for gas sometimes. Surely, they'll know him. Stop there."

Matt pulled into the small two-pump station, and they heard the ding-ding as the truck tires ran over the air hose. A man in gray coveralls and a gray cap strolled out of the station and to Matt's window. He rolled it down.

"Can I help ya, sir?" The man in his mid-fifties smiled around a wad of chew beneath his lower lip. He twisted to the left and spit a string of brown juice onto the ground.

"Yes, please. Ten gallons and an oil check. Then I have a question for you when you're finished."

The man gave Matt a quick two-fingered salute. "Ya got it." He headed to the back to add the gas then hurried to the front of the truck and lifted the hood. After he checked the oil, he wiped his hands on a rag and made his way back to Matt's window. "Oil looks just fine, sir. Don't need any. I added ten gallons o' gas as ya asked." He spit another stream of chew to the side and waited.

Skylar tried not to stare. There were hands at Scott ranch that chewed tobacco, but she didn't care for the habit. She was thankful Matt didn't chew.

Matt handed the man some cash, then he sauntered inside for change and returned to hand it to Matt. Matt gave the man a tip, then asked, "We're in town to visit someone. Do you know Eli Harding?"

One brow lifted, then the man's eyes narrowed. "What ya lookin' for him for?"

Skylar's heart began to sink. *Please Lord, we need to find Deputy Harding. Please let this man help us.*

Matt chuckled. "Nothing bad, I can assure you. We simply want to visit with him." He tossed a thumb in Skylar's direction. "Her dad used to know him. She wants to find out some things about her dad that Eli might know." Matt shrugged. "We're not out to bother him or bring him trouble."

The man spit again, never taking his eyes off of them. "Well, don't suppose it would hurt none. Y'all don't look like you're trouble." He shifted on his feet then turned to point back the way they'd come. "Turn down that road to the left. Take it about five miles...."

Skylar hurriedly jotted the directions on a notepad from her purse. Matt thanked him then started the truck and turned back the way he'd directed them and headed out of town.

"I wasn't so sure he was going to help us out there for a minute." Matt shifted in his seat.

"Agreed." Grandma Etta sniffed. "I was praying though."

"You and me both." Skylar leaned her head against Grandma Etta's.

"Make that three of us," Matt chuckled.

"I'd say we had our own little storming-the-gates-of-heaven session, and we didn't even know it." Grandma Etta slapped her knee with a cackle. "There's nothing like prayer to move the heart of God."

The road to Former-deputy Harding's house led them back up into the Georgia mountains. His address might be Calhoun, but it was nowhere near town.

"I don't think Mr. Harding wants to be found easily," Skylar said as Matt turned the truck from the paved road onto a dirt track. "Didn't the man at the gas station say once we hit the dirt road, it would be another couple of miles?"

"Yeah, he did." Matt swung the steering wheel to miss a pothole. "It makes me wonder why this man left Oliver Springs right after your dad did, and why he moved out in the middle of nowhere."

"Good question." Grandma Etta grabbed the armrest to steady herself. "If Bufford wants us to talk to this man so much, then he must know something. I'm wondering if he'll talk. If he's out here in the middle of the mountains, is he hiding? And if he is, why?"

Skylar turned her eyes on her grandmother. She hoped the older woman wasn't right about her suspicions.

"That must be it." Matt's words brought Skylar's attention back to stare out the front windshield. A small log cabin sat back off the right side of the road a couple hundred feet. Matt pulled into the dirt driveway but stopped just off the road. Dust swirled around the pickup as he turned off the engine.

*Lord, only You know what we'll find here.* Skylar's silent words lifted heavenward. *Guide us and protect us. And please help us find the information we seek.*

~

Matt climbed from the pickup and went around to help Grandma Etta and Skylar out. They cautiously approached the cabin, but when they were about halfway to the front porch, the cabin door flew open and a man in his mid-sixties stood in the doorway, a double-barrel shotgun aimed at them.

"Don't come any closer," he called. "I won't hesitate to shoot."

Matt inhaled a deep breath. What was it with these people who lived in the back of nowhere? Were they all suspicious of strangers? "Deputy Harding?"

"I ain't a deputy no more. Besides, I don't know you folks. How do you know who I am?" He closed an eye and took better aim.

"Please don't shoot." Skylar lifted her hands in the air. "We're not here to hurt you. We only want to ask you some questions. My name is Skylar Simpson. My dad was Brodie Sawyer." She slowly pointed at Grandma Etta. "This is my grandmother, Etta Sawyer, Brodie's mother. And this is my boyfriend, Matt Scott. Matt and I live in Wyoming, and we came to fine out some information about my dad. He's no longer living."

Harding lifted his head and opened his eye to stare at Skylar. "Brodie left here a long time ago. What could ya possibly need to know about him? If you're his daughter, you should know everything ya need to."

"I don't know everything. My uncle Bufford Sawyer sent us to talk to you. He said you could help me. Someone in Wyoming has accused my father of murder. I know he wasn't a murderer, but I need to prove it." Skylar paused. "Please, Mr. Harding. Help me."

After several moments, Harding uncocked his shotgun and lowered it. "Come on in. I don't think I can help, but I'll hear ya out." He stood by the open door. "And don't move fast. I'll be keeping my eyes on the lot o' ya."

Grandma Etta propped her hands on her hips and raised a brow. "You know me, Eli. You and Sheriff Baker have been to my house on more than one occasion."

A ruddy tinge brightened Harding's cheeks. "I know who ya are, Mrs. Sawyer, but I don't know them." He tilted his head in Matt and Skylar's direction. Matt forced himself not to roll his eyes.

"Maybe not, but they're with me, you idiot. They're not going to hurt you, and neither am I. We just want some answers about Brodie."

Harding sniffed and moved out of Grandma Etta's way. "Have a seat." He shuffled over and leaned the shotgun against the stone fireplace.

It was a simple cabin with simple amenities. Matt and Skylar sat on the overstuffed couch, Grandma Etta took the wooden chair, and Harding took what must be his favorite recliner.

"Where's Betty?" Grandma Etta shifted on her seat. Matt doubted it was comfortable, but she'd left the couch for Skylar and him.

Harding stared into the dying embers of the fire. "Betty's been gone nigh on ten years now. She died of a bad case of pneumonia. Couldn't shake it."

"I'm sorry to hear that, Eli. After you moved away, I had no way of knowing. I didn't even know where you moved to."

Harding clasped his fingers across his stomach and twiddled his thumbs. "I know. It's what I wanted. I didn't want...." He glanced at his hands and swallowed hard.

"You didn't want what?" Grandma Etta asked.

He shook his head. "Nothin'. It don't matter." Harding avoided their eyes and kept looking at either his hands or into the fireplace. He certainly wasn't relaxed. He didn't want to talk to them, that was for sure.

"Mr. Harding—" Skylar leaned forward. "I have a newspaper article from 1945 that says my dad was arrested for murder but little else. I grew up in Wyoming with him always there. He told my mother he never committed that murder, although he never talked with her about the night the sheriff was killed. You were there, weren't you? Can you please tell me what happened? Please tell me why Dad was arrested for murder then released. Why is Uncle Bufford serving in prison?"

Harding ran a palm down his face. "Yeah, I was there, but I was shot. I passed out before the state troopers arrived. Can't tell you much." He clasped his hands together then unclasped them and smoothed them down his overall legs. "All I remember was there was chaos goin' on and...a lot of shootin'."

"Who was there, Eli? Surely you remember who all was present at the time." Grandma Etta's voice was soft without a hint of accusation.

Harding's shoulders relaxed, and he met Grandma Etta's eyes. "Yeah, I remember. I was goin' through the woods with Brodie after Sheriff Baker had deputized him. The sheriff went around another way. We were at Griff Jenkins' place in the woods out back o' his house. We came upon Griff Jenkins, and one o' his buddies makin' moonshine. Bufford was there too. They come up shootin', and I got shot and the sheriff got shot, only he got killed. I was leanin' up against a tree when I saw Brodie and Bufford still there. The other two must've skedaddled out o' there. I passed out, and they took me to the hospital. I was told the state troopers arrested Brodie for murdering the sheriff and took him to jail."

Matt leaned forward. "You're saying Skylar's dad, Brodie, was deputized then arrested for the murder of Sheriff Baker. What motive do you think Brodie would've had to murder the sheriff? Didn't Brodie just arrive home from the war that evening?"

Harding averted his eyes and shrugged. "Just tellin' ya what happened. I don't know what motive he would've had, but I know he was released soon after he was taken to jail."

"Was Dad carrying a gun that night, Mr. Harding?" Skylar asked, her words hardly above a whisper.

His eyes swerved to hers and held for a moment before diving away. His fingers fidgeted then he reached up and wiped sweat from his brow. "I don't recall."

"You can't remember if Brodie carried a weapon out with him after he was deputized?" Matt propped his arms on his knees and clasped his hands loosely together. "That would be an important thing to remember, wouldn't it?"

"That was over twenty-five years ago. How can I remember everything?" Harding's gaze once again settled on the flames dancing in the fireplace.

"When did you leave your job as deputy, Eli?" Grandma Etta shifted on the hard wooden seat.

"Right after I got out of the hospital. I went back and resigned, then Betty and me moved down here. We didn't tell nobody where we was movin' to."

"Why not?" Matt asked.

Harding's eyes shifted to Matt then away. "I was done with being a deputy."

"What about your family? And Betty's? Surely you told them where you were moving to." Grandma Etta shook her head. "You're not making sense, Eli."

"Maybe it's just 'cause we wanted to get away, Miss

Etta." He pushed to his feet. Frustration marred his features. "I'm gettin' tired of these questions. You said you wanted to ask about Brodie. Quit askin' about me."

"We simply want to understand what happened that night, Eli." Grandma Etta lifted a hand toward him. "I don't think you're telling us everything. You seem…nervous. What are you holding back?"

Harding stomped over to the fireplace. He laid an arm across the mantel, his gaze on the burning embers. "I'm not hidin' nothing."

"Did I say you were? I asked if you were holding back."

"It's the same thing, ain't it?"

"I don't know, is it?" Grandma Etta's words were soft.

Harding jammed his hands into his overall pockets, and he swiveled from the mantel. "Look, why don't you look up Griff Jenkins and talk with him. Maybe he can tell you somethin'. That is if you can pin him down."

"What do you mean, pin him down?" Skylar asked. "Wasn't Griff Jenkins one of the moonshiners that ran away that night?"

Harding gave a nod and glanced at Skylar. "Yep. He and his buddy, Harper Kent, are on the Nascar circuit now. Jenkins is a race car driver, and Kent's his crew chief. It's hard to pin 'em down 'cause o' their racing schedule. I don't have no 'letricity way out here, so I don't have no TV, but I hear things in town when I go in for supplies. Folks there follow NASCAR. I hear there's only a couple more races in the season. Not sure what the rest o' the schedule is. You'll have to find that out fer yourselves." The first bit of mirth they'd seen from Harding since they'd arrived erupted in a chuckle. "Where do you think Griff learned to drive so fast? Answer—driving moonshine down mountain roads, trying to evade the law on his way to the honkytonks in Georgia and North Carolina."

Grandma Etta's brows met in a frown. "Yeah, and they got my Bufford involved in making that hooch. He went to prison for it."

"So they did, Miss Etta—" Harding turned to face the others, "—once the state troopers caught up with 'em."

"I know. They served for a time for making the hooch and transporting it across state lines, but I always wondered if they didn't have something to do with the sheriff's death." Grandma Etta stood and straightened her back. "The killer was never caught, was he?"

Harding glanced away. "I wouldn't know nothin' about that."

"No?" She strode over to stand in front of him. "Are you sure about that, Eli? Are you sure you didn't move down here to hide out? If we found you, I bet the killer could too."

Harding's face blanched. "I keep to myself, and I don't know nothing. Remember, I passed out. I didn't see nothin'."

"Mmm-hmm." Grandma Etta patted him on the shoulder. "If anybody asks me, I'll tell them that, Eli. Your secret's safe with us."

He took a deep breath and swallowed. "Thank you."

"We'll see ourselves out."

As the trio climbed into the pickup truck and Matt started the engine, Skylar stared out the front windshield at the cabin. "Do you believe him? Do you believe he didn't see who killed the sheriff?"

"Not on your life," Matt scoffed. "He knows something, but he's using that passing-out story to protect himself."

"Can you blame him?" Grandma Etta sighed. "If word got out that he saw something, he'd be a dead man. Even twenty-five years later, it's likely the murderer would be charged, so they'd come after Harding."

"Most definitely." Skylar shifted her eyes to her grandmother. "There is no statute of limitations on murder."

Matt avoided a pothole on their way back. "We have to look up this Jenkins guy, but we can't tell him where we got his name."

"Exactly." Grandma Etta leaned forward and eyed Matt.

"But we have to talk to Bufford again before we look up those two yahoos. We need to get his perspective of what they did that night."

"You know, Grandma Etta, Dad wouldn't be carrying a gun when he accompanied the sheriff to Griff Jenkins property." Skylar swiveled her gaze between Grandma Etta and Matt. "Deputy Harding was evasive about that question. He wouldn't answer either way."

Matt maneuvered a sharp mountain turn. "That's what I thought. 'I don't recall' leaves a lot of questions unanswered."

"Now that I think of it, when Brodie left the house that night, he didn't have one." Grandma Etta crossed her arms and stroked her chin as if in thought. "The sheriff hadn't given him a gun. So why would they accuse him of murder?"

"Unless he gave him one on the way to Jenkins' property." Skylar rubbed her temples. "Oh, I don't know. This is all so confusing. I feel like we're just going round and round in circles and getting nowhere. All I know beyond a shadow of a doubt is the fact that Dad didn't do it, but there are so many missing pieces."

Grandma Etta slipped her arm around Skylar. "I know, child. Your daddy had the answers. It's too bad he never shared more with your mama, but I'm sure he wanted to put that night behind him. Rest assured, the answers are out there, and the good Lord will help us find them. Don't give up."

Skylar turned a weary smile on her grandmother. "You're right. As you say, we'll talk with Uncle Bufford again and get his perspective on what the deputy told us."

"That's a good next step." Matt piped in. "After we eat and get a good night's sleep. Agreed?"

"Agreed," the two women said in unison.

"But first, we eat." Matt's stomach growled as if to emphasize his words.

~

Eli Harding paced in front of his fireplace after his visitors left. His life had settled down without a worry for the last two and half decades. Why all of a sudden had that young upstart woman dragged her grandma and boyfriend out here to stir up trouble? That's exactly what their nosing around would do. Stir up trouble.

Eli marched over to the cabin window and stared out. His mind revisited that night years ago when his boss was shot. He squeezed his eyelids closed, but he couldn't erase what he'd seen. Yes, he'd passed out. That was true. But the visit to his hospital room—he couldn't forget that. And he couldn't tell anyone. Or his life was over.

Eli swallowed hard. What should he do? Should he make a phone call? He didn't have a phone. Service didn't reach out here in the middle of nowhere. That was the way he wanted it. But he could make a trip to town. He could warn the person those three were searching for. Searching? Yeah, and he gave them a lead, didn't he? Eli shook his head and a sigh whooshed out. It was a lead he hadn't meant to give but a difficult one to follow. Maybe they'd give up when they found out just how difficult it was.

Eli strode to his kitchen woodstove where his percolator coffee pot sat on the back keeping hot. He grabbed the mug he'd used that morning and filled it. Leaving it black, he headed back to the front window and took a long draught of the hot brew. He jammed his other hand into his overall pocket. Nah, they wouldn't be able to follow that lead. Nascar drivers were too hard to pin down. You couldn't get close to 'em. No, he'd hold off on making that call just yet. Feeling better about his decision, Eli took another drink of his coffee and strolled over to grab his shotgun. It hadn't been cleaned in a while. Maybe it was time.

~

Later that evening while Matt helped Grandma Etta clean up after the supper meal, Skylar slipped out the front door. She'd grabbed a crocheted throw from the back of the couch and tossed it around her shoulders. Tiptoeing across the front porch and down the steps, she meandered across the yard. Silence filled the chill autumn air as she stared up into the inky sky sparkling with stars. There was the Milky Way. The Creator's design of the heavens always amazed her.

*You did that not for Yourself but for us, didn't You, Lord? How marvelous and beautiful is Your creation.* Skylar paused, unsure how to continue. *That's silly, huh? You already know what's in my heart. You know I'm feeling discouraged right now. This whole search feels like we're butting against a wall. Deputy Harding gave us little information to go on. Only a name of someone we may or may not be able to find. Some big-name celebrity that's not going to be easy to contact. And when we visit Uncle Bufford, we have so little time to glean anything from him. Only a few minutes then his time is up.*

Skylar waited for several moments. For what she wasn't sure. A still small voice? Clear directions? She didn't know. *We need Your guidance, Abba.* Then a disturbing thought occurred to her. *Is this a fool's quest? Should I not have come at all? Should I have simply ignored Gina's accusations and trusted Matt?* Doubts began to assail Skylar, and tears burned behind her eyes. *What, Lord? What do You want me to do?*

"Hey, what are you doing out here in the cold?" Matt's voice sounded from beside Skylar just before he slipped his arm around her shoulders drawing her close.

Skylar jumped. "You startled me." She leaned into him.

"I'm sorry. I thought you heard me come out of the cabin. Are you all right? What are you doing out here?" He kissed the top of her head.

"Staring at the stars and praying. Wondering if perhaps this whole search is a fool's quest. Maybe I should've stayed home and told Gina to mind her own business then simply trusted you." She gazed into Matt's face. "I wanted to prove my dad wasn't a murderer, but in reality, I don't have to prove anything, do I?"

Matt cupped Skylar's cheek and rubbed his thumb along the edge of her lips. "To me? Of course not. But this isn't a fool's quest, my love. Gina is from a rich and powerful family, and she'll do everything in her power to smear your family's name in Casper, Gillette and the surrounding countryside. She started this dance, but we're going to end it. And you needn't worry. I'll be here to help you with this search every step of the way."

He lowered his head, his lips touching hers softly at first. Then Matt drew Skylar more firmly into his arms, and his kiss deepened. This amazing man took Skylar's breath away. Oh, but she felt safe in his arms. And loved.

After several moments Matt lifted his head a few inches. Even in the moonlight, she could see his dark eyes staring into hers. "I love you more than you can know, Skylar Simpson. You never have to worry about Gina or anybody else. Hear me clearly. You are the only woman for me. Got it?" His lips twitched into a smile.

Skylar leaned forward, her hand pulling his head back to her. She placed a deep kiss on his lips, taking her time to ensure he knew she got it. Then she released him, to find him breathing heavily. She smiled and whispered, "I got it."

Matt kissed her temple. "I believe you do, sweetheart. Now, maybe we better head back inside before I double-check—you know. Just to reassure myself."

# Chapter Eight

The next morning Skylar waved back at Matt who waited in the pickup while Grandma Etta and she went inside the prison to visit Uncle Bufford. As much as Matt wanted to meet the man, visitation was restricted to family.

"So, Harding saw you after all," Bufford spoke into the handset from behind the bulletproof glass. "I'm a little surprised but glad nonetheless."

"He did." Grandma Etta once again held the phone handset between her and Skylar so they could both hear Bufford. "He wasn't overly helpful. I think he's hiding something. He wouldn't say whether Brodie carried a gun that night. Do you remember?"

Bufford took a deep breath then shifted his gaze to the ceiling as if attempting to recall memories from long ago. He shook his head. "No, Brodie wasn't carryin' one when he burst onto the scene with the sheriff and Deputy Harding. When the gunfight broke out between those two, Jenkins and Kent, Brodie rushed over to me and shoved me to the ground. He covered me with his body to protect me from gunfire. Jenkins and Kent drove away after one of 'em shot the sheriff and the deputy. I would think it had to be one of 'em." Bufford stared at the two women. "I remember Deputy Harding warnin' Brodie not to pick up a gun left lyin' near the sheriff."

"And did he?" Skylar asked.

"I'm pretty sure he did. That's probably why they tried to pin the murder on him. The state troopers showed up just then."

"So why did they let him go?" Grandma Etta asked.

"I have no idea. I was arrested for moonshinin' and aidin' and abettin' the moonshiners." He sighed. "Back then, I was young and startin' a family. I needed money. Jenkins and Kent came home from the war and started up their moonshine business again. They were making money hand over fist, and they paid me well." He shrugged.

"Is it worth talking to Jenkins and Kent?" Grandma Etta shifted in her seat. "Surely they can tell us something."

Bufford's brows raised. "Are you serious, Mom? One of them is likely the killer. You don't need to be talkin' to no killer. Besides, I heard tell Griff Jenkins is now a big NASCAR racer and Harper Kent is his crew chief. You'll never catch up with 'em. The NASCAR circuit is a busy place, and it's hard to get close to those guys. Griff Jenkins is a celebrity, you know."

Grandma Etta released a mirthless chuckle. "He may be a celebrity in man's eyes, but in God's eyes, Griff Jenkins is just a man. God looks on the heart, and if there's evil there, He'll deal with it."

"That's right, Mom, but it don't mean you have to be in the middle of it. You gotta be careful. Those men might be dangerous, especially if they're killers."

She smirked at him. "We'll see."

Bufford rolled his eyes then stared at Skylar. "I hope you got better sense than my mama."

Skylar nodded. "I hope so too. I'm counting on the Lord to guide us. Is there anything else you can tell us about that night that might help us in our search?"

"Like what?"

"I don't know. Anything. Something you can remember about Dad and his actions. We'll take whatever you can give us."

"One-minute warning, Bufford." The guard at the back of the room said through the handset.

Bufford heaved a heavy sigh. "Y'all are going to find Jenkins and Kent, aren't you?"

Skylar and Grandma Etta nodded.

He shook his head. "Well, seein' as how I can't stop you, check the NASCAR racin' schedule to see where they're racin' next. The season should be comin' to an end soon. You might check North Wilksboro racetrack or Charlotte speedway. Both are in North Carolina."

"Hang it up, Bufford." The guard headed his way.

"Please, please, be careful. Love y'all." Bufford hung up the phone and placed his hand on the glass.

Both women placed theirs on the glass opposite his as Grandma Etta hung up the receiver. They watched as the guard led Bufford away, then they left the prison and returned to the pickup where Matt waited for them.

Once they settled in their seats, Matt asked, "Did you discover anything new?"

"Uncle Bufford confirmed that Dad wasn't carrying a gun when he arrived at the scene that night." Skylar met Matt's eyes. "He also stated that a gunfight broke out between the lawmen and Jenkins and Kent. That means they had weapons, but he didn't know who killed the sheriff. Dad protected Uncle Bufford during the gunfight by covering his body with his. Uncle Bufford heard the deputy warn Dad not to pick up a gun that lay near the sheriff's body. Apparently, it was left at the scene when the other men took off, leaving the sheriff and the deputy dead and injured. The warning came too late. State troopers arrived and found Dad holding the gun."

"So they arrested him," Matt stated more than questioned.

"Yes. Uncle Bufford has no idea why Dad was released though." Skylar shook her head. "It makes no sense."

"I think it goes back to Eli Harding. He knows more than he's saying." Grandma Etta glanced out the windshield as two guards passed by. "We'd best head home before the guards get edgy and think we're planning an escape. I doubt they'll think too kindly to us sitting in the prison parking lot."

Matt started the engine. "You got it."

~

"I have no way of knowing what a NASCAR schedule is." Grandma Etta straightened the lace doily on the table. She patted the pillows on the love seat and refolded the crocheted afghan. "You don't see a TV here, do you? We're going to have to go into town to find out that information."

Matt sat in the rocking chair with one leg crossed over his knee, enjoying the view of Skylar helping her grandma dust. "Then let's go. I'll take you to find a racing schedule. And if we grab supper after that, more's the better."

Grandma Etta propped her hands on her hips. "Is that all you ever think about? Food."

Matt grinned at her, but before he could answer, Skylar stopped dusting and placed a hand on his shoulder. His heart picked up a beat at her touch.

"Growing boys need to eat, Grandma Etta." Skylar leaned down and touched her lips to Matt's cheek.

He caught his breath. Matt hadn't yet asked this woman to marry him, but he would. He wanted her in his life permanently—in his life, in his arms, in his.... *Whooee!* He shoved that thought away. *Settle down, heart. Stick to the safe topic of eating. Yeah, eating. Or NASCAR. Either one will do.* Matt heaved a sigh and reached up to stroke Skylar's cheek. "Little darlin', I'm hungry all the time." Had his voice been just a mite too husky?

Skylar's cheeks flared, and her eyes grew round.

*Oops, that didn't come out right.* Matt cleared his throat. "Um, is it too early to grab a bite in town while we go look for that schedule?"

"I hope that's what you were talking about." Grandma Etta murmured as she turned away. "I'll grab my purse, and we can go."

Skylar started to turn away, but Matt snagged her wrist between gentle fingers. "I'm sorry, Skylar." He shook his head. "I was just thinking moments before what your touch does to me, and…well, I…."

A soft smile lifted the corners of Skylar's lips. "I get it." She gathered his hand in hers. "We're human, but we have to be careful. We want to keep our relationship pure and—"

"The way God would have us to." Matt lifted their hands and placed a kiss on her knuckles. "I love you. Don't forget that."

"And I love you."

"Can we go?" Grandma Etta asked from beside the front door, her toe tapping. "If I have to listen to any more of this syrupy love talk, I'm going to lose my appetite. And I was looking forward to supper." She posted hands on her hips. "Where are we going to eat anyway?"

~

By popular consent, they chose Reaves Café for supper.

Helen Carter stood behind the hostess counter as usual. "Well, well. If it ain't our newcomers to town. I see you found the young lady you were lookin' for, young fella. Good for you." She tilted her head as a wide grin stretched her lips, theN peered at them over her readers. "Y'all make a cute couple, if I do say so."

Skylar slipped an arm through Matt's. "Am I ever glad he showed up."

"I'm sure ya are." Helen's eyes shifted to Grandma Etta. Her brows furrowed for a moment then they lifted. "Etta Sawyer? As I live and breathe, I ain't seen you in a few years. How ya been?"

"Better than I deserve, Helen. And you?"

Helen grabbed menus from the side of the counter. "Fair to meddlin', I suppose. Sure can't complain. Nobody'd listen anyway. Guessin' you folks are here to eat, not chat. Come on over and have a seat."

She led them to a booth and placed the menus on the table. "Etta, your granddaughter's workin' this evenin'. I'll send her over. Y'all enjoy your meal." With a wink, Helen hurried away.

As they perused their menus, Ruthann rushed over, leaned in, and gave Grandma Etta a hug. "Hello. How is everyone?"

"Hello, sweetie. Are they keeping you busy?" Grandma Etta's face lit up at the sight of the teen.

"It hasn't been terribly busy yet, but it'll pick up in a while." Ruthann removed her order pad from her apron pocket. "Have you had a chance to look over your menus or do you need more time?"

"Ladies?" Matt's eyes shifted between Skylar and Grandma Etta. "Are you ready to order?"

"I am." Skylar glanced at her grandmother. "Are you, Grandma Etta?"

"I will be by the time you two kids tell her what you want."

They gave Ruthann their orders then she slipped the order pad into her pocket. "I'll be right back with your drinks."

"Good, then if you have a few minutes, we have something to tell you." Grandma Etta patted the girl's arm.

Ruthann gave her a curious smile. "Oh yeah? Okay. I'll be right back."

A few minutes later, she returned bearing a tray with glasses of beverages. Placing them in front of the three seated at the table, she asked, "So what did you want to tell me?"

"We visited your daddy this morning. He looked great." Grandma Etta smiled and reached for Ruthann's hand.

Ruthann's lips broadened into a smile. "I'm not allowed to visit him yet. You know, my age and all, but Mama visits him as often as she can get there. He told her some good news the last time she went."

"Oh?" Grandma Etta's brow shot up. "What kind of news?"

"He's going to be paroled again soon." She giggled. "I think he learned his lesson this time. He'll not be going anywhere."

"That's wonderful news, sweetie." Grandma smiled, then her smile faded. "I wonder why he never told us about that."

Skylar reached across the table and laid her hand on her grandmother's. "He didn't have a chance. We kept him busy with questions about Dad, Deputy Harding, and everything to do with that night in 1945. He only has a limited amount of time to visit with us, and he answered everything we asked as best he could."

Grandma Etta gave a slow nod. "I suppose you're right. Other than the first time we went together, and I asked how he was doing, I never gave him a chance to tell me anything."

Ruthann slid an arm around Grandma Etta's shoulders. "It's all right. He won't be getting parole right away. It's not for another month or so. You'll be back to see him, won't you?"

Grandma Etta patted Ruthann's cheek. "You bet I will, sweetie. And I'll make sure I ask him about it too."

Ruthann gave the older woman another hug then stepped back. "I'll go check on your food, and then I have another customer I have to see to. I'll be back."

They watched her slip away toward the kitchen, then Matt shifted in his seat. "That's another sweet granddaughter you've got there."

"Don't I know it." Her eyes shifted to Skylar. "I only wish I'd known this one and her three sisters while they were growing up. If that awful night hadn't happened, then—"

"You can't change the past—" Skylar picked up Grandma Etta's hand and held it between her own, "—but you can move on from now into the future. When this whole debacle is behind us, we'll make sure you meet your other granddaughters."

Grandma Etta's eyes brimmed with tears. She averted her eyes to their hands. "I would dearly love that." Her words were little more than a cracked whisper.

Matt decided right then if there was anything he could do to make it happen, he would. This dear, elderly woman had been robbed of four of her granddaughters long enough. She had one back now. He'd make sure she'd meet the other three.

They took their time enjoying their meal, and settled back to relax and chat.

When Ruthann returned to remove their plates, Matt asked, "Would you mind sending Helen back over?"

"Of course. I'll get her as soon as I take these dishes to the back." She hurried away with the load of plates.

Within a few minutes, Helen strolled over and propped her fists on her hips. "Did you folks enjoy your meal?"

Matt patted his stomach. "It was delicious, just like the last time I was here."

Skylar and Grandma Etta agreed.

"Well, if it's not about the food, what can I help you with?"

"Do you happen to have a Nascar race schedule for this season?" Matt leaned his elbows on the edge of the table and clasped his fingers.

One of Helen's brows shot up as her eyes shifted to Grandma Etta. "Well, I know you don't have cable TV out your way, Etta. They're just now talkin' about gettin' it t'other side o' town." Her eyes moved back to Matt. "You plannin' on goin' to a race?"

He nodded. "Thinking about it. Do you have a schedule?"

She screwed up her face. "You know, Danny, our cook, is a big NASCAR fan. He might have one. Let me go ask him."

Matt turned to catch Skylar's eye, and he winked. "We'll find one. If he doesn't have one, someone else will. This is the south, you know. NASCAR's big around here."

Grandma Etta scoffed. "Like you wouldn't believe. If they don't have cable to tune in, their antenna or rabbit ears will bring it in. Don't believe what Helen says. Cable isn't the end all out in these parts."

"Got one!" Helen yelled all the way across the restaurant. It was probably good they weren't busy yet. She slapped the shiny trifold brochure onto the table. "Danny didn't have one, but our dishwasher, Franklin, did. He said keep it. He's got another one at home."

Matt picked it up and slipped it into his shirt pocket. "Be sure and tell Franklin how much we appreciate it, will you?"

"You bet I will, handsome." She gave him a wink then turned her eyes on Skylar. "You hang onto this fella. He's a keeper, gal."

"Thank you. I think I will." Skylar met Matt's gaze when Helen hurried back to the front of the restaurant.

The look in her eyes turning his insides to goo. Oh yeah. She was a keeper too. He would hang on to her, no matter what. Then doubt set in.

*I can't be the man I want to be for her by myself, Lord. One thing I've learned since I put my trust in You is I'm not as strong as I think I am. My strength comes from You. I need You to help me hang onto Skylar. I love her. More than life itself. Please give me wisdom. Help us find what we need to prove her dad isn't a murderer. We don't have to find the killer. That's the job of the law, but please keep us safe.*

~

That evening after they returned to Grandma Etta's cabin, Matt studied the NASCAR race schedule and discovered the next race would be held at North Wilkesboro Speedway in North Wilkesboro, North Carolina, that weekend. That was fortunate. He borrowed an old travel atlas that Grandma Etta had tucked away in a closet and determined the distance from Oliver Springs to North Wilkesboro. Given the age of the map, he hoped the roads were better now. After adding up the road distances, he figured it was about a five-and-half to six-hour drive.

"If we start early tomorrow morning, we can be there sometime early afternoon." Matt leaned back and stretched his back. "What do you think?" He eyed the two women who had sat down at the table while he made his calculations.

"I can be ready to leave whenever you want to." Grandma Etta shrugged. "It's getting dark early now, so we have to be careful about creatures on the roads, but the earlier we leave the better."

"Agreed." Skyler nodded.

Grandma Etta scooted her chair back. "Then I'm heading to bed. See you young folks in the morning at the crack of dawn. Er…before the crack of dawn." She waved a hand. "Oh, whatever. Don't stay up late. Especially you, young man. You're driving. Good night."

Skylar stood and wrapped her arms around her grandmother before she could leave the room. "Good night, Grandma Etta. I love you."

A gentle expression softened the wrinkled features of the older woman. "I love you, too, darlin'." Her arms tightened around Skylar. "I'm glad you're here even if the reason isn't the best one."

"Me too." Skylar kissed her cheek. "Sleep well."

Grandma left and Skylar leaned over Matt, wrapping her arms around his shoulders from behind, her cheek next to his. "I think she's genuinely glad we're here."

Matt chuckled while taking her hands in his in front of his chest. "I agree, and she sure likes to pick on me."

"But you've got broad shoulders." She gave them a squeeze.

"Sure, I do, and I get a kick out of her. She's a tough old bird. Your grandma's been through a lot in her life."

"Yes, she has, and it's all made her the strong woman she is today."

Skylar straightened, slipping her hands from his. "We need to get some sleep. Don't forget, you're driving." She imitated her grandmother's words then laughed softly.

Matt shoved his chair back and stood, drawing Skylar into his arms. "Come here, missy. Don't think you're going to get away that easily."

Skylar's giggle grew louder, then she covered her mouth with her hand to stifle the sound.

Matt lifted a finger to his lips. "Shhh. I bet she's not asleep yet. She'll be out here in a skinny minute telling us to shush and get to bed."

"It's all your fault, mister, making me laugh out loud like that." Skylar poked a finger in his chest. "You are going to get me in trouble. Now, good night. I'll see you in the morning."

"Uh-uh. Not without a goodnight kiss first." Matt drew her closer within his arms. "All joking aside, I need a kiss. From you, sweetheart."

The smile on Skylar's face softened. Her eyes skimmed his features and landed somewhere near his mouth. He swallowed, and his heartrate picked up as her gaze lifted back to his. A flame lit in the depths of hers even as the tip of her tongue darted out and licked her lips. As Matt lowered his head, Skylar's eyes drooped closed, and she lifted her face. Her lips met his, and his breath caught. Oh gracious, what this woman did to him. Matt kept his kiss gentle, at a cost to himself, but that's how he'd keep it. For now. He wanted to make this woman his wife someday. Then…. He lifted his head and heaved a heavy breath. "Good night, love. I'll see you in the morning."

Skylar's eyes drifted open. She gave him a beautiful smile. "Good night. Sleep well."

He flashed her a grin. "You know who I'll be dreaming of."

"Oh?" One delicate brow lifted as she stepped back and out of his arms, her eyes never leaving his.

He gave her a wink. "You, darlin'. Good night."

# Chapter Nine

The trio found the North Wilkesboro Speedway easily enough, and since the race wasn't until Sunday, parking wasn't difficult. Matt had read that qualifying began Saturday afternoon, but although it was Friday, race fans were already making their way to stake their claim for their seats. Drivers had been making practice runs all day and still were. The trio soon discovered that tickets for the race sold months in advance.

"We don't intend to stay for the race," Matt explained to the guard at the entrance to the speedway. "We'd like to talk with one of the drivers if at all possible. We came all the way from Wyoming. Her dad—" he tossed a thumb over his shoulder toward Skylar "—used to know Griff Jenkins back in the day after the war."

The guard crossed his arms over his chest and smirked. "Yeah? He and everybody else's dad. Get lost, buddy."

Skylar pushed in front of Matt. "Please, sir. My dad was accused of a terrible crime, and I need to clear his name." She omitted the fact her dad had passed away. "I'd really like to talk to Mr. Jenkins. He may be able to help me clear my dad's name. Please. If you'll simply tell him I'm here and ask if he'll see me."

The smirk on the guard's face slipped a smidge. He sighed and propped his hands on his hips. After a moment he said, "All right. I'm not making any promises, but I'll call over to his trailer and see if he's in. If he is, I'll ask him. I'm not chasing him down though. This speedway is a big place, and the drivers don't sit in their trailers holding court with race fans."

Skylar gave a brief nod and breathed a sigh of relief. "Thank you. Whatever you can do to help is greatly appreciated." *Please, Lord. Let Mr. Jenkins be in his trailer then allow him to agree to see us.* She watched as the guard stepped into the little guard booth and reach for a phone. *You are in control, Abba. Not us. Not the guard and not Griff Jenkins. Only You. Thy will be done.*

"Yes, sir. I understand." The guard hooked his thumb into his utility belt. "Right. I'll tell them. Thank you." He hung up the phone and stepped out of the booth, one brow lifted as his eyes shifted among the three. "Well, I'll be doggoned, if Griff Jenkins didn't tell me to send you folks right on down to his trailer." Disbelief had replaced his smirk. "There's no way you can find it on your own, so he's sending a fella with a golfcart to drive you down there." He tipped his service cap back and scratched his head before replacing it.

Skylar smiled as sweetly as she could. "Thank you for calling. I'm sure you hear all kinds of stories from race fans who come through here wanting to talk with the drivers."

"Lady, you have no idea. That's why I was so skeptical of your story, but I guess this will teach me to check things out a little more."

Several minutes later, an older man with gray hair sticking out from beneath his ball cap rolled up beside them in a golfcart. A broad smile lifted his lips. "You folks need a ride to see Griff Jenkins?" His eyes turned to Grandma Etta and he winked. "How about you ride up here with me, darlin'?" He patted the seat next to him.

Grandma Etta huffed then pursed her lips and stared down her nose at the driver. "You keep your hands to yourself, old man. I don't have time for fresh flirts."

Skylar chuckled as her grandmother met her eyes. She and Matt had already made themselves comfortable on the rear seat, Matt's arm around Skylar's shoulders. Grandma Etta frowned at Skylar as if to say, "thanks a lot for nothing." Skylar curbed her laugh as Grandma Etta climbed onto the front seat as far from the driver as she could get.

The driver leaned toward Grandma Etta. "Don't worry, darlin'. I got a wife at home. But if I didn't…. Mmmm, I'd sure think about pursuing you, honey."

Grandma Etta cast him a withering glance then turned her gaze toward the front, her body ramrod stiff.

Skylar buried her face in Matt's twitching shoulder to keep from bursting out laughing. Matt appeared to be struggling to contain his own laughter. Poor Grandma Etta.

Once she had her laughter under control, Skylar glanced around to see the crowds of people walking in every direction. There were food vendors, T-shirt vendors, and souvenir vendors with lines of people at each. Not to mention lines at the bathrooms.

"Can you imagine what it'll be like on race day?" Skylar's head swiveled in every direction.

"Oh, you have no idea, Miss," the old man turned his head to speak over his shoulder. "It gets downright crazy here on qualifying and race days. Y'all sticking around for them?"

"No, we don't have tickets." Matt shifted his arm to draw Skylar closer. "We weren't planning to come until yesterday."

"I see." The man drove the cart into a long lane of RVs and camping trailers.

"These are some fine rigs." Matt pointed out a couple. "They must have cost a pretty penny."

"Oh, they sure do, but then again, the race drivers can afford 'em." The old man shook his head. "Most have luxury interiors and conveniences the average camper can only dream of."

He stopped the golf cart beside a long trailer and hopped out. Before Grandma Etta could make a move, he held out a hand. "My dear lady, let me give you a hand out."

"I'm not crotchety, you old fool." Grandma Etta stared at his hand and didn't move.

"Grandma!" Skylar couldn't believe her ears. "Our driver is simply trying to be a gentleman."

Grandma Etta sniffed and paused for a moment. Skylar couldn't see her face, but she had a feeling her grandmother was regretting her harsh words.

"I apologize, sir. I realize you were simply being a gentleman. Forgive my unladylike…words." She put her hand in his and allowed him to help her from the cart. When she stood beside him, she tugged her hand from his and added, "Thank you." She folded her hands in front of her.

"I understand, ma'am. Well, I did come on a little strong earlier, so perhaps it should be me who is apologizing." He tipped his ball cap. "I don't even know if you're married or not."

"Thank you." Grandma Etta tilted her head. "For the apology." She waited as Matt helped Skylar from the cart, then the man led them to the door of the trailer. He knocked three times, and they waited.

The door opened to reveal a tall man with a bit of a paunch wearing a ball cap with the number 25 embroidered on the front. Skylar had noticed a silk flag embedded in the ground beside the front of the trailer with the same number surrounded by flashy colors swaying in the breeze.

"Is this them?" The man eyed Skylar, Matt and Grandma Etta.

"Yep." The old man stepped back. "Folks, this is Harper Kent, Griff's crew chief."

The man standing in the trailer door nodded, a half-grin lifting one corner of his mouth. "Come on in. Griff's waitin' inside."

Matt helped Grandma Etta up the steps then Skylar before following them into the trailer. Skylar glanced around as she stood to the side. Their driver had been right. This wasn't merely a camping trailer. Every surface bespoke luxury. From the hidden lighting along the edges of the ceiling to the solid oak cabinetry to the fireplace to the leather furniture in the living area. The kitchen had beautiful marble-like counters, a three-burner stove, and a full-sized refrigerator. Skylar had no idea campers had such things. She wondered what the bathroom and bedroom were like.

"Folks, this is Griff Jenkins." Mr. Kent's voice drew Skylar's attention to a man entering from the rear of the trailer. He, too, was tall but slimmer. She supposed that racing required staying fit. Both men were about Matt's height of six foot two inches.

Mr. Jenkins held out his hand. "Welcome." His eyes stalled on Grandma Etta. "Mrs. Sawyer. Nice to see you again. It's been a long time."

Grandma Etta shook his hand, her chin lifting slightly. "Indeed, it has, Griff. I see you've done well for yourself. Except for some gray in your hair, you're looking good."

He shrugged, a smile on his lips. Skylar noticed a deep dimple in his cheek. "Thank you. I haven't done too badly." His gaze moved on to Skylar. "And you must be Brodie's girl." He shook her hand. "I'm sorry your dad's been accused of another crime. He's had a rough time, hasn't he?" Mr. Jenkins led them to the sitting area where they all sat down. "You've come a long way to talk to me. Tell me what's happened to Brodie."

Skylar clasped her hands in her lap and took a cleansing breath before delving into her story. "It's not a new crime, Mr. Jenkins. It's the crime from 1945. The murder of Sheriff Baker. Only it was proven that Dad didn't kill him." Mr. Jenkins' brow furrowed, and his lips clamped into a thin line.

"Please, call me Griff. Go on with your story." Griff crossed one leg over the other knee and leaned his chin on his fingers, his pointer finger along his cheek.

Tension hovered over the man like a heavy blanket. For what reason? "Dad's name was cleared back then before he moved our family out west. But someone in Wyoming has recently come across a newspaper article from 1945, written before he was released. They've decided to make things miserable for my family."

"Why doesn't Brodie deal with it? Why come to me?" Griff shrugged.

"Dad died several years ago." Skylar swallowed hard, twisting her fingers together. "He never told mom much about that night, except that he didn't kill the sheriff and that he was released. Since I've come to Tennessee, I've talked to Uncle Bufford. He thought perhaps you would be able to tell me more about what happened. He could only tell me what happened from his point of view which was that Dad protected my uncle during the shootout. He didn't see anything else. I also talked to Deputy Harding who told me he passed out from the injury he received during the shootout, but he couldn't tell me who shot him. Only that it was your gun left on the ground next to the sheriff."

Griff swiped a hand down his face and gave Skylar a mirthless grin. "Yeah, it was. I went to jail once the state troopers caught up with us, but it wasn't for murder." He pointed at his crew chief who had pulled up a dining chair and straddled it, his arms across the chair back. "No, I went to prison for moonshining and transporting moonshine across state lines. I never fired that gun. I always carried it with me when I was running liquor. It stayed in the glovebox of my car. I must've dropped it, although I don't recall taking it out of the car that night. Anyway, Harper and I took off in my souped-up 1940 Ford with a flathead V-8 engine. When the sheriff and the deputy burst onto the scene, we skedaddled it out of there, didn't we, Harper?"

"Sure did," the crew chief nodded. "We had a load, and we weren't interested in the sheriff finding it or us."

"But the moonshine still was on your property, wasn't it?" Matt asked.

Griff chuckled. "Can't say we were all that smart in those days."

Skylar leaned forward. "Then who else was at the shootout? Who could have killed the sheriff?"

Griff shrugged. "I have no idea. All I know is the sheriff was alive when we ran."

The trailer door opened just then, and a woman entered. She stopped and turned to stare at the group, slipping sunglasses from her eyes and letting them dangle from her fingers. Surprise etched her delicately made-up features. Her short blonde curls peaked from beneath a leopard toque hat. A matching fur scarf wrapped high beneath her chin accessorizing her tan wool suit. Matching leopard high heels encased her feet, and a leopard bag hung from her elbow. After a moment she asked, "What is this, Griff?"

The race car driver surged to his feet and stepped over to the woman who Skylar guessed to be around her mother's age. He dropped a kiss on the woman's cheek.

"Ah, darlin', you're back." He turned to his guests. "You might remember Etta Sawyer from the hollow. And this is her granddaughter, Skylar… um…." Griff glanced at Skylar. "What did you say your last name was?"

"Simpson."

"Oh, yes. Skylar Simpson. And her boyfriend…." He pointed at Matt. "Sorry, I'm terrible with names."

Matt grinned. "It's not a problem. Matt Scott."

Griff snapped his fingers. "Right." He turned back to the woman. "This is my wife, Elizabeth Jenkins."

"Elizabeth?" Grandma Etta chuckled. "I always knew you as Beth Ann. You changed your name. And your clothes."

Elizabeth raised her chin slightly, her smile not quite warm and welcoming. "Hello, Mrs. Sawyer. It's…a pleasure to see you, I'm sure. Yes, I used to be called Beth Ann, but since Griff has made something of himself, I need to…maintain a certain respectability due the position he now finds himself in. My given name is Elizabeth. I simply choose to use it now."

"Seems to me you're putting on airs."

"Grandma!" Skylar elbowed her grandmother. "Please."

Elizabeth gasped, her hand flying to her chest. "How dare you?"

Grandma Etta heaved a sigh. "I apologize, *Elizabeth*. It seems that since I've grown old, I sometimes don't know when to keep my mouth shut." She held out her hand to the younger woman. "It's not any of my business what you call yourself. Your husband has done well for himself. Running moonshine might've been a bad start for him and sent him to jail, but he turned it into something good, it seems. I'm happy for y'all. Please forgive my judgmental comment." She glanced at Skylar. "I seem to be making far too many of them lately."

Skylar slipped her arm around Grandma Etta's shoulders. "We all say far too many things we shouldn't, Grandma Etta." She turned her eyes to meet Elizabeth's. The other woman swallowed and nodded.

"It's all right. Don't we all say the stupidest things sometimes?" She reached out a hand and squeezed Grandma Etta's. "Now, what are you folks here for?"

Griff led her to the couch beneath the window. "Have a seat, darlin', and I'll explain."

And he did. A discussion ensued until a knock sounded at the door. Harper rose to answer it.

"Honey, what are you doing here?" he asked.

Another woman stepped hesitantly inside but before she could answer, Elizabeth snapped her fingers. "Oh, no. With the company being here, I forgot to tell you your wife was looking for you, Harper."

The woman who had just arrived looked troubled, her

shoulders slumping. "I've been looking for you everywhere, Harper." She turned to stare at Elizabeth, accusation in her eyes. Her voice remained low as she asked, "Why didn't you tell him?"

"When I saw there was company here, it flew right out of my head, dear. I'm so sorry."

"What's wrong, honey?" Harper slid his arm around his wife's shoulders.

Mr. Kent's wife wasn't flamboyant like Elizabeth. Her eyes skimmed shyly over the group, a tension furrow between her brows. She half turned away from them and lowered her voice, but not low enough they couldn't hear her say, "I'd rather not talk here."

Harper's head tilted. "Sure thing, honey."

Without another glance at the group, she opened the door and fled. Harper turned to them, a sheepish expression on his features. "I'd better see what the problem is, folks. It was nice meeting you. Hope to see you again sometime." He tossed a wave and followed his wife out the door, closing it firmly behind him.

"Any idea what that's all about?" Griff turned to Elizabeth.

She gave a careless shrug. "No, but Sharon seemed distracted while we were in town shopping. She's generally quiet anyway. Doesn't share much. Sharon's always been that way, you know. She's the shy type."

Griff reached over and took her hand, giving it a squeeze. "Your opposite, darlin'."

Elizabeth cast her eyes heavenward and gave him a pretty smile. Turning toward their guests, she leaned forward. "So, what's your next move? It seems you're no closer to finding the truth about who killed the sheriff, are you?"

Skylar shook her head. "It's rather discouraging, truth be told. Everybody we've talked to can't, or won't, tell us much about that night."

Griff tossed a hand in the air. "Why is it so doggoned important to prove Brodie didn't kill the sheriff? He was released which should've proved him innocent. That should be enough."

"Because the person who's trying to ruin Skylar's family used to be my girlfriend, Gina," Matt said, "and she wants me back. When I broke up with Gina, it was because I'd spent time with Skylar on a trip to Europe with my dad and a group of friends. I fell in love with Skylar. I discovered what I'd been missing and just what kind of selfish person Gina is. This act of revenge proves it. If we can't find a way to redeem Skylar's dad, Gina will do everything in her power to ruin Skylar's family."

"Gina can weave whatever kind of story she wants to back up the newspaper article she handed over to me." Skylar piped in. "I have no doubt she made a copy, or she wouldn't have relinquished it so easily."

"You're probably right there." Griff rubbed his chin. "Have you been to the county courthouse in Kingston to check out the court records from 1945? I don't know if there'll be anything more than what everybody has already told you, but you never know."

Matt met Skylar's eyes. He shrugged.

Skylar returned her eyes to Griff's. "No, we never thought of that, but I suppose it's a good idea."

She turned to Grandma Etta. "Is it far?"

"It's not that far for us to go."

Griff leaned forward, elbows on his knees and his fingers clasped together. "Look, folks. I've done some things I'm not overly proud of in my time. And maybe not just the moonshining. I'm not the only race car driver who got his start in racing by making moonshine and driving loads of it by the hundreds of gallons to honkytonks. Legal bars put moonshining out of business. It went the way of the dodo bird, but we all found a new way to live, and it got me where I am today. All that's behind me now."

Skylar nodded. "That's wonderful. But simply quitting doing something illegal or something that's wrong isn't enough. Have you ever given your life to Jesus Christ?"

Griff shrugged, spreading his hands wide. "We go to chapel every Sunday. All the racetracks have a chapel service for the drivers and their families before the races. We almost always attend, don't we, honey?"

Elizabeth tilted her chin upward a tad. "But of course."

"Like the Good Book says, going to church is important, folks, but it isn't going to get you into heaven." Grandma Etta crossed her arms over her chest and stared down the couple. "It takes more than that."

"Um, I don't know…" Elizabeth began then hesitated.

Skylar cast a glance at both Elizabeth then Griff. "Jesus Christ died on Calvary's cross for the sins of all mankind. Those who accept his gift of salvation are forgiven their sins. Those who don't accept His gift will one day stand before God and answer for what they've done in this life. They'll have to pay for their own sins by being separated for eternity in hell. The ultimate sin is not accepting Christ as Lord. Simply going to church or doing good things isn't enough to get into heaven."

Griff leaned forward. "You know, the chaplain on Sunday mornings has never mentioned any of this. He basically talks about doing good things and how it makes God happy."

Skylar nodded. "It's important to do good things and to please God, but first you have to come to know Him as your personal Savior. You need a relationship with Him. How can we please Him if we don't know Him? How can we do what He wants us to do, if we don't get to know Him first?"

Griff exchanged looks with his wife. "I've heard of hell, but mostly as a cuss word. I've even used it myself."

Elizabeth rolled her eyes. "More than a time or two."

Griff cast her a withering glance then returned his eyes to Skylar. "As I was saying, I don't know anything about what the Bible says concerning these things. I suppose I'd be interested in finding out more. Not sure I'm ready to commit, but I'm ready to listen."

Skylar turned her eyes toward Elizabeth.

"I don't know." Elizabeth sighed. "My mama and daddy used to go to the little church back up in the hollow, and they took us when my sister and I were young. In fact, it was Preacher Sawyer that preached at that little church." She smiled at Grandma Etta. Then her smiled faded as memories seemed to flood her mind. "I didn't put much stock in it because my daddy was an alcoholic. He had his own moonshine still. Although he didn't sell it, he sure did drink it. Mama, well, she was a good Christian woman. She tried to do good by us girls and raised us right, but she wasn't happy when I married Griff." She turned to stare at her husband, a soft smile lifting the corners of her lips. "Mama's happier now that Griff's a race car driver and not a moonshiner." She turned her eyes back to Skylar. "Mama used to tell Daddy if he didn't mend his ways, he'd end up in hell-fire. She was a quiet-spoken woman, and I believe she loved him with all her heart, but that was one thing I remember her telling him in her soft voice while tears poured down her cheeks." Elizabeth stared into space as if looking into the past. "Daddy drank till his dying day, to Mama's sorrow."

Skylar reached over and laid a hand on Elizabeth's arm. "I'm sorry, but your mama knew what was right. I'm sure she prayed for your father as well as you and your sister."

Elizabeth's eyes returned to Skylar's. "Oh, she did. All the time. I suppose it worked for my sister. She married a man who became a missionary. They went to Thailand." She sighed. "I believe they're happy there." She shuddered. "I couldn't do it."

"You could if you had a relationship with the Lord and that's what He wanted you to do." Skylar smiled. "But just because someone gives their life to Christ doesn't mean He calls them to serve on a foreign field as a missionary. He uses people in all walks of life, and he can use you right here on the race track if that's what He chooses."

Griff glanced at Elizabeth and chuckled. "You know Cole Howard, honey? He's a Christian. So is Pete Martin. They're not shy about it either. Both are good men and good drivers."

Elizabeth's brow furrowed. "I don't ever see them or their families in chapel."

Griff shook his head. "I heard they find a church in town to go to wherever the race is."

"Hmm." Elizabeth shifted in her seat. "I didn't know that."

Griff glanced at his watch. "I've got to get ready to go to a race meeting shortly, folks. Wish I could visit longer. Will you be staying in town for the qualifying race tomorrow or the race on Sunday?"

"No." Matt stood. "This was a quick-decision trip, and we don't have tickets. Besides, we need to get back to Oliver Springs."

Jenkins stood and helped Elizabeth to her feet, pulling her arm through his. "Well, I could probably find some seats for you for the qualifying race tomorrow, but it would be nearly impossible for you to find lodging in town or even in the surrounding area. Everything books up months in advance."

"Oh, please. Don't think another thought about it." Skylar waved a dismissive hand. "As Matt said, this was a last-minute trip, and we need to get back. We hadn't planned to stay."

Elizabeth turned to stare at Griff with a smile on her face, then she gripped his arm. He returned her smile, winked, and nodded.

"My wife has a great idea."

"How'd you know?" Matt's brow furrowed. "She didn't say anything."

"Son, when you've been married as long as I've been, you'll know too." Griff laughed out loud.

Elizabeth's chin lifted, and her smile grew. "He reads me quite well."

"So, what's her idea?" Skylar reached for Matt's hand and twined her fingers with his.

Griff wrapped his arm around Elizabeth's shoulders. "The Daytona 500 race in Daytona, Florida, is coming up in the spring. Why don't you folks come? I'll arrange tickets for you and even see if I can arrange some lodging. That part might be tricky, but I'll see what I can do. Have you ever been to a race before?"

They all shook their heads.

"Florida?" Skylar asked. "But that's…that's so far."

"Maybe. But you came from Wyoming, didn't you?" Griff held up a hand. "Florida's a lot closer than Wyoming."

"He's got a point," Grandma Etta eyed her granddaughter, "but I'm too old to be making such a trip."

Griff chuckled. "Not from where I'm standing, you're not, Miss Etta. I plan on seeing you there, and a ticket will be waiting for you." He checked his watch. "Gotta go. I'll be in touch. Great seeing y'all."

Griff laid a kiss on his wife's lips and gave the others a wave before charging out the door.

Elizabeth sighed. "That man can still stir this heart of mine." She turned to the trio and grinned. "You heard him. He's making plans for y'all to attend the Daytona 500, and my Griff won't forget."

She called the man with the golfcart to return them to their vehicle, and while they waited for him to arrive, Elizabeth pulled a slip of paper from a drawer and wrote on it. "Here's our phone number. We have one of those newfangled Motorola handheld mobile phones. It's all the rage. Griff just had to have one. It feels like a brick when you hold it up to your ear, but it sure comes in handy. Give us a call if you ever need anything." She slipped the paper into Skylar's hand. "It was a pleasure to meet you, sweetie. I'm sure we'll see you again. In the meantime, I'll think about what you said. It reminded me of my mama and what she believed. I'd forgotten, but…maybe I need to remember."

"I'll pray for you and Griff that you'll come to know Christ." Skylar wrapped the older woman in a hug.

Elizabeth stepped back. "I believe you will. Thank you." She turned to Grandma Etta and gave her a hug. "It was good to see you again, Miss Etta. It's been far too long. I've been reminded of my roots today. It was almost like old-home week."

"It was good to see you, Beth Ann." Grandma Etta whispered the name.

Elizabeth smirked. "You're the only one I'll let get away with that." She shook Matt's hand and glanced in Skylar's direction. "You take good care of that young woman. She's priceless."

Matt grinned. "Don't I know it, ma'am. I'll take great care of her."

"Wonderful." She patted his hand.

A knock sounded at the door.

"Safe travels, and I'll plan to see y'all in Daytona, Florida."

# Chapter Ten

**Matt turned the** pickup truck west out of North Wilkesboro and lowered the sun visor above the driver's side of the windshield. The sun sat on the rim of the mountains and would soon drop below the other side. Until then, it's brightness was nearly blinding.

He couldn't believe how long they'd visited with Griff Jenkins and his wife, Elizabeth. Griff turned out to be a down-to-earth kind of man, and his wife, although she seemed uppity at first, turned out not to be. Did she put on airs, as Grandma Etta had accused her of? Perhaps, but she wasn't that bad. They hadn't discovered what they had hoped to about Brodie Sawyer, and that was disappointing, but the visit wasn't a total loss.

Matt was proud of Skylar and her boldness in sharing Christ with the race couple. Perhaps one day the seed she had planted would come to fruition. Griff had also made the suggestion that they visit the county courthouse to find out further information about the night Brodie was arrested.

"Are either of you hungry?" Matt glanced at the two silent women at his side. "Now that we've left the busyness of North Wilkesboro and the crowds, we can stop at an exit and grab a bite at a restaurant if you'd like." His stomach rumbled.

Skylar laughed. "I think it's more a necessity for your

sake. Why don't you stop at the next exit you see with a place to eat?"

"You realize it's going to be super late when we get home, don't you?"

"Who cares?" Grandma Etta leaned forward to talk around Skylar. "We can sleep in tomorrow morning."

"Your wish is my command."

Traffic on the highway had spread out, and Matt noticed a large dark pickup truck seemed to keep pace with them from about fifty feet back ever since they'd left town. The driver appeared to be the only occupant. Once the sun descended over the other side of the mountains, Matt dismissed it as someone simply traveling in the same direction.

He spotted a sign for a family restaurant off the next exit then a quick ride into town to the right. After he exited, he had to wait at the stop sign for an oncoming car. The dark pickup truck exited behind him and stopped too. Dusk had already settled over the countryside and darkness edged in. The truck's headlights prevented Matt from seeing the driver clearly. Once the oncoming car passed, Matt turned right and accelerated. A left curve lay ahead, and just as Matt began to turn through the curve, the truck sped up and began to pass him on the left.

"What…?" Shock filled Matt as the truck suddenly rammed into Matt's pickup. Matt slammed on his breaks and veered to the side of the road—anything to avoid hitting the truck. A loud bang sounded, and he lost control of the pickup. "A tire's gone down. I can't control it." Matt yelled. "Brace yourselves." The pickup careened over the edge of the road, down, down, down.

~

The truck stopped along the side of the road, and a dark figure climbed out. Walking to the edge of the road, he aimed a bright flashlight down into the deep ravine where the crumpled pickup truck rested against a copse of shrubs and trees. Steam hissed and oil leaked even as the passengers inside the cab remained unmoving. Good. That should take care of them. No more questions. No more worries. With a sneer, the figure turned and climbed into the pickup and headed back to the highway.

~

Owww. Skylar's head pounded so much. But why? Oh goodness, she hurt all over. She had no desire to open her eyes, but her ears picked up the sound of a moan, and it hadn't come from her. She forced her eyes open and glanced around, nothing registering at first. She tried to move her appendages one by one. Everything moved except her left foot. It wouldn't budge.

Where was the moaning coming from? Her right? Turning her head in that direction elicited a terrible pain in her neck and head, but she had to find out who was moaning. Glancing out of the corner of her right eye, she spotted…Grandma Etta? Then Skylar's surroundings began to register. She was in a pickup truck—Matt's rental pickup truck. They'd gone over the edge of the road. No, they'd been forced over the edge of the road.

One of the headlights was still on, giving enough light for her to see the dimly lit interior of the truck cab. Matt sat behind the steering wheel, his head lolled sideways. He was unconscious. Or so it seemed. But…Grandma Etta. She turned back to her grandmother and gasped. One thing at a time as she attempted to ignore the raging throb in her head.

"Grandma Etta?" Her voice strained as she lifted a hand to touch her grandmother. "Grandma Etta, are you awake?"

"Yes, I'm…awake. My arm. Something's wrong. It's…painful." Grandma Etta's voice sounded weak and breathy.

"Sit tight and don't move. I need to try and wake Matt." Skylar reached over and touched Matt's neck. His heartbeat was strong. *Thank you, Lord. Please help me wake him.* She raised her fingers to his cheek. "Matt, sweetheart, wake up."

She patted his skin. "Come on, Matt. Please wake up. We need you with us."

Matt's head barely moved at first, a gentle rock back and forth on the headrest, then back and forth harder as if attempting to escape Skylar's assaulting fingers. "I'm awake. Leave me alone. My head hurts."

"Join the club," Grandma Etta's words were acidic.

Matt's eyes opened and stared around. He closed them with a heavy sigh. "Please tell me this is a nightmare."

"I wish it were." Skylar attempted to shift in her seat, but her left foot was held firmly by something solid. She stared into the darkness under the dashboard. "Something's holding my foot, and I can't move it."

Matt lifted his head and groaned. "Give me a sec to get my bearings and take stock." He stared out the front windshield. "Did you notice that?" He pointed out the glass.

"What?" Skylar stared where he pointed. "I've been a little busy taking stock myself."

"We're facing almost uphill. It's how we landed. We must've slid down that way."

"So?" Grandma grumped.

"Think about it. If we'd come down face-first and come to a sudden stop, we'd be in much worst shape. I'd have a steering wheel implanted in my chest, and you two would have landed on the dashboard. As it is, we were all forced back into the cushioned seats. Yeah, we have a terrible case of whiplash, some bumps on the back of our heads, and whatever else we haven't discovered yet—"

"Grandma's arm is injured, and I'm not sure what's going on with my left foot." Skylar placed a hand on the back of her head and eyed her hand—no blood, thank goodness.

"Okay, but it could've been a lot worse." Matt bent his elbow back and forth.

"You're right," Grandma Etta murmured, "but how do we get out of this mess? Tell me that."

"Who would deliberately do this to us?" Skylar couldn't

begin to imagine.

~

Matt leaned his head back and stared out the cracked windshield. He attempted to ignore the throb in his head. *Both are great questions, Lord. I'll add another. Is the person who ran us off the road gone? And what if they're not? We could use Your help to take stock and try to get out of this mess, as Grandma Etta so eloquently stated.*

"I have no idea who would do this, but it had to be someone who knew we were at the racetrack today and knows we're looking for information about your dad." Matt reached for his door handle and gave it a shove. The door opened with little resistance. "That's encouraging." Next, he shifted out of his seat and tested his limbs by taking a few steps. "I don't seem to have any injuries other than a whopping headache. Let me climb beneath the dashboard and see what's holding your foot, Sky."

Matt knelt on the ground beside the truck and leaned in under the steering wheel. "Looks like something from under the dashboard shifted in the impact. We must have hit something, turned, and landed face forward. All I know is, it wasn't a fun ride down. When I rented this truck, I found a crowbar with a tire jack behind the seat. I'll see if I can find it and get you out. You ladies are going to have to lean forward so I can pull the seat up. Hold tight, sweetheart."

Skylar gave a mirthless chuckle. "I'm not going anywhere."

Several minutes later, Matt had wedged a crowbar beneath the dashboard under the shifted piece holding Skylar's foot in place. Leaning all his weight onto the bar, he asked between clinched teeth, "Can you pull your foot out?"

Skylar tugged her foot, but it wouldn't move. Shaking her head, she groaned. "It won't budge."

Matt eased up on the crowbar and took a deep breath. "It's hard to get leverage with the steering wheel in the way."

He heaved a heavy sigh then repositioned the crowbar. "Let's try again, sweetheart. If you feel it give some room, try and yank your foot out."

"I will."

Whispering came from Grandma Etta, and he knew she was praying. The poor woman had an injured arm and was in pain, yet she had the presence of mind to pray for the release of her granddaughter's foot. Bless the woman!

"All right. Here we go." Matt leaned in again, bracing his feet against a rock beside the truck, and placed all his weight on the crowbar. He felt a shift in whatever was pinning Skylar's foot. Was it enough to free her? Holding his breath, he laid on the bar and gave it a bounce, hoping it would help.

"My foot is out." Skylar patted Matt's back. "You can let it go now."

Matt lifted himself off the crowbar and rolled onto the driver's seat drawing deep breaths. Where tension like wound springs had been moments before, he lay with every muscle spent.

Skylar rubbed his head. "Matt, are you all right? Is your head exploding?"

"How'd you know?" It felt like hammers beating from the inside out. The pressure of putting all his weight into the crowbar had only made the pounding worse.

"I have some aspirin in my purse, Skylar," Grandma Etta piped in, "but there's no water."

"I don't need water." Matt's voice sounded muffled against the seat. "I'll get 'em down."

"Well, okay. Skylar, if you can find my purse, you're welcome to find the aspirin. It was on the floorboard before we started down the hill. No telling where it is now."

"I'll find it."

Skylar rummaged around the truck cab. *Hurry up, sweetheart.* He had no idea if aspirin would touch this headache and how soon, but if he had any hope of getting them out of this situation, it was the first place to start. What time was it? It had been just after five o'clock when they'd pulled off to find a restaurant, and the sun had dropped behind the mountains.

The pounding threatened to rob his thoughts. *No, you have to think.* Matt didn't know how long he'd been unconscious. It could've been minutes or it could've been hours. Working on the ranch wasn't conducive to wearing a wristwatch, but he sure wished he had one now. The sign at the exit said they were only three-quarters of a mile from town. If they could all walk, they needed to stay together. He didn't want to leave the women here at the truck to fend for themselves. No. Not happening.

"Here, Matt. Take these aspirin." Skylar held out her hand to him.

That meant he had to move. That thought alone was daunting. Inhaling deeply, he heaved himself off the seat and climbed back into the truck. He leaned his head back and closed his eyes. Oh, if the pounding would just stop. Was it a concussion? He'd better not go to sleep.

Skylar placed a hand on his arm. "I know you're in severe pain, but if you take the aspirin, it should help."

He opened his eyes and met hers, even managing a slight grin. "Yeah. Thanks, Grandma Etta. Thanks for having aspirin in your purse."

"Oh, pshaw. It's nothing. Just take 'em so you can get some relief, and we can get out of here."

The light from the headlight had grown dim. Not good. Before long they'd be in the dark. They needed to climb that hill while they still had light to see.

Matt accepted the pills from Skylar and popped them in his mouth. With a little difficulty, he swallowed them dry. Anything to try and rid himself of this pounding.

"Ladies, our headlight isn't going to last much longer. It'll light our way up the hill, but we need to get a move on. Grandma Etta, I know you were praying for me to get

Skylar's foot out. Now I need you to pray our predator isn't waiting for us at the top of the hill."

~

Grandma Etta's door wouldn't open. On its descent, the truck had settled with her door and the tailgate against a copse of shrubs surrounding bigger trees. Skylar and Grandma had to slide across the bench seat to get out—not an easy thing for Grandma with her injured arm.

Skylar tore off the hem of her shirt to fashion a makeshift sling for her grandmother. After tucking the truck rental papers into his jacket pocket, Matt helped the older woman up the hill while Skylar managed on her own. By the time they reached the asphalt road at the top, the headlight on the pickup had died.

"Well, at least it lasted until we reached the top." Grandma Etta eyed their former ride.

Skylar glanced around them. "And it doesn't look like our pursuer is anywhere in sight."

Matt released a grunt. "Whoever it was is probably long gone. They likely thought they left us for dead."

"They almost did." Grandma grumbled as she glanced in both directions down the road. "So, which way to town?"

"That way. It's not even a mile. First stop, something to eat, then the police station."

Skylar tucked her arm within Grandma Etta's good one. "Lead the way, Matt. We'll follow you." *Lord, we could sure use some help in this little town.* Small towns could be finicky when it came to strangers. Even talking to the police was the best idea.

"Matt, what do you think about calling Griff and Elizabeth Jenkins instead of talking to the police? You know how small-town police can be sometimes, especially when it comes to strangers."

Matt stopped and turned on the darkened road. "But what if it was Griff or Elizabeth who sent the attacker after us? They'll know we're not dead."

"Hmm. I'm not so sure about that." Grandma Etta shifted her arm in the sling. "They were sure accommodating by the time we left. Why would they invite us to Daytona if they were planning to kill us?"

"To throw us off maybe?" Matt turned and started walking again. "Let's keep moving. I'm still starving. If I eat, that might help my headache."

Skylar chuckled. "I'm sure it would."

"I'll think about the police thing," he added as he strode onward.

*Lord, give him wisdom. We need to make the right move and trust the right people. We're at a loss here. Who do we trust? We trust You absolutely. Show us who we can trust here for help.*

It wasn't long before the lights of a little town came into view, and relief filled Skylar. Whatever lay ahead, getting something to eat would help Matt make decisions. Skylar chuckled inwardly. For such a handsome grown man, he ate like a growing boy. Her heartstrings tugged at the thought that this man was hers. No matter what Gina tried to do, Matt loved *her*, Skylar Simpson.

"You all right, child?"

"Of course. Why, Grandma Etta?"

"You just squeezed my arm. You sure you're all right?"

Oops. She must've grown a little fervent in her thoughts about Matt. "I-I must've had a chill. Yeah, that's it."

"Mmm-hmm. Sure it was." Her grandmother didn't pursue the matter. In the short time they'd known one another, Skylar's Grandma Etta had come to know her well.

"There's a family restaurant." Matt pointed to a little diner on the corner of the street. "Let's eat there. Maybe they'll have their own Helen to welcome us."

"Sounds good. Even I'm hungry." Grandma Etta waved a hand in the direction of the diner. "Lead on."

Skylar realized once they sat down that she wasn't hungry. To tell the truth, she felt a bit nauseated. She ordered a cup of chicken noodle soup then picked at it. Her own headache hadn't subsided, but there were only two aspirin in the container from Grandma Etta's purse, and she wasn't about to deprive Matt of them. He was in far worse shape than she was. She would simply make do for now.

Once Matt and Grandma Etta had sated their appetite with a delicious homecooked meal, they all sat for a few moments at the table to decide what to do.

"I'm happy to find it's not as late as I thought it might be, and that this restaurant was open." Matt patted his filled stomach. "My head's feeling much better, and I can actually think straight." He glanced at the clock on the wall. "It's only nine-forty. If asked, I'd have said it was after midnight, but then I wasn't thinking straight."

Skylar rubbed his arm. "No, my darling, you were in sad shape. I'm glad you're feeling much better. So, what's the plan now? Do you still want to talk to the police or call Griff Jenkins?"

"I have to talk to the police to get a police report for the rental truck. Then I'll have to call the rental company too. They're not going to be happy, but I need a new ride at some point. I suppose we'll spend the night in this little burg. I'm seriously thinking of calling Griff as well, if nothing more than to get his reaction. That should tell us something."

Grandma Etta lifted a shoulder. "I think that's a fine idea, and Beth Ann, er Elizabeth, gave you their telephone number for that newfangled whatever it's called. Use it. Call 'em."

A variety of emotions vied for a place on Matt's features. "All right. The police first. I have to report the incident with the truck and being run off the road. Second the rental company. Then we have to find a place to stay for the night. Tomorrow morning I'll call Griff."

"Wonderful." Grandma slapped her hand on the table then grimaced.

"Oh my, we forgot about getting Grandma some

medical help." Skylar slipped a gentle arm around her grandmother. "We'll have to see if there's a hospital around here."

Grandma waved her words away. "Not, necess—"

"Of course, it's necessary," Matt said. "That arm might be broken. Come on, let's head to the police department then they can tell us where there's a hospital. That's next on the agenda. I can call the rental company from a payphone at the hospital."

The restaurant hostess directed the trio to the police station only a block away. Skylar kept her arm around Grandma Etta's waist and helped her along. She could tell the older woman's strength was fading.

Matt held the door open for the women then led them to the desk sergeant on duty. "Hello, sir. I'd like to report being run off the road about three-quarters of a mile back toward the highway just off the exit. My girlfriend's grandmother has been injured."

"And my boyfriend may have a concussion, but he's not going to mention that, sir," Skylar piped in, her eyes on Matt. He quirked her a lowered brow then turned his attention back to the uniformed man behind the counter.

The officer eyed the three then nodded slowly. "I assume you mean it was a hit-and-run."

"Yes, sir. Whoever it was ran us off the road and down the embankment. We landed in a copse of trees. It took us a while to get my girlfriend freed from being stuck beneath the dashboard. I had to use a crowbar to free her. We climbed up the hill and walked into town. My truck is a rental, and I need a police report to share with the rental company." He tugged the rental paperwork from his jacket pocket and laid it on the counter. "Do you think you could help us out, sir?"

The officer slid the paperwork toward him and glanced through it. "You rented the truck in Knoxville?"

"Yes, sir."

Skylar noticed Matt was being as polite and respectful

as he could be.

The officer eyed Grandma Etta with her makeshift sling. "Would you like to have a seat over there, ma'am? I'm sure after your rough evening and walk into town, a chair would feel good right about now." He pointed toward a row of chairs against a wall.

"Thank you, young man. I certainly would."

"We'll see about getting you some medical attention shortly." He aimed his attention back to Matt. "Sir, I'll get an officer to take you back out to the site of the incident. First, we have to make sure you aren't under the influence. Of alcohol, that is. I'm sure you understand."

Matt's eyebrows furrowed, but he didn't argue. It wouldn't do any good, after all. Skylar was sure the officer had to follow protocol.

Matt heaved a sigh but complied when the officer stepped around the counter and administered several sobriety tests. He had Matt count backward from a hundred. Flawlessly. Then he walked a line toe to toe. Flawlessly. Matt balanced on one leg for a full minute. Again, flawlessly. The officer narrowed his eyes at Matt as if he couldn't believe he was actually sober. For the last test, he told Matt to hold his finger in the air at arm's-length in front of his face and look at it. Then he told him to bring his finger to his nose. Matt did this without a hitch.

"Well, sir," the officer grinned, "I'm sure you understand why I had to test you."

Matt chuckled. "Of course, I do, but now you know I didn't run off the road because I was drunk. Sir, someone ran me off the road. It was a dark pickup truck. We came off the exit to come into town to get something to eat. The pickup truck had been following us since North Wilkesboro and came off the exit right behind us. At the left curve, he forced us off. I tried to stay on the road, but my tire blew. I lost control and went over."

"Why would someone do that?" The officer peered at

Matt after jotting down some notes.

"I'm not sure." Matt met Skylar's eyes. She nodded.

"Where were you coming from?" The officer glanced up at Matt.

Matt sighed and turned his gaze back to the officer. Skylar could tell he was hesitant to tell him the whole story, but he had to, or the officer wouldn't take this situation seriously.

"Tell him, Matt. Tell him everything." Skylar placed a hand on his arm.

"Tell him, son," Grandma Etta said from where she sat.

"Is there something you're holding back, sir? You need to tell me what's going on." The officer leaned on the counter. "If you want help, you need to talk."

Matt shook his head. "It's just such a long story."

The officer smiled. "I'm not going anywhere since I don't get off until eight tomorrow morning, but I think that little lady over there needs medical attention before that. So, talk."

Matt spilled the story. The officer remained silent only nodding occasionally as Matt talked. When he was finished, the officer chuckled. "You mean to tell me you met Griff Jenkins today? That's about as cool as it gets. He's my favorite NASCAR driver. He's fast and a true winner. I'm a little envious of that, you know. You say he invited y'all to Daytona for the Daytona 500? Well, you'd better go."

"That's what I said." Grandma Etta sniffed."

Skylar turned and raised a brow at her. The way she remembered it, Grandma Etta had said she was too old to go. Skylar turned back to the officer. "What do you think?"

"That's quite a story." He shook his head.

"You don't believe it?" Skylar gasped.

"Oh, yeah, I believe it. It's just incredible, that's all." The officer held up a defensive hand. "Look, I can't go out there with you. I have desk duty, but I'll get Patrol Officer Lane to head out to the wreck site with you. If it's the way you said, there'll be skid marks and plenty of other evidence to check out. I'll have another officer take this dear lady and your girlfriend to the hospital over in the next town. When you're finished, Officer Lane will take you to the hospital. You need to be checked for a concussion. He'll also arrange for the rental to be hauled out of the ravine to our impound lot until you can call the rental company. I'll call over to the hotel next to the hospital and reserve you a couple rooms for the night. I'm sure some rest will help you all. You can take care of the rental in the morning. Sound like a plan?"

Before Matt could open his mouth to speak, Skylar piped in. "It's a great plan. Thank you, sir. More than you know."

"Here's the desk number. Everything that's happened tonight will be in the police blotter, and the morning desk officer will have access, so you can talk to him when you need to."

Matt held out his hand. "Thank you. I appreciate all of your help, sir."

"No problem." The officer offered them a half-grin and shook Matt's hand. "The two officers will be here shortly. Have a seat and take a load off until they arrive."

# Chapter Eleven

**Matt and Officer** Lane, a lean fiftyish man with a crewcut, scanned the asphalt road with bright, wide-beamed flashlights in hand.

"Do you see the two sets of tire tracks?" Matt turned toward the uniformed man who was staring at the pavement.

"I do indeed." Officer Lane straightened and pointed at the road. "Take a look at this. Here it looks like a set of tires braked then got kinda squirrely before heading over the edge of the road, skidding as it went. The second set of tire marks are in the left lane as they brake hard then turn toward the right. From the amount of rubber they left behind on these tracks, I'd say they were stepping on the gas to use force. Then here, just in front of the other vehicle's skid marks, they brake again. Sudden, like they came to a stop to keep from going over the edge. Then if you look around the ground, there are bits of chrome and what looks like a broken headlight cover and shattered yellow sidelight cover fragments. I'd say the chrome is possibly from the wheel-well trim. It's curved like that."

"Yeah, well, that other vehicle was my rental." Matt waved a hand. "Come over here, sir." Matt strode toward the edge of the road and stopped. He pointed his flashlight beam into the ravine. There sat the sad remains of his rental pickup truck. It nearly broke his heart. That truck had become his vehicle away from home. He still had to deal with all that entailed.

A soft whistle escaped the officer beside him. "Whooee. Now that's a sorrowful sight. No wonder you sent your ladies to the hospital. We need to wrap this little investigation up and get you there too."

"Do you believe what I said happened?" Matt turned to face the officer.

"There's not a doubt in my mind." Officer Lane propped his fists on his hips. "I'll get you over to the hospital, then I'll come back out and run the measurements before writing up my report. I'll also arrange to have the truck pulled out o' there and hauled back to the impound lot. Don't worry. You won't be charged anything. It'll sit there until the rental company can arrange to have it picked up. I'm sure they'll work something out to get you another vehicle."

Matt heaved another sigh. "Let's hope so. I appreciate your help out here. Believe me, it wasn't a fun ride down that hill when that truck struck us and pushed us over the edge."

"I can only imagine. I've covered a lot of accidents in my time but never anything like this. I'm just thankful y'all walked away with only the injuries you received and nothing worse."

Matt turned and strode toward the officer's squad car. "You and me both."

~

"Check her out too," Grandma Etta demanded. "I heard her moaning after the truck came to a stop down that hill. I'm pretty sure her head was hurting."

The doctor finished bandaging Grandma's left forearm then placed a new sling around her neck and slipped her arm inside. Fortunately, her arm wasn't broken but severely sprained and had a deep laceration. "If she's had a headache and feels she needs to be seen, I'll be happy to take a look at your granddaughter, Mrs. Sawyer. That's what we're here for." He gave the older woman a tolerant smile and turned to

Skylar. "Would you like for me to take a look at you, young lady? Did you hit your head? Have you had a headache since the accident?"

Skylar started to say no, but her head had been throbbing since they landed in the ravine. With her concern for Grandma Etta's arm and for Matt's pounding head, she'd pushed her own discomfort to the background. Eating hadn't helped, and the nausea hadn't subsided. She must have hit her head in the impact somehow, and the pain persisted. "Yes, I have a throbbing headache. Maybe I hit my head during the truck's descent into the ravine or on impact with the copse of trees."

"Ah," the doctor removed his stethoscope. "Then exchange seats with your grandmother. She's all finished." Once they'd done so, he listened to her heart and breathing then draped the stethoscope once again around his neck. "Were you unconscious at all?" He removed a small reflex hammer from a drawer in the cabinet on the wall and checked her reflexes.

"Maybe for a few minutes? I'm not actually sure."

"She was unconscious, but it wasn't for long," Grandma Etta spoke up. "I was never unconscious, but she and Matt both were."

"Who is Matt?" The doctor stepped back and crossed an arm over his chest, propping the elbow of his other arm on it.

"My boyfriend." Skylar leaned forward on the examination table. "He should be coming in soon. I believe he, too, has a concussion. He had a terrible headache, although after taking some aspirin and eating, he started feeling better."

The doctor chuckled. "Food can do that for some folks. When he gets here, we'll take a look at him. For now, I'm concerned about you. Do you have any other symptoms besides the throbbing headache?"

Skylar closed her eyes. "Yes. I'm nauseated, and I lost

my appetite. We went to a restaurant to grab a bite before we went to the police station. Matt was starved. He and Grandma ate fine. I tried to eat a bowl of soup but couldn't get it down."

"Hmm. I wondered about that." Grandma said from her chair. "She's got a concussion, hasn't she, Doc?"

He chuckled. "It's looking that way." He turned to Skylar. "Any vomiting or dizziness?"

"No."

"Good. Do you have any pain relievers to take?"

"No."

"Then, I'll prescribe you some along with an anti-nausea medicine, and I recommend someone stays with you tonight. Get plenty of rest and don't overdo. Think you can handle that?"

When Grandma harumphed, Skylar waved a dismissive hand. "I'm sure I can."

He wrote the prescription on a script pad and tore it off before handing it to her. "You can fill that at the hospital pharmacy."

Skylar reached for it. "Thank you."

"I'll see if your boyfriend has arrived yet." The doctor excused himself and left the room.

Skylar turned her eyes on grandmother. "What was that skeptical sound for?"

"You might get some shut-eye tonight once we get to the hotel—" Grandma Etta shrugged, "but I'm not so sure about the 'plenty of rest and don't overdo' orders the doc gave you. Do you think you're really going to slow down while you're searching for Sheriff Baker's killer so you can clear Brodie's name?" A doubtful expression settled on the older woman's features. "We both know that's not going to happen. And if Matt has a concussion? Well, that's double trouble."

Skylar leaned back, resting her head against the pillow on the exam table and closed her eyes. She willed her head to stop pounding. *Lord, this is not a good situation we find ourselves in. We're in a strange town. We're injured in one way or another with no vehicle to take us home. Hopefully, the police have worked out a place for us to stay for the night. We don't know what tomorrow will bring, and to top it off, someone is trying to…kill us. Or maybe they think they already have. Things look rather bleak.* A sigh escaped as Skylar paused to take stock of their situation. *I don't know what's happening with Matt right now, but he's in your hands, Lord. We all are. Only You know what lies ahead. Please light our path and guide our steps.*

The curtain to the cubicle swished back and a nurse strode in. "Ladies, the doctor has written out your release orders. He's also written another script for meds for each of you. Something for that arm, Mrs. Simpson, and for your headache and nausea, Miss Sawyer. He's just finished up with Mr. Scott in the cubicle two down from here. If you're ready to go, I'll take all three of you down to the pharmacy. If you'll follow me."

Within a half-hour they had prescriptions in hand and were standing at the entrance to the hospital.

"What's next?" Grandma Etta turned to face Matt, the chill in the autumn air causing a puff of vapor in the air as she spoke.

Matt glanced around the short distance in front of the hospital. "The desk sergeant reserved us rooms at the hotel next to the hospital." He pulled a slip of paper from his jacket pocket and read it. He glanced around again. "That's the hotel just over there." He eyed the two women with him. "Can you both walk that distance? We'll take our time and go slowly."

"It's not like we have much choice, is it? I'm fine." Grandma Etta adjusted her new sling. "I'll take something when I reach the hotel, but I can walk over without a problem."

Skylar met Matt's eyes. She didn't dare nod with the

pain shooting through her skull. She simply plastered a weak smile on her lips. "I'll make it. Let's just go. I have something to take when I get to our room."

Matt nodded and took her hand. He slipped his other hand in the crook of Grandma Etta's good elbow. "Okay, ladies. Let's make our way over and check in. We all need a good night's sleep."

Skylar was thankful for the brightly-lit sidewalk that led to the hotel, and it didn't take long to walk there and checked in. The desk officer had reserved two rooms for them. Skylar and Grandma Etta shared a room, and Matt was right next door in an adjoining room. Skylar and Grandma took their pain meds and went straight to bed.

It didn't even matter that the bed felt like she was sleeping on a table. The pillow was soft, and that was all Skylar cared about. *Thanks for that, Lord. Please help my headache to go away and help us all to sleep well. Take care of all the details that need worked out, especially the need for a vehicle to take us home. Please give Matt wisdom to know what to do. I...love You. Amen.*

Within minutes Skylar faded into sleep. Not even the pain throbbing through her head kept her awake.

~

"Yes, that's great. Thank you. I'll be waiting." Matt hung up the room phone and stood. His stomach growled. Time to eat. Were Skylar and Grandma Etta up and ready to grab breakfast? He padded to the connecting door between their rooms and tapped lightly. When there was no response, he tapped a little harder. "Hello? Good morning, ladies. Are you awake? It's time to grab some breakfast."

The knob turned and Grandma Etta swung the door wide. "I'm in total agreement. Let's eat."

Matt grinned at the older woman. "Where's Skylar? Is she up? How's she doing this morning?"

"Better, I think. We both slept like proverbial logs."

Skylar stepped out of the bathroom and gave Matt a

tired smile. "Good morning."

Matt wrapped an arm around her waist and tugged her close for a gentle kiss. "Good morning, beautiful. How'd you sleep?" He couldn't miss Grandma Etta's eye roll.

Skylar gave him a hug then stepped back. "I slept well. Still have a bit of a headache, but it's nothing like I had last night. I've taken another pill. Hopefully it'll knock the rest out."

"Are you hungry?"

"I could eat." She reached for her purse.

"Then let's go. This hotel serves a hot breakfast." He locked up after the women stepped into the hallway. They made their way to the breakfast area and perused the available foods. Once they'd served themselves, found a table, and said a blessing, they began eating.

"So, what's the plan for today?" Skylar sipped her coffee then set down the mug.

"I've already called the car rental company, and they're on their way from Knoxville to pick me up and take me to the police station where the pickup truck is sitting in the impound lot. When they receive the police report, they'll look the truck over. They've already made an initial call to the police station and will bring another vehicle along with the plan to replace the truck. We'll see how it goes, but they should turn over the second vehicle to me."

"Sounds good." Grandma Etta passed the butter to Skylar.

"It certainly does." Skylar spread butter on her pancakes then poured syrup over them. "What's next?"

"I also gave a call to Griff Jenkins but couldn't reach him. I got Elizabeth and told her what happened last night. She was shocked and couldn't imagine who would follow us and do such a thing. Elizabeth said she'd pass my message on to Griff."

"Did you believe her?" Skylar forked a piece of pancake.

Matt shrugged and picked up his coffee mug. "Her shock seemed genuine."

"I doubt the woman could be that good of an actress," Grandma Etta chuckled. "She may put on airs, but she's just a country girl at heart."

"I still can't figure out who would follow us then run us off the road." Skylar popped another piece of pancake into her mouth and chewed.

Matt had wracked his brain to come up with the answer to that same question. The only people they'd talked to were Skylar's Uncle Bufford, Deputy Harding, Griff Jenkins, and his wife Elizabeth. Oh, and Harper Kent was present when they visited Griff and Elizabeth. Matt took another swallow of coffee. Harper Kent? Now that's someone he hadn't thought about before now. He was there the night the sheriff was killed and when they visited Griff Jenkins. Could he…?

A gentle finger touched his forehead, and he turned toward Skylar. She grinned. "What's that pucker sitting between your brows for? You look like you're a million miles away. Where did you go?"

Matt set his mug down and leaned his arms on the edge of the table. "Oh, I was just contemplating your comment about who ran us off the road. It's something I've been thinking a lot about."

"What have you come up with?" Grandma Etta dabbed her mouth with her napkin.

"Not much. I've gone over everyone we've talked to about this case, and unless Deputy Harding, the Jenkins, or Harper Kent sent someone after us, it's hard to say who it could be." Matt shook his head despondently.

"That does leave a lot of doubt, doesn't it?" Skylar agreed.

Matt glanced at his watch. "I need to go. The agent from the rental company will be here soon to pick me up. You two take your time. Hang out in the lobby until I come pick you up in the new rental, but keep your heads on a swivel. We may be presumed to be dead, but…you never know."

~

A chill surged through Skylar at Matt's words. They were presumed to be dead. She didn't like the sound of that, but after last night's events, she supposed it to be true. What if someone wasn't sure they'd finished the job? As she and Grandma Etta sat on a loveseat in the lobby behind a pillar, she couldn't begin to get engrossed in the news on the TV station. She took Matt's advice and kept her head on a swivel. She watched every person that passed by and listened to every conversation around them.

"Would you settle down, child?" Grandma Etta patted Skylar's arm. "You're making me nervous."

"Sorry, but what Matt said before he left has made me nervous."

Grandma Etta returned her attention to the TV, and Skylar returned her surveillance to her surroundings. Suddenly, a voice from the front desk said her name, along with Matt's and Grandma Etta's. She peered carefully around the three-quarter wall behind their couch to see a tall man in a leather coat and a knit slouch cap with a visor. He stood in front of the counter talking to the desk clerk. Skylar yanked back. Why would a strange man be asking about them?

Skylar leaned toward Grandma Etta and whispered in her ear. "Grandma Etta, we have to go. Now. There's a strange man asking about us at the front desk. Let's go out the back way. Hurry."

Skylar helped Grandma Etta to her feet and took her good arm, making sure she had her purse, then hurried her to the back exit. They slipped out the door and ran as quickly as they could around the side of the building. Where should they go? They stopped for a moment to get their bearings. The only place she knew was the hospital. Would they be safe there?

A gunshot sounded a second before a bullet hit the

building right next to them.

"Come on. Let's go." Skylar grabbed Grandma Etta's arm, and they ran around the building. Not toward the hospital. They'd be sitting targets. Too much open space. They made for the building next door and kept moving until they saw a sign that read Police Department. Great. They'd head there. Another shot rang out. Keeping as low as possible, they made their way toward the police department and yanked the door open.

Skylar shoved Grandma Etta in first against the wall and dove in after her. No sooner were they inside when the door shattered. A bullet had struck the glass. Both women shrieked as they pressed further into the room. A policeman appeared from behind the counter and yanked them behind it.

"Thank you, young man." Grandma Etta breathed as she lay on the floor wrapped in Skylar's arms.

After a moment there were no more shots. More police swarmed the area as the first officer helped the two women to their feet.

"I'm Officer Moreno, ladies. Are you all right?" The tall, dark-haired officer held Grandma Etta's arm and pulled a chair over for her to sit on. "Did the glass get on you? Let's take a look."

Skylar stood and carefully helped Grandma Etta remove her coat. "I hope it's not all in your hair. Let's see." She parted the strands of the older woman's hair to look at her scalp. "Oh, dear. It looks like there are shards on your scalp, especially toward the back."

"It's all over her coat too." The officer held up Grandma Etta's coat then met Skylar's eyes. "I'll bet it's all over yours and in your hair as well, ma'am. I want to send you both over to the hospital, but not until I find out what happened to cause this. Can you tell me?"

Skylar sighed. "I can, if you've got time for a story."

He eyed her through narrowed lids. "A story?"

"A true story."

"Shoot. I'm not going anywhere, and something tells me it's going to be interesting."

Grandma Etta released a snort. "Hmm. You have no idea."

Skylar started from the beginning with the 1945 newspaper article. By the time she finished, Officer Moreno wasn't the only officer listening to her tale.

"Wow, you met Griff Jenkins?" one officer asked. "For real?"

"Hey, Kowalski," Officer Moreno turned to the young man, "You and Myers go see if you can hunt down this nut case who's trying to kill these ladies. See if he's still hanging around the streets. Bring him in if he is."

"Yes, Sarge." Kowalski crunched through the glass then disappeared out the door followed by another officer.

"If you ladies can hang out here a little longer, I'd rather not send you to the hospital in case the gunman is still around. Give my men a chance to find him." Moreno turned toward the desk behind the counter. "You said your boyfriend is in the next town at the police station. I'm going to call over there. What did you say his name is?"

"Matt Scott."

"Right." He turned toward another officer. "Grab these ladies some coffee, would you?"

"Sure, Boss."

"Thank you," Skylar and Grandma Etta replied in unison.

Skylar's scalp began to itch but she didn't dare scratch it. She didn't want to cut her scalp or her fingers. Oh, just the thought…. She concentrated on drinking her coffee. It was nice and hot if not the tastiest, but considering her situation, she'd enjoy it. *Lord, this day went south rather fast. And it's not over, is it? Please help us.*

"Your boyfriend is almost finished." Officer Moreno dropped the phone handset back on the receiver and turned back to them. "He'll meet you at the hospital."

Skylar grinned. "See, I was telling you the truth."

A ruddy tinge colored the officer's cheeks. "You have to understand that as an officer I must verify all information, Miss Simpson."

"Of course you do. I understand perfectly."

Officer Kowalski and the other officer strode through the door before the janitor finished cleaning up the shattered glass. The officers carefully made their way to Moreno's desk.

"What'd you find?" Moreno's eyes ping-ponged between the two men.

The officers exchanged a glance before Kowalski answered. "We spotted a guy in a black leather coat jump into a black pickup truck and hightail it out of town."

Grandma Etta turned to Skylar. "Do you think that's him?"

Skylar cocked her head to the side. "I would think so. The guy at the hotel front desk had on a black leather coat. He's the one that came after us and shot at us. The truck that ran us off the road last night was dark."

Grandma Etta frowned at the officers. "Why didn't you bring him in before he could skip town?"

Kowalski's expression turned sheepish. "We were on foot, ma'am."

"All right. Take these ladies over to the hospital and have them checked out for cuts." Moreno ordered Kowalski. "Also, ask to have them cleaned of any glass. They'll have to have new clothes and coats. What they're wearing are covered in glass."

"But—" Skylar began.

"The hospital has contacts with agencies, Miss Simpson." Moreno tucked his thumbs into his utility belt. "They'll help out with clothes until you can do better for yourselves."

"I see. Thank you." She cast him a grateful smile.

He waved a dismissive hand. "No problem. Go along with Kowalski. Your boyfriend will be there shortly. You and your grandmother will want to have all the glass removed by the time he arrives. I think I've got all I need as far as a report. We'll keep our eyes open for this guy, but you all need to be careful."

"You bet we do." Grandma Etta followed Officer Kowalski out the back way to his cruiser.

Skylar once again thanked Officer Moreno then caught up with her grandmother.

# Chapter Twelve

A few hours later, they were finally on their way back to Grandma Etta's house. It seemed more like a week since they'd left her house rather than yesterday morning, Matt thought as he settled behind the steering wheel of the new rental pickup truck. He was happy the rental company had brought another truck instead of a car. This one was a little bigger with a wider bench seat. It gave Grandma Etta more room for her injured left arm.

Skylar scooted a bit closer to Matt to ensure her grandmother had plenty of room. He didn't mind. A glance to the right showed both ladies had their heads back and eyes closed. What was supposed to be a quick trip to find out information from Griff Jenkins had turned into a nightmare. Skylar and Grandma Etta were worn out. For them, the nightmare had continued today.

Matt stared down the highway as he racked his brain to figure out the puzzle of who would want them dead. It was obvious that whoever had killed Sheriff Baker so long ago still didn't want to be discovered. But things didn't start happening until they'd gone to see Deputy Harding, the Jenkins, and Harper Kent. It had to be one of them or someone connected to one of them.

Deputy Harding had passed out at the time of the shooting, or so he'd said. Bufford seemed to back that statement up. So that left Griff Jenkins or Harper Kent.

Matt smacked his palm against the steering wheel. Skylar jumped and sat up.

"What? What happened? What's going on?" She glanced around, confused.

"Aw, sweetheart. I'm sorry for waking you." Matt clasped her hand and gave it a gentle squeeze. "It was just me. I was running the last two days over in my head and got frustrated. I slammed my hand on the steering wheel. Sorry. Why don't you put your head on my shoulder and go back to sleep."

Skylar rubbed Matt's arm. "No, I'm fine. I don't want to leave you to frustrating thoughts. It's not fun to be alone when you're feeling that way." She glanced around, more awake now. "Where are we?"

"We're back in Tennessee. It won't be long before we'll be in Oakridge, then on to Oliver Springs then home."

Skylar released a soft chuckle then whispered. "You mean home away from home?"

Matt tossed her a grin. "Yeah, I suppose so. Grandma Etta makes it feel like home, doesn't she?"

"Yes, she does."

~

Neither of them spotted the soft smile that lifted the corners of the older woman's lips, her face turned toward her window. It pleased her old heart to know these two young people felt at home in her little old cabin in the back woods. *I don't know how much longer they'll be staying, Lord, but thank You for sending them my way even for a little while.*

~

"You know, I was just thinking, every one of our suspects knows where we're staying." Skylar dropped her purse on the couch once they'd entered the cabin later that evening. She turned to the others as Matt closed the cabin door behind him. "Whoever is after us knows where Grandma Etta lives."

Grandma Etta opened the woodstove door. Nothing but cold ashes lined the bottom of the fire box. Matt stepped over and gently lifted her out of the way. He gathered kindling from the wood box against the wall and began to build a fire.

Skylar could tell her grandmother was still tired from their adventures when she didn't put up a fight with Matt over building the fire but rather settled so quickly in her rocking chair.

"That thought has crossed my mind too." Matt tossed on more kindling when a flame leaped higher then added a couple of larger pieces as the flames licked the dry wood. He turned and met Skylar's eyes. "I'm not sure it's going to be safe to stay here for long."

She turned her eyes on her grandmother. "They all know you, Grandma Etta. They know where you live, and I wouldn't be surprised if the guy who's after us heads this way. Now that whoever killed the sheriff knows we're looking to clear Dad's name, they'll be coming for us."

Grandma Etta stopped rocking as Skylar's point must have hit home. "Where will we go?"

"I've been thinking about that." Matt tossed on one more small log. "We should gather some things and head into town. I doubt they'd think to look for us at Mrs. Hildebrand's. Why would they? They have no idea that we know her."

Skylar paced back and forth a few times. She stopped and met Matt's gaze. "I can't think of a reason why they would come looking there. We can tell Mrs. Hildebrand what's going on. She won't say anything." She paused then frowned. "As long as Helen at Reaves Café doesn't catch wind about us being there and why."

Matt chuckled. "Yeah. Everybody in the county will know."

"Helen Carter?" Grandma Etta once again put the brakes on the rocker. "That gossip at the café in town?"

"Yep." Matt reached for the fire poker and stirred the

fire. Warmth filled the chilly room.

"Heaven help us if that woman gets wind of anything you don't want the town to know. That woman is a blabbermouth." Grandma Etta's eyes turned heavenward. "Forgive me, Lord. That was unkind, even if true."

Skylar covered her mouth and turned away to keep from showing her mirth. Grandma Etta was a dear but lacked a filter. Skylar would sure miss her when she returned to Wyoming. The thought brought a pang to her heart.

"All right then, it's a plan." Matt closed the woodstove door as the light of leaping flames shone through the glass. He stood and stretched his back. "Let's gather our things together and plan to leave as soon as possible."

"But you just started the doggone fire." Grandma Etta stood and warmed her hands before the woodstove.

"I know." Matt propped his hands on his hips. "It was cold in here. Don't worry. I didn't put on much wood. Just small pieces. We'll enjoy the warmth while we can, then I'll put it out."

It wasn't long before they'd gathered their belongings. Grandma Etta went to the kitchen and collected some food items and bread she'd made two days earlier. She wanted to contribute something for their stay at Mrs. Hildebrand's. When she asked Matt how they would pay for staying at the B&B, he patted her shoulder and told her not to worry about that. He had it covered. She walked away shaking her head and muttering about how expensive it was going to be. Skylar smiled and glanced at Matt. He simply gave her a wink.

When the fire was banked and their suitcases and the food were stowed in the back of the pickup truck, they locked the cabin, once again settled in the truck cab, and drove into town. Matt remembered exactly where Mrs. Hildebrand's house was located and before long parked in her driveway. Leaving their things in the truck, they made their way up the walkway to the front porch.

"This is a lovely place as far as I can tell in the dark. I'm sure the daylight will give me a much lovelier view." Grandma glanced around. "I don't believe I've ever met Mrs. Hildebrand."

"It is a pretty place, and I'm sure you'll like her. She's a nice lady." Skylar spoke in a low voice as Matt rang the doorbell. "Please be on your best behavior."

"Hmm. I'm always on my best behavior," Grandma Etta responded with a sniff.

Skylar placed an arm around her grandmother's shoulders. "Of course you are."

The porch light turned on, then the front door opened a crack. An eye peered out at them. "May I help you?" A timid feminine voice spoke from behind the door.

"Mrs. Hildebrand, it's Matt Scott and Skylar Simpson. You do remember us, don't you?" Skylar noted Matt's bright smile as he nodded toward Skylar. "We also have Skylar's grandmother, Etta Sawyer, with us. Remember I asked about finding her home a couple weeks ago? You helped me find where Skylar was heading?"

They waited as seconds ticked by hoping that Mrs. Hildebrand would remember them. A gasp sounded from behind the door, then it closed and a chain latch was released before the B&B proprietress swung the door wide and stepped back.

"Yes, yes. I remember you both. Please do come in." She held her arm out. "I see you caught up with each other." Glancing down at her purple bathrobe, she tugged the belt tighter. "Please pardon my attire. I wasn't expecting anyone this evening, and it's later than I usually expect guests."

Mrs. Hildebrand closed the door when they'd all stepped inside.

Matt removed his cowboy hat. "Yes, I apologize for coming so late. You see we have a bit of a dilemma. First, I have to ask if you might have a couple of rooms we could stay in for a few nights."

Surprise lifted Mrs. Hildebrand's brows. "Oh, well, of course. I only have one guest for tonight, so I have plenty of room. I'm expecting two other guests over the next two nights, but that's not a problem."

Skylar spotted the relief on Matt's features even as she heaved a sigh of relief. *Thank you, Lord. That's one problem solved.*

"After we settle in, we'd like to have a talk with you, if you don't mind." Matt turned back toward the door. "I'll grab the suitcases."

"Certainly." Mrs. Hildebrand clasped her hands in front of her full waist. "Whenever you're ready."

"Mrs. Hildebrand, let me introduce you to my grandmother, Henrietta Sawyer." Skylar wrapped an arm around her grandmother's waist, being careful of her injured arm.

"Ah, Mrs. Sawyer, it's a pleasure to meet you. Please call me Martha." Their hostess held her hand toward Grandma Etta, a welcoming smile on her face.

Grandma Etta smiled in return and shook the extended hand. "It's nice to meet you, Martha. Everyone calls me Etta. I'd like it if you would too."

"Why certainly, Etta." Martha turned toward the staircase at the side of the entryway. "Please follow me, and I'll take you ladies to your room."

"I'll wait here for Matt so I can help him carry the bags upstairs." Skylar waved them along. "Please go ahead. We'll be up in a few minutes."

It wasn't long before Matt returned with three suitcases and the bag of food. "Here, let me help." Skylar grabbed the bag of food and set it on the floor then grabbed the suitcase tucked beneath his arm. "They've gone on upstairs." She chuckled. "From early appearances, I'd say they're going to hit it off."

"That's a good thing. Grandma Etta could use a friend."

"Yes, maybe she could." Skylar nodded toward the

stairs. "I'll carry these up. Let's go find them, but we should be quiet. She has another guest."

"Right."

Matt followed Skylar up the staircase to the hallway above, their feet sinking into the thick carpet lining the stairs. They found Martha and Grandma Etta at the end of the hallway in a larger bedroom than the one Skylar had stayed in before. There were twin beds in this room.

"I hope you ladies will be comfortable in here." Martha clasped her fingers together in front of her and beamed at them.

"Oh, this will be wonderful, Martha." Grandma Etta flashed her a smile as she glanced around the pastel floral room. "This is lovely. We'll be quite comfortable here, won't we, Sky?"

"Yes. I'm sure we will." Skylar remembered the comfortable mattress in the room she'd stayed in before. She hoped the ones in here were the same.

"Splendid. Then, Matthew, please follow me, and I will show you to your room. It's just across the hall." Martha handed Skylar her room key then stepped across the hall and opened the door.

"I'll be right back," Matt whispered and hurried after her with his suitcase.

"What do you think?" Skylar turned to Grandma Etta.

Her grandmother shook her head. "I've never stayed anywhere so nice. Even back in teaching school, it wasn't anything like this." Her eyes were as round as proverbial saucers. She met Skylar's gaze. "And Martha is quite the hostess, isn't she?"

"Oh, you haven't seen anything yet. Wait until breakfast."

Martha stepped back into the room followed by Matt. "Young Matthew tells me there's something we need to discuss."

Matt closed the door behind him and offered a seat for

Martha on one of the beds before he took a seat on the wooden chair at the desk. Skylar and Grandma Etta were already sitting on the other bed.

"Please tell me what's going on." Martha glanced from one to the other in the room. "I'm growing quite concerned."

"To be honest with you, there is some cause for concern. There's someone after us." Matt leaned forward, clasping his hands together. "But let me go back to the beginning." He started with the 1945 article and Gina and the threat to Skylar right through to the shot fired into the police station that morning. Was it really just that morning?

"We couldn't stay at Grandma Etta's, Martha. Whoever is after us knows where she lives. We had to hide somewhere." Skylar shifted on the bed.

Martha covered her mouth with trembling fingers. "Oh, my goodness. That's a terrible story, dear Skylar. But have you brought danger to my door? Will they trace you here?"

Skylar shook her head. "No, we don't think so. They don't have any way of connecting us with you. I don't see how they could find us here as long as we stay low. At least it'll give us time to come up with a different plan."

"Martha, we had nowhere else to go." Matt shrugged. "We returned to Grandma Etta's cabin this evening to the realization we weren't safe staying there. But we have to ask you not to say anything to anyone. I mean anyone. Especially anyone like…Helen Carter." He eyed Martha for several seconds.

A slow smile crept over her lips until she burst into tinkling laughter. She put her hands over her mouth as her shoulders shook. It was several moments before she controlled her mirth. Wiping the tears from her cheeks, Martha heaved a sigh and turned to Matt. "Oh, my dear boy. That was a good one. There's no way on God's green earth I would share anything with that woman that I minded getting out to the public. She can't keep a secret about anything. It would simply kill her to keep her mouth closed.

I don't think she knows how." Another chuckle slipped from her again, and the others joined in. "Oh, forgive me." She planted her hand over her ample breast. "I haven't had that good of a laugh in…well, a long time. That felt good. No, I wouldn't trust Helen Carter with anything."

Grandma Etta chuckled again. "That's not exactly how I put it, but it's more or less the same."

"Oh, you know her?" Martha turned lifted brows toward Grandma Etta.

"Yeah." Grandma Etta made a sour face. "I do."

"Well, it's getting late. We all need to get to bed and let Martha do the same. We've kept her up long enough." Matt stood and headed toward the door. "It's been a long two days, and I'm extremely tired. What time is breakfast, Martha?"

She told them when breakfast would be served. "But I can extend it if you'd like. Just for tomorrow." She smiled.

"Don't think of it." Grandma Etta stood and slipped her good arm through Martha's. "We'll be there." She reached for the food bag. "I brought some food from my kitchen to help. There's some bread I made a couple days ago. Should still be fresh enough, I'd think. Even if it's only for French toast or toasted sandwiches. There are other things in there like soup and canned fruit and veggies. I also brought along my homemade apple butter."

Martha accepted the bag. "Why, that's thoughtful of you, Etta. Thank you."

"Think nothing of it." Grandma Etta waved a dismissive hand

Martha headed toward the door. "Everyone sleep well. I'll see you in the morning."

"You too," a chorus of voices replied.

After Martha had left, Matt tugged Skylar toward the door. He glanced back at her grandmother. "Good night, Grandma Etta. Rest well."

"Oh, I'm sure I will. You do the same." She turned

toward her suitcase and hummed softly as she ignored them.

Skylar allowed Matt to grip her hand and tug her into the hallway, quietly closing the door behind them. He glanced down the hall before wrapping her in his arms. She met his eyes and saw a flame kindled there. Her heartbeat picked up. With everything that had happened over the last few days, they'd had precious little time for themselves. It felt so good to be back in Matt's strong arms again. She'd missed this. From the flame in his eyes, apparently, he had too. As he lowered his head toward hers, she felt her breath catch. Oh, what this man did to her. His lips ignited a flame deep within that warmed her all over. Reaching up to clasp her arms around his neck, she splayed her fingers through the hair at the nape of his neck.

Matt groaned and lifted his head to rest his forehead against hers. "Girl, you know you hold my heart in your hands, don't you?" He laid a kiss on her cheek beside her ear and chuckled. "I think it's time for you to go back inside. I love you, Sky. Don't ever forget that."

Warmth rushed through Skylar once again at the huskiness in Matt's voice. She smiled softly and gave him a tender kiss on the lips. "I won't forget. I love you, Matt Scott. Sleep well."

"Darlin', after that kiss, I'll be dreaming of you and sleeping like a baby." Matt slid his arms from around Skylar and stepped away toward his room. "Good night," he whispered. "See you in the morning."

She blew him a kiss and stepped inside her room, closing the door behind her.

Grandma Etta had picked her bed and tucked herself in. She'd left the soft bedside table light on and faced the wall. Skylar locked the door and tiptoed across the plush carpet to her suitcase to gather her things to head toward the bathroom.

"Did you kiss your Prince Charming goodnight, sweetie?" Grandma Etta's muffled voice was still clear.

Skylar paused. "But of course."
Grandma Etta chuckled. "Good night. Love you, dear"
"I love you, too. Good night."

# Chapter Thirteen

For the next few days, Matt, Skylar, and Grandma Etta simply stayed inside Martha's B&B and went nowhere. A few out-of-town guests stopped overnight then went on their way the next day. The trio felt it was safe enough to chat with them at breakfast and simply state they were from Wyoming when asked where they hailed from. Easy enough. They avoided deeper questions. Also, easy enough. There weren't that many.

Martha cooked all three meals for them, which she normally didn't do for guests but didn't mind doing for them. Matt paid her extra for that so she could purchase groceries she didn't have on hand for the additional meals. Grandma Etta did what she could one-handed to help her.

Skylar wasn't sure how it was going to work out with two cooks in the kitchen but was completely surprised when they worked so well together. They chatted amiably as they divvied up meal preparation, and when it came time for kitchen clean up, they shared that too. They wouldn't hear of allowing Skylar to help. It was *their* job and that was that. She pitched in with dusting and vacuuming the guest rooms while Martha stripped and remade the beds. Martha's back was more than happy for the help.

One afternoon Skylar sat at the kitchen table reading a book from Martha's small library while the two older ladies prepared supper. Matt had been up to his own devices out in the garage behind the main house. Martha allowed him to work on her deceased husband's old cars. She could never bring herself to get rid of them and gave Matt permission to tinker away.

It was quiet in the kitchen with the older women talking softly until Matt strode in the back door and plopped onto a kitchen chair. All eyes turned in his direction.

"You look like a man with deep thoughts on his mind." Skylar inserted a scrap of paper in her book and laid it on the table. "What's going on?"

Matt removed his cowboy hat and ran a hand through his hair, and as he did, Skylar noticed his fingers were clean. Hmm. Apparently, he hadn't been working on the car out back. At least not on any greasy parts.

"I've been thinking about what Griff suggested when we visited him last week."

"What was that?" Grandma Etta turned from the counter where she was patting out homemade biscuits. She'd removed her sling and begun using her arm more. She wiped her hands on a cotton dishtowel.

Matt dropped his hat on the table and met her eyes. "Griff suggested we go to the county courthouse over in Kingston and see what we can dig up about the court case regarding the night Brodie Sawyer was arrested."

Grandma Etta propped her good wrist on her hip. "You know, with everything that's happened after our visit with Griff, I completely forgot he suggested that."

"So did I." Skylar leaned an elbow on the table. She turned a furrowed brow toward Matt. "You can't seriously be thinking of going to the courthouse now."

Matt glanced at the wall clock above the table then back at Skylar. "Of course, not now. It's almost suppertime."

Skylar cast a withering eye at him. "You're so funny. I meant, you can't seriously consider going now while we're in hiding. If we go into any town, we'll obviously not be in hiding anymore."

A grin lifted the corners of Matt's lips. His gaze slid from Skylar to Grandma Etta.

The older woman lifted a brow. "She's got a point."

"She does." He tilted his head. "I was thinking of enlisting some help."

The room grew silent for several moments before Grandma Etta asked with narrowed eyes, "Who?"

"Perhaps Martha wouldn't mind going down to the courthouse and asking for a couple of documents for us."

Martha, who had been stirring a stew on the stove, suddenly stopped and laid down her spoon. She turned and wiped her hands on her apron. The expression imprinted on her features appeared as if she'd just been asked to rob a bank. "You want me to…to do what?"

"Martha, can you please put your stew on the back burner for a couple of minutes?" Skylar pulled out a chair and patted the seat. "This won't take but a moment. Matt will explain."

Their hostess slid the pot to the back burner and turned off the flame. She hesitantly strode toward the chair and took a seat. Skylar swallowed the chuckle that threatened to emerge. The poor woman looked like she was expecting an interrogation.

Matt leaned his elbows on his knees and smiled at the older woman. "It's not a difficult thing, Martha. Nothing illegal at all. I would do it myself except exposing me or any of us still puts us at risk of the folks who are after us discovering we're here. So, what I need you to do is go to the courthouse and ask for a couple of documents concerning Skylar's dad from the night the sheriff died. Mostly police and court reports. I'll write it all down, so you don't forget. If for any reason those documents are sealed and they won't give them to you, then say thank you and walk away. Think you can do that?"

Martha gave a hesitant nod. "I'm sure I can. As long as

you write down exactly what you need."

"Of course." Matt patted her fidgeting hands.

"Shall I get back to the stew?" she asked.

"Certainly." He leaned back and gave her space to stand. He turned to Skylar and met her eyes, holding them.

"That's not all, is it?" She stretched her arm along the table and held her hand out.

Matt shook his head and, reaching out, clasped her fingers in his. "Afraid not. I've been thinking about other things too."

"Like?"

"Like the fact we can't remain in hiding forever. We can't continue to take advantage of Martha's hospitality."

"Oh, I don't mind." Martha spun around, her stirring spoon in the air. "I've so enjoyed you all being here."

Grandma Etta placed a hand on Martha's arm. "And we've enjoyed being here, but Matt's right. We can't stay here forever."

Matt stood and faced them all. "We have to draw the murderer out, ladies."

"What?" All three women chorused at once.

"What do you mean, draw the murderer out?" Grandma Etta asked. "You mean like use us for bait?"

Matt's features screwed up in thought. "That's not exactly what I had in mind, but we have to test the waters and discover who's behind the guy who's after us. My gut's telling me somebody sent him. Nobody was following us or trying to kill us until we went to see Deputy Harding and the Jenkins."

"And Harper Kent," Grandma Etta piped in. "Don't forget he was there the night Sheriff Baker was murdered."

"And he was there when we visited with Griff and Elizabeth," Skylar added.

"Agreed." Matt crossed his arms over his chest. "They all have alibis for that night, at least according to them. That's why it's so important to get police and court reports if possible."

"It's a start." Skylar leaned back in her chair. "I'm not sure how you're planning to draw the murderer out, but if we can get more facts in hand, that'll help."

"*Do* you have a plan?" Grandma Etta narrowed her eyes at Matt.

He strode over to the older woman then wrapped an arm around her shoulders. "I'm working on it. Let's see what the courthouse has or doesn't have as far as documents. They may give us something to go on that no one has mentioned. Then we'll go from there." Matt gave Grandma Etta's shoulders a gentle squeeze. "In the meantime, pray. Hard."

~

After breakfast the next morning, Grandma Etta promised she would take care of washing the dishes as she urged Martha to put on her hat and make her way to the courthouse.

"Etta, the courthouse isn't going anywhere." Martha reached for the bottle of dish detergent. "It'll still be there after the dishes are washed."

Grandma Etta plucked the bottle from Martha's hand and untied the strings of her apron. She hung it on the peg where Martha kept it. "There's no need for you to put it off another minute. I'll take care of the dishes. Matt has asked you to take care of this important assignment, and he's depending on you, dear." Grandma Etta turned Martha by the shoulders toward the door. "He's waiting for you in the dining room with the directions of what he needs for you to ask for. It's all quite simple."

Martha attempted to stop and turn around. "Oh, but—"

"No buts. This is important. Now, go." Grandma Etta gave her friend a gentle shove through the kitchen door.

~

Matt glanced up from the paper he was perusing and set his coffee cup down. "Ah, there you are, Martha. I've got everything you need right here." He lifted the paper and gave it a wave. Worry lines crossed the woman's forehead. It was the first time he'd ever seen them there. A pang of concern hit him. Would she be able to do this? It wouldn't be that hard, but Martha was afraid it would be. He needed to go over the paper with her so she could see what she was asking for. He patted the seat beside him. "Martha, please have a seat. I'd like to review this with you so you can see that it's not hard or illegal or anything like that."

She gave a weak smile and nodded as she took the chair. "That certainly would be reassuring."

"I'm sure it would be." Matt read through the page with Martha and pointed out exactly what she would need to ask for at the courthouse. She finally understood that all she had to do was ask for the documents for a friend who lived in Wyoming. Matt gave her money to pay for copies, since the court clerk would likely charge for them. By the time he was finished, Martha had relaxed and was ready to go.

"I've already pulled your car out of the garage, and it's sitting out front." Matt held up the keys. "I hope you don't mind. I even checked the oil for you."

He dropped the keys into Martha's hand. She gave him a sweet smile. "Well, if that isn't wonderful service, I don't know what is. Thank you. And thank you for explaining everything to me. I feel much better now."

Matt patted her hand. "I wish I could go instead of you, but it's not wise. We appreciate all that you're doing to help us. You've been amazing." He leaned forward and placed a kiss on Martha's cheek.

A flood of color surged across her features as she released a soft laugh. "Oh, it's been my pleasure. I've enjoyed the company. Now—" she retrieved the paper, "—let me get on with my errand. I'll be back soon."

Matt stood when she climbed to her feet and left the room. Martha was a plucky lady. Although afraid, she pulled herself together and marched off to do as he'd asked.

Matt's eyes strayed toward the ceiling. *Lord, help her.*

~

Martha parked her car as close to the county courthouse as she could, but unfortunately, she still had to walk about a block. She wondered at the number of cars parked around the old red brick and clapboard building. Court must be in session or something.

As she neared the tall, fat white columns that held up the front entrance to the courthouse, Martha heard a voice she didn't want to hear. Helen Carter. No! "Oh, dear Lord. Please not now." Martha whispered. She glanced around and spotted the restaurant hostess talking with another lady as they crossed the street and headed in her direction. *What do I do?* Martha froze for a few seconds before her feet took action, and she climbed the few steps to slip behind the last column. She hoped Helen wouldn't go into the courthouse because she couldn't afford to run into that woman. Helen would attempt to drag out of Martha what her business was at the courthouse. *Oh Lord. Hide me.*

Helen's voice rang out as the twosome drew nearer. Martha hugged the column with her back, preparing to slip around it in either direction depending on which way the women went. Martha held her breath lest they detected her presence. Every muscle clamped tight, ready to move.

The women climbed the steps and came into view. Martha froze, afraid to move lest she draw their attention. They headed straight into the courthouse never noticing her. For a moment Martha remained where she was, not moving a muscle. She couldn't go inside. Not while Helen was in there. *Now what, Lord?*

*Think, Martha. What would Matt tell you to do?* He'd likely tell her to find a much more out-of-the-way spot to watch for Helen to come back out. Glancing around, Martha realized she couldn't go inside any of the businesses on the street. Helen might come in any one of them after her time in the courthouse. Okay, so perhaps the alley across the street behind the dumpster. That offered a great view of the front of the courthouse. She crinkled her nose at the thought it would probably smell atrocious. She glanced around some more. *Hurry, Martha. They'll be out again before you find a hiding place.* Then she spotted it. The small park cattycorner from the courthouse. A grouping of bushes and shade trees surrounded several benches. She'd put on her sunglasses and the roll-up sunhat she kept in her purse. Martha kept a small devotional tucked away in there for appointment visits too. She'd pull it out and pretend to read.

Hurrying from behind the column, Martha dashed across the street and over to the park where she set up surveillance from a park bench for the restaurant hostess and her friend. When Helen Carter had vacated the vicinity, then Martha would feel comfortable to head into the courthouse. This was difficult enough of a task for her. She simply did not need to be grilled by Oliver Spring's nosy body.

After about five minutes of watching, she glanced at the devotional in her hand and realized it was upside down. "Oh Lord," she mumbled. "I'm not cut out for espionage."

Ten minutes passed quickly. If the women didn't come out soon, she'd have to abandon her post and find a bathroom. Her bladder was talking to her. She might even have a few things to say to Matt by the time this experience was over.

During her surveillance several people had come and gone through the immense tall white doors of the courthouse entrance. She'd dismissed them all and was growing more and more frustrated when suddenly the doors opened and out walked Helen and her friend.

Martha sat up straight then remembered to act like she was reading but spied them over the top of the devotional. The women once again crossed the street and strolled back in the direction they'd come. All the while Helen's voice could be heard loud and clear. Martha rolled her eyes and shook her head. She appreciated all the B&B business Helen sent her way. She simply wished the woman wasn't so nosy.

When they'd disappeared down the block and around a corner and Helen's voice could no longer be heard, Martha stashed her devotional, sunglasses, and her hat back into her purse and headed toward the courthouse. Time to get this assignment over with and head home.

The first place she headed was the lady's room, then she made her way to the record's office. Hopefully that's where she'd find what she needed. With a deep breath, she pasted a smile on her face and yanked open the glass door. *Lord, give me strength. Again.*

~

"You've got to be kidding." Matt laughed out loud as he leaned his arms along the edge of the table. "The one person you wanted to avoid, and that's the one person you almost ran into."

Martha giggled softly then heaved a heavy sigh. "Oh, my goodness. What an ordeal. And I thought simply walking in to ask for the documents would be difficult enough."

Skylar covered her mouth to suppress a laugh. "I'm sorry, Martha. I have a mental picture of you skulking behind that column, then hiding in the park with your hat, sunglasses, and book. Talk about secret agent stuff."

"She's missed her calling." Grandma Etta chuckled, waving a theatric hand. "Martha, you should've been in spy movies."

"Perhaps I should've been." Martha leaned back in her chair, her giggles growing. "You would've been impressed. They never spotted me. Even when I was behind the column."

Matt shuffled through the papers on the table. "Well, I'm impressed. Look at the documents you received. I've only glanced through them, but these are the state police reports and the court documents from that night in 1945 and the days after. I can't wait to read them. Hopefully they'll shed some light on things."

Skylar sobered. "Hopefully they'll prove Dad's innocence."

"Amen to that." Grandma Etta reached over and squeezed Skylar's hand.

"Indeed." Martha clasped her hands on the tablecloth.

Matt grinned. "Especially after all our Martha went through to get them."

Martha's cheeks flushed. "Other than the fact I had to go to the lady's room while I was sitting out there, for the most part it wasn't…terrible."

"So you're going to read through all that then finish coming up with your plan?" Grandma Etta aimed her question at Matt.

"Yep. Honestly, I don't think I'll find anything earth-shattering, but something may pop up. Who knows?"

Skylar stood and walked around and placed her arms around Matt's shoulders. She leaned in to prop her cheek next to his. "We're praying for wisdom for you, sweetheart. You're in a tough spot, and you need it. We're depending on you, and you're depending on the Lord. So, we pray." She dropped a kiss on his whiskered cheek.

Grandma Etta rolled her eyes and pushed her chair back. "Oh my goodness, it's time to leave. The love talk has started, and I don't think I can stomach it." She stood and patted Martha's shoulder. "Come on, my friend. Let's go start some supper and leave these two love birds to sweet-talk each other all they want to. Just not in my presence."

Martha smiled and joined her friend. "Perhaps not, but I'm happy they're in love, Etta. They make such a beautiful couple. I do believe the Lord has His hand on their relationship."

Matt watched as the women left the room. He pushed his chair back and pulled Skylar onto his lap then wrapped his arms around her waist. Her face rested mere inches from his. "You know? I do believe Martha's right."

"About?" Skylar smiled as she traced a finger from

Matt's temple down to his chin.

He closed his eyes for a moment as he attempted to take a breath of air. This woman stole his breath more than he'd ever admit. His eyes opened again and met hers, spotting a teasing light in their depths. "She's right about the fact that we make such a beautiful couple. At least half of us." He slipped a hand behind Skylar's neck. "Your half." He sighed. "You are the most beautiful woman I've ever met, and I thank God that you love me. Because, darlin', I love you. More than I'll ever be able to tell you or show you. But I'll try."

Matt tugged her head forward, finding her lips with his. He placed gentle pressure on them at first, tasting the sweetness that he always found when he kissed her. Skylar slid her fingers through his hair and Matt groaned, increasing the pressure slightly. His heart raced, or was that hers or both their hearts? He tugged her closer to him as he deepened the kiss but only for a few seconds, then he pulled away. As much as he wanted to keep on kissing this woman that he loved with all his heart, he had to stop. They had to stop.

"You know something, Matthew Scott?" Skylar's voice was barely above a whisper as she leaned her head against his shoulder.

"What?" Matt swallowed, his voice husky.

"You're a wonderful kisser." Skylar sighed.

Matt wasn't exactly sure what to say to that. No one, not even Gina, had ever told him that. "Thanks. You're pretty amazing at it yourself. In fact—" he whispered, "I…uh,…I had a hard time…."

"Stopping?"

"Yeah."

"I know. Me too."

# Chapter Fourteen

**Later that night**, Matt studied the state police and court records from 1945. Although originally arrested for the murder of Sheriff Baker, Brodie was later found not guilty and released due to a lack of evidence. The gun found at the scene was proven not to be Brodie's, and although he'd picked it up, his brother Bufford gave a sworn statement before a jury that Brodie protected him with his body during the shootout. They were nowhere near the sheriff at that time. Only after the shootout when Griff Jenkins and Harper Kent drove away had Brodie gone over to find the deceased body of Sheriff Baker. Unfortunately, he'd picked up the gun, and that's when the state police discovered him holding it.

Further state police reports indicated that state troopers eventually caught up with Griff Jenkins and Harper Kent. The gun had been identified as belonging to Griff Jenkins. He, however, had fled the scene before the sheriff was killed. Deputy Harding made a sworn statement in court to this effect, but he'd passed out due to his gunshot wound before he could make a statement to the state police defending Brodie's innocence at the scene. He'd sworn in court that he did not see who killed the sheriff during the gunfight as he himself was shot.

Matt heaved a heavy sigh, shuffled the papers, and

dropped them on the dining room table. The reports proved Brodie was innocent, but nowhere did anything lead to who might have killed the sheriff. He rubbed his eyes and leaned back in his chair. Frustration surged through him. Everybody knew Brodie didn't commit the murder. Bufford didn't do it. Griff and Harper didn't do it because they'd fled the scene prior to the sheriff's death, and apparently Deputy Harding didn't do it. So, who killed the sheriff?

"Want some hot chocolate?" Skylar set a cup of the steaming beverage on the table in front of Matt then lowered herself into the chair next to him, her own cup in front of her.

"Oh, that smells wonderful. Did you make it?" Matt pulled the mug closer.

Skylar shook her head and lifted her mug. "Nope. I can't take the credit. Grandma Etta made it. She thought you might need something sweet to get your thinking juices flowing. Those are her words. Not mine."

"That was thoughtful of her." Matt took a sip then licked his lips. "Mmm. Delicious. I just wish it would give me some answers."

"Having trouble?"

He tapped the pages on the table. "I've read through every one of these, and the only thing I've found for sure is that your dad was innocent."

"That's a good thing."

"Yes, it is, but it's also something we've known all along. It just gives us written proof. Which again is a good thing." He released another heavy sigh. "The problem is, there's nothing for us to go on that would lead to the killer. If there were something like that, they'd have found him or her a long time ago."

"True." Skylar placed a hand on his. "So, what's the plan?"

Matt entwined his fingers with hers. "As I mentioned to you all earlier, it's time to draw out the killer."

"How do you plan to do that?"

"First, I'm going out to the cabin. If someone's been there looking for us, I'll know."

Skylar gave him a questioning look.

"We locked the cabin, remember?"

She nodded. "This sounds dangerous."

"I doubt they'll still be there. It's been over a week."

"I still don't like the sound of it. So, you go out and nobody's there. Then what?"

"I'll come back here and test the waters by giving Griff Jenkins a call, first to see if he's behind it. Then I'll head back to the cabin and wait. If he or Harper Kent are involved, somebody's bound to show up."

"I don't like that plan at all."

"We have to do something, sweetheart. We can't sit here forever doing nothing."

"What will you tell Griff?"

Matt thought for a moment. "I suppose that depends on what I find out at the cabin. I'll take it a moment at a time."

"And pray." Skylar squeezed his fingers.

He smiled, and with his free hand slid a gentle finger down her cheek. "You know, our trip to Germany was the best thing to ever happen to me."

"Oh, yes? Why?"

"First it made me see what I was missing in my…association with Gina. I saw what a selfish person she is, and what an amazing woman you are. But more than that, I realized my need for Christ. It was truly special that Dad and I came to Christ at the same time. Since then, I've grown in my relationship with the Lord. Even on this journey with you to find out about your dad, I'm learning to lean more on Christ, and my faith is growing stronger. It's easier to lift a prayer no matter what the situation is."

Skylar leaned forward and laid a quick kiss on Matt's lips. "I love you. I love that you're God's child, and that we can grow in our faith together."

*Lord, one of these days I'm going to ask this woman to*

*marry me. I assume we both want to get married, but I need to make it a fact. I just don't want to ask in the middle of all this trouble. Help us solve this so we can move on.*

Matt tucked a stray tendril of hair behind Skylar's ear. "You and me both, sweetheart. Now, let's pray we can find the killer and turn them in. We need to settle this once and for all."

Skylar dropped her gaze to the pages on the table. "Agreed. What if it isn't Griff or Harper? What if it's still Deputy Harding? You know how suspicious he was acting when we visited him. He lives so far out it's doubtful he has a phone. You won't be able to draw him out."

Matt quirked his mouth sideways. "No, he doesn't have a phone. There were no lines to his house, and I don't want to go back down there. Not unless I absolutely have to. If he's involved…well, I'll have to think of something else after we give the first plan a try. But when you think about it, he could've taken us out when we were there."

"That's true." Skylar glanced at her wristwatch. "It's getting late. You should tell the ladies your plan in the morning."

Matt stood and pulled Skylar to her feet. He gathered her within his arms. "I'll do that. Keep praying, my love. I need wisdom to carry out this plan. The cabin could still be locked, and no one has shown up."

"What will you do then?"

"I'll still call Griff. It's possible he and Harper could very well be innocent. If no one shows up, then we're back to square one. We need God to open a door for us and lead the way through."

Skylar wrapped her arms around Matt's neck and searched his eyes. "Yes. This is a cold case for a sheriff that needs to be resolved. Soon."

~

"Good morning, Martha." Skylar strolled into the kitchen to find Martha and Grandma Etta fast at work preparing breakfast.

"Good morning," Martha's voice sang cheerfully from the kitchen stove.

"Good morning, sweetie." Grandma Etta sliced homemade bread and slipped it into the toaster on the counter.

"You two keep this kitchen humming." Skylar perused the food cooking on the stove. "I see there are a couple of guests waiting in the dining room. They appear to be enjoying their morning coffee. May I help with anything?"

Grandma Etta grabbed the slices of toast as they popped up from the toaster. "Here. Swipe a healthy dollop of butter across those and plate them."

Martha slid scrambled eggs and hash browns onto two plates then added bacon. "Once the toast is added, I'll take them out to the guests. Thanks for your help."

"I haven't done much, but okay, you're welcome." Skylar laughed.

Matt walked in as Martha walked out. "Coffee smells good. Is there plenty?"

"What do you think? Does Martha ever go short on coffee?" Grandma Etta gave a short laugh and reached for a mug. She filled it and handed it to Matt. "Black as usual, I presume."

"The only way to drink coffee." He took a deep draft of the hot brew. "Mmm. The best way to start the day."

"I guess you want some bacon, eggs, hash browns, and toast to go along with that." Grandma Etta grabbed a plate and began dishing it up.

"Yes, ma'am. Please and thank you." Matt pulled out a chair at the kitchen table and dropped onto it.

Martha rushed into the kitchen and fanned herself with her apron. "Our guests seem happy. I'll check on them again shortly." She glanced at Matt then Skylar. "I see you're eating, Matt. Skylar, you must eat, too, dear. Let me get you a plate."

"Oh, no, you don't." Skylar turned the woman around and gently pushed her toward a chair at the table. "You sit for a few minutes while I fix my own plate, thank you. Besides, Matt has something to tell you ladies this morning. I'm sure he can tell you between bites. What do you think, Matt?"

He nodded and swallowed a bite. "Most definitely." He laid down his fork and downed a swallow of coffee. "I've come up with a plan."

Grandma Etta slid into a chair and placed an arm on the edge of the table. "Oh, this should be good. Do tell."

"I'm heading out to the cabin today to check it out. I have a feeling whoever was after us probably went out there looking for us sometime since we left. I'll find out."

"Are you sure that's safe?" Twin frown lines formed between Grandma Etta's brows as they dipped low.

"Maybe not, but I have to find out. The cabin could very well still be locked up like we left it."

"But it might not be," Martha piped in. "My husband used to have a handgun of some kind. I still have it upstairs with the ammunition it used. You should take it with you. I don't know what caliber it is, but it's better than going unarmed into an unknown situation."

Matt grinned and forked another bite of food. "I'll take you up on that offer, Martha. I'll sure feel safer having it along."

Martha gave a decisive nod. "And so will we."

"What if you go out and find no one's been there? Then what?" Grandma Etta tapped a finger on the table. "Whether someone's been there or not, you still have to have a next step."

"Sure, I do. The next step is to return here and call Griff Jenkins. If someone's been there, I'll tell him that. Hopefully, he'll mention it to Harper Jenkins. Then I'll head back to the cabin and wait around to see if someone shows up. It'll likely be the killer or the killer's accomplice. Maybe the guy who came after us last week."

"Shouldn't you get the police involved in this?" Grandma Etta asked.

"If I get them involved too soon, they won't allow me to do this."

"Maybe that's a good thing," Martha suggested. "It could be dangerous for you. You're not a professional."

"Perhaps not, but I do have a vested interest in finding the killer."

Grandma Etta circled the rim of her coffee mug then lifted her finger into the air. "I have an idea."

"What's your idea?" Skylar wrapped an arm around her grandmother's shoulder, being careful of her injury.

"We should call my brother Jimmy. He has six sons. They'd bring out enough fire power with their shotguns and rifles to take down a whole passel of bad guys. My nephews could camp out back out of sight and be there if and when the killer or the bad guy shows up. You wouldn't be on your own. Then they could help haul him off to the police.

Skylar spotted the wheels turning as Matt was quiet for a few seconds.

"It's...definitely a thought. Let me think about that for a bit. We're not to that step yet, but it's a good idea." Matt patted Grandma Etta's hand. "The best thing I can ask of you ladies right now is to keep praying."

"You know we'll be doing that." Grandma Etta sniffed and rolled her eyes.

"When are you leaving?" Martha asked.

"After breakfast." Matt lifted his empty coffee mug. "Until then, may I have some more, please?"

~

With the knowledge the three women would be praying for him, Matt tucked the Colt .45 semi-auto and two extra magazines Martha loaned him in the pickup truck's glovebox and headed out. When he neared the cabin, he slowed to almost a crawl and stopped just within sight of the cabin. There was no vehicle in Grandma Etta's driveway, and there didn't seem to be any sign of life on her property, but he didn't care to take any chances.

Matt slipped the gearshift into reverse and backed up the truck until it was out of sight of the cabin. He parked it off the side of the road and killed the engine. Grabbing the Colt and the mags from the glovebox, he climbed out of the pickup and gently closed the door. He pocketed the truck keys and the two mags then slipped the handgun into his jean's waistband at the small of his back. He'd hefted the weapon in his hand while still at Martha's and liked how the grip had fit in his hand. Dad had rifles, shotguns and handguns on the ranch in Wyoming, so Matt was used to shooting almost anything. The Colt .45 wasn't new to him, although he'd never shot this particular model. He hoped upon hope he didn't have to shoot it at all.

Matt slipped into the woods next to the truck and quietly approached the cabin from that direction. Although he hadn't seen any indication that anyone was there, he'd rather play it safe. An old outhouse sat between the cabin and the woods. It made a great blind, and Matt ran for cover behind it.

The windows on this side of the cabin were obscured. As long as he stayed low and approached the porch carefully, he should be able to reach the door without being seen. He glanced around the edge of the outhouse to see if there was any movement. Still nothing. Good. He sprang forward and headed for the front steps. Keeping to their right, he crept up to the porch, his steps quick and light.

Matt stifled a gasp. The wooden door stood half ajar, hanging half off its hinges. His heart missed a few beats. That didn't bode well. It was the first sign someone had been here. Standing to the right of the open doorway, he waited for several seconds listening. A couple of late autumn birds chirped in the trees even as the wind gently stirred the remainder of the dry, rustling leaves. Other than the birds and the leaves, the only other sound was his own heartbeat.

He focused on the cabin's interior. Something stirred inside. Footsteps scurried across the wooden floor of the cabin. Did they belong to a person or an animal? He drew in a deep breath then released it all at once. Silence ensued. His bet was on an animal. The footsteps were too light to belong to a human.

Just in case he was wrong, Matt slipped the Colt .45 from his waistband then gripped it in his hand. He carefully pushed past the half-open door to prevent ripping it from its bottom hinge and stepped inside. The cabin stood cold and semi-dark, but from the minimal morning light that made its way in from the doorway, Matt could plainly see the room had been tossed. The love seat and the overstuffed armchair had both been sliced and the stuffing torn out. The rocking chair lay broken, and the old piano in the corner had been tipped over. The wood box sat empty. The woodstove's door was open, its ashes spread everywhere. The keepsakes from the mantel had been either smashed or scattered around the room. Family pictures had been ripped from the walls and the glass shattered. Matt felt sick at the destruction. Poor Grandma Etta. This had been sheer meanness, plain and simple. He reached down and picked up an old, framed photo of Grandpa Sawyer. Bits of broken glass dropped to the floor and tinkled in the silence. The photo seemed to be intact. Matt removed it from the frame and tucked it into his shirt pocket. He found more of the same destruction in the kitchen and the bedrooms. In one bedroom he found a message written in red lipstick on the mirror.

*Go back to Wyoming and leave the past alone.*

The message from the killer was clear. He or she wanted them to stop their search for Sheriff Baker's murderer. It wasn't enough that they'd proven Brodie Sawyer innocent, but then, the murderer didn't know they'd discovered that. It was enough that they were searching for the murderer.

Matt surveyed the destruction around him. He would

make this right for Grandma Etta if it was the last thing he ever did.

The question was, who did this? And the next question was, how was Matt going to tell Grandma Etta about it?

~

With a heavy heart, Matt drove back to Martha's B&B and parked near the garage. He turned off the engine and sat for a moment. *Lord, I'm going to need Your help breaking the news to Grandma Etta about how bad her cabin is. I feared someone would toss it, but I had no idea they'd be so destructive. Please give me the words to tell her, and help her to take it...Lord, just help her. I can't imagine how I would react if someone told me my home had been destroyed.*

Matt scrubbed a hand down his face and opened the truck door to go inside. He found the women in the kitchen as he expected. A delicious aroma filled the room—fresh baked bread for sure. And something savory. He was starved. His stomach growled. The women's chatter silenced as they became aware of Matt's presence.

Skylar made a dash for him and wrapped her arms around his neck. She planted a quick kiss on his lips. "You're back."

Matt returned her kiss and wrapped his arms around her waist. "Mmm. That's a right nice welcome. And something smells tasty."

Martha giggled. "It sounds like you're hungry. I could hear your stomach growling way over here."

"Yeah, well, I missed lunch, you know." He gave Skylar another hug then released her.

She plucked his cowboy hat from his head. "Why don't you have a seat. Supper's ready. You can tell us how your day went while we're eating."

Matt drew out a chair at the table and dropped onto it. "Actually, I think I'd rather eat first then talk about my day after, if you don't mind."

Grandma Etta turned from stirring a pot on the stove. "That good, huh?" She lowered a brow at him. "I'm not liking how that sounds."

Martha swatted a hot pad at Grandma Etta's shoulder. "Oh, leave the fellow alone and let him eat first. He's famished. Here." She picked up a ladle and handed a bowl to Grandma Etta. "Serve the stew while I put the bread on the table. It's still nice and warm. Skylar, will you put the butter on the table, please?"

Matt was grateful for the reprieve, and within minutes they'd said grace and were digging into the delicious beef stew and fresh homemade bread. For a short time, Matt was able to put aside the difficult task he had, enjoy the company of the three women, and hear about their day. Once the meal had finished, he gathered the plates and carried them to the sink. Grandma Etta eyed him curiously.

"Want to wash them too?" Her eyes narrowed.

He cast her a sheepish grin. "If you'd like me to."

She chuckled. "No, I'll take care of them. It's just that you usually disappear about now."

Matt stuffed his hands into his back pockets. "Yeah, I guess you're right."

"Something didn't go well today, did it?"

"Are you sure you don't want me to wash the dishes?" He angled his gaze toward the kitchen sink.

"Matthew Scott. What aren't you telling me?" Grandma Etta crossed her arms over her flat chest.

He heaved a heavy sigh and met her eyes. "Do you want me to tell you now or after you do the dishes?"

Grandma Etta's features turned to stone. "Okay, everybody to the parlor. Now." She turned on her heel and led the way to the front of the house.

"Shall I bring coffee, Etta?" Martha called to Granda Etta's retreating back.

"Forget the coffee, Martha."

Their host's brows shot toward the ceiling as she met

Skylar's eyes. Skylar wrapped an arm around the older woman's shoulders.

"This can't be good, Sky." Martha glanced at Matt.

"It's not." He shook his head.

Once they'd made themselves comfortable on the soft furniture in the parlor, Grandma Etta wasted no time getting to business. "So, tell me. What happened?"

Matt leaned forward on his chair, his hands clasped between his knees. "There wasn't anybody there when I arrived, but the place was trashed through and through. I'm sorry, Grandma Etta. They destroyed the place. They tore up the furniture and broke dishes and pretty much everything you own. There's not much left." He slipped the photo of Grandpa George from his shirt pocket and handed it to Grandma Etta.

She reached for it with trembling fingers. "I take it the picture frame was broken."

Matt nodded. "I'm afraid so. Along with all the other family pictures. I didn't go through the other ones, but I will. I'll go through everything else and see what can be salvaged. Don't' worry. If it can be fixed, I'll fix it."

Grandma Etta stared at the picture of her husband then lifted saddened eyes to Matt. She shook her head. "You needn't worry. They're only earthly things, after all. I can't take them with me when I die, you know."

A brief smile flashed over Matt's lips then faded away. "No, but you can still enjoy them while you're here. Let me see what I can do." He ran a hand around the back of his neck. "There's one more thing."

"What is it?" Dread filled Grandma Etta's words.

"Whoever was at the cabin wrote a message on a mirror in one of the bedrooms." Matt paused.

"What did it say?" Skylar's voice was a mere whisper.

"It said, 'Go back to Wyoming and leave the past alone.'"

Skylar gasped. "This is all my fault." She turned to her

grandmother who sat beside her on the couch. "If I hadn't come here looking for proof that Dad was innocent, I wouldn't have gotten you involved." She took Grandma Etta's hand. "It's because of me that your home's been destroyed."

Grandma Etta wrapped an arm around Skylar and tugged her close. "No, child. It's not your fault. There's a sheriff who's dead because someone killed him. That same person did this, or had someone do it." She sighed. "Just because you came back here looking for answers about your dad's innocence doesn't make what happened your fault. There's a guilty party out there still doing wrong.

"Matt's right. It's time to finish this and draw the killer out. As much as I don't like Matt being in danger, we have to put a stop to this." She looked Matt in the eye. "It's time to call Griff Jenkins and make sure he and Harper Kent know about what happened at the cabin. Make sure he knows how we were run off the road and nearly killed. Ask him if he knows how to get hold of Deputy Harding."

Matt thought for a moment then gave a slow nod. "I'll call him first thing in the morning."

# Chapter Fifteen

"Good morning. Is this Griff?" Matt shifted on his chair, gripping the phone handset tighter.

"Yes, it is." Griff Jenkin's cheerful voice came over the line. "May I ask who this is?"

"Hi, Griff. This is Matt Scott. You may remember Skylar Simpson, Etta Sawyer, and I came by your trailer at the Wilkesboro Speedway a little over a week ago. We were searching for information about Brodie Sawyer."

"Yes, of course. I do remember y'all. How are you doing?"

"Well, honestly, we've been better."

"Elizabeth told me you'd called after your visit to Wilkesboro. She said something about you'd been run off the road and nearly killed. I wanted to call and see how you're doing, but I had no way of contacting you."

"I know. Grandma Etta doesn't have a phone at her cabin, and besides that, we're not staying there. After we were run off the road, we went into hiding."

"I see." Griff's voice sounded contemplative. "I'm sure that was the best thing to do under the circumstances. Elizabeth mentioned the next day somebody caught up with you and shot at you. Is that right?"

"Whoever it was fired at Grandma Etta and Skylar. Fortunately, they made it into a police station before the shooter could harm them. Or worse."

"Thank goodness."

"Exactly." Matt measured the tone of Griff's words, and they seemed genuine.

"So, what are your plans? I'm not going to ask where you're staying."

"I appreciate that. I drove to Grandma Etta's cabin yesterday to check it out. Somebody had been there and had trashed it. They completely destroyed Grandma Etta's things. All of her belongings are shattered or torn apart. Whoever went through the house was thorough."

"That's awful," Griff gasped. "Who would do such a thing to an old woman?"

"That's what I want to know because I'm going to deal with them when I find out." Matt read genuine shock and disappointment in Griff's voice. If he was acting, Matt would be surprised.

"There's more."

"Tell me."

"A message was written on a mirror with red lipstick in one of the bedrooms. It said, 'Go back to Wyoming and leave the past alone.' Do you have any idea who would do a thing like this?" Matt asked.

After several moments, Griff released a heavy sigh. "I don't, but I'm sure you realize y'all stirred up a hornet's nest by asking questions about Brodie. Somebody killed Sheriff Baker. That somebody don't like it that y'all are asking questions."

"And you have no idea who that might be? My family's been threatened, Griff. I take that personally."

"I know you do, son. I would, too, if I was in your shoes. As much as I don't want to, I'll ask around."

"Do you know any way to get a hold of Deputy Harding? When we visited him, I had the feeling he wasn't being straight with us, and he was there the night the sheriff was killed."

"I don't know where he lives, Matt. I've been told he lives somewhere down in the Georgia mountains, but that's all I know. I haven't seen him since we were in court back in the day."

Matt drew in a deep breath and released it slowly. "All right. I appreciate your help."

"What's your plan? Can I help you in any way? Can I send a car for you and your family and put you up somewhere?"

Matt hesitated. "It's best that I keep them in hiding for now. I'm going to stay at the cabin for a while. I want to try and fix some of the things that were broken. I don't want Grandma Etta to see it the way it is."

"I understand. If I can help in any way, let me know. And remember. Y'all are still invited to the Daytona 500 in the spring."

Matt chuckled. "Let us get through all this mess, and we just might take you up on that invitation."

~

Skylar slipped into the room and dropped onto the couch beside Matt. She'd heard him hang up the phone and knew his conversation with Griff was over. He barely reacted when she drew her arm through his and leaned against his shoulder.

"Matt? Are you okay?"

He heaved a heavy sigh and turned to glance at her. "Yeah, I'm fine."

"And Griff? What did he have to say?"

"I don't think he's the murderer, just as we've believed all along. But—" Matt paused, scratching his chin, "he said he'd ask around. That may get us some results."

"What do you mean?"

Matt turned to look at Skylar more fully. "He said, 'as much as I don't want to, I'll ask around.' That almost sounds like he's afraid of talking about this. Like he's afraid of opening up a can of worms."

"So, you don't think he's involved? He's not the murderer, is he?"

Matt grinned at Skylar and traced a finger down her cheek. "No, sweetheart, I don't, but Griff may realize that someone near him is the murderer, although he may not know who it is. By talking to folks around him, he'll likely send the murderer our way."

"And did you tell him where we are?"

"No. I told him you and Grandma Etta are in hiding, but I told him I'll be at the cabin trying to put things to rights for her. He'll share that, so hopefully they'll come."

Skylar wrapped her arms around Matt and held on tight. "I'm praying the Lord protects you."

Matt pulled her close. "You and I both, sweetheart."

~

Matt packed a small leather satchel he'd borrowed from Martha with clothes for a few days and tucked the Colt .45 semi-auto and the two extra magazines on top then zipped it closed. Martha sent a large picnic basket of food for him that would feed an army. He borrowed a toolbox from the garage as well as glue, screws, and nails of various sizes and tucked them into the floorboard of the passenger side of the truck. After saying his goodbyes, he once again drove toward Grandma Etta's cabin. No doubt someone would show up, but until then, he hoped to make a few repairs for Grandma Etta. There was an awful lot he wouldn't be able to fix, but some things he could.

When he reached the cabin, Matt pulled the Colt .45 from the satchel and took a look around to ensure no one had arrived before him. Satisfied no one was there, he slipped the weapon into the back of his waistband and the magazines into his back pockets. He wouldn't be caught unprepared. He parked the pickup truck with the back bumper facing the house then brought the satchel, the toolbox, and the fasteners inside. Dropping the truck keys into his front pocket, the first thing Matt did was repair the front door which still hung by one hinge. Once that was done, he made sure the doors were locked then closed the curtains over all the windows, except the one in the living room.

Matt sat a table where he could see the road from the window and began working on some of the smaller items like the picture frames. He could replace the glass later. Although he'd considered parking the truck behind the cabin, he'd told Griff he was here, and Griff would pass on that information. Whoever was coming would expect his vehicle to be out front. He needed to be vigilant in watching for…who? He had no idea who his enemy was, but he'd be watching for them. He stared at the road for several moments. Would they approach from the road? Or would they do like he had yesterday and park down the road then approach through the woods? Matt's gut tightened. *Lord, I have no idea what to expect. All I know is they want to cause harm. Please protect me. Protect Skylar and Grandma Etta and—*

A sound at the rear of the cabin sent Matt's heart to lodge in his throat. Peering out the front window, he spotted nothing out of the ordinary. With the Colt in hand, he rushed to the kitchen and slipped the curtain aside a sliver to peer into the back yard.

A racoon meandered across the grass away from the back door. Apparently, the little scoundrel had attempted to gain entry but had given up when he couldn't. Matt released the curtain with a chuckle. His heart rate began to slow. He glanced at the floor and realized why the racoon wanted in. Although Grandma Etta had taken most of her foodstuffs to Martha's, she'd left behind a few things. In his rush, he hadn't noticed the smell of food from some broken jars. Boy, he did now. That racoon could smell it all the way outside.

Matt grabbed a broom and a couple of rags and began cleaning up. Just as he'd tied the mess into a garbage bag, tires crunched on the dirt and gravel road out front. Leaving the bag on the floor, he hurried to the living room and peered out the front window. A black pickup truck sat idling on the road a short distance from the driveway. Matt couldn't tell if it was the same black pickup that had run them off the road over a week ago. It was too far away to tell if there was damage to its front right fender, and it had been too dark that night to tell what kind of vehicle it had been. As Matt watched the idling pickup, it suddenly did a three-point turn and sped away.

Strange. Could it have been someone who realized they had taken a wrong turn? Or was it the guy in the black pickup who had run them off the road after all? Had he come to get the lay of the land and would return later? After dark perhaps when Matt couldn't see which way he was coming from? Matt scrubbed a hand down his face. *Dear Lord, I've got a bad feeling about this. I hope You've got a plan to protect me. Right now, I'm not so sure my plan is working out as well as I thought it would.*

~

"He's there."

"Is he alone?"

"How should I know? Do you think I have x-ray vison or somethin'." The young man took a last drag on his cigarette then dropped it on the ground and crushed it under his shoe. "A pickup truck was there. I'd done a number on the other one. Pretty sure he got another truck, and that's what's sittin' in front o' the cabin."

"It doesn't matter if he's alone or not. Better if he isn't. We'll take them all, or we'll have him take us to the others. One way or the other, we'll get them all."

"Yeah, yeah. Whatever you say."

A heavy sigh sounded through the telephone line. "Nephew, sometimes I don't think your heart is in this. You know you'll get paid. Just do the job."

"My heart doesn't have to be in it. I just want the money. Same as you, I got debts to pay, and I don't wanna go back to prison in the process."

A long pause then a response through gritted teeth, "You don't have to remind me of my gambling debts."

The young man's voice took on an appeasing tone. "Look. I'm sorry, okay? I'll take care o' whoever's in that cabin."

"I know you will." The answer was frosty. "And I'll be there to see that you do."

~

Grandma Etta stood at the kitchen window with her arms crossed over her chest. Skylar had seen her standing there for quite a while. She'd learned one thing about her grandmother in the short time she'd known her. Although she was a bit on the gruff side, she had a heart of gold and took everything to the Lord. Unless Skylar missed her guess, Grandma was pouring her heart out to the Lord over Matt and his safety at the cabin. Was she worried about him? More than likely. But if you asked her, she'd say no. Only concerned. Worry was a sin. Worry meant you weren't trusting the Lord like you should.

Maybe she was right, but Skylar was more than concerned. She'd done her fair share of praying ever since Matt had left Martha's. In fact, she hadn't stopped praying.

Skylar slipped to Grandma Etta's side and placed an arm around her shoulders. "Can I get you a cup of tea or coffee to help in your prayer vigil? That's what you're doing, isn't it?"

Grandma Etta gave Skylar a side-eyed glance. "You're onto me, aren't you, sweetie? A cup of hot tea would be nice."

Skylar patted Grandma Etta's arm and strode to the stove to put the teakettle on. "I suspected you'd been praying. I have. Why wouldn't a prayer warrior like you be doing the same?" She filled a tea ball with tea leaves and dropped it into the kettle.

Grandma Etta rubbed her upper arms. "I wouldn't call myself a prayer warrior, but I do spend a fair amount of time in prayer. When you live alone, the Lord's a good companion and the perfect One to talk to. I can talk to Him about anything, you know. "

"That's true." Skylar took two teacups from the kitchen cabinet. "Do you ever doubt when you pray?"

"What do you mean, child?" Grandma Etta pulled out a chair at the table and took a seat.

Skylar brought the cups to the table and gathered the bowl of sugar cubes from the cabinet and lemon wedges from the fridge. "Do you ever doubt the Lord hears your prayers?"

Grandma Etta gave an emphatic shake of her head. "Why, I never do. There are times when my prayers go unanswered, but it's not because He doesn't hear them. He simply chooses not to answer right away, and sometimes His answer is no. But unless there's sin in our lives, and we need to make things right with Him, He hears our prayers, child. We need to be faithful, read His word, and talk to Him. He'll make it known what His answer is."

Skylar turned back to the kitchen and turned off the flame on the stove. She picked up the teakettle and carried it to the table where she set it on a trivet.

"You already knew all that, didn't you, Sky?" Grandma Etta's voice was gentle.

Skylar nodded. "I suppose I needed a reminder."

Grandma Etta poured the tea into the cups, doctored her tea, and took a sip. "Don't we all need a reminder every now and then?"

"Do you ever decide to help God out?"

Grandma Etta cleared her throat and stared innocently into her cup. "Whatever do you mean?"

~

Matt spent the day at the cabin working on a few small trinkets and household items that he could fix, his ears attuned to any strange noise. The racoon never made another appearance, fortunately. The wind rustling through the treetops caused Matt's heightened senses to hear things that weren't there. He kept checking the various windows around the house when he thought he heard something. The nerve-racking sounds kept him on his toes.

He ate some lunch then supper from Martha's picnic basket. She'd sent a thermos with soup and sandwiches piled with roast beef and cheese. There were also thermoses of iced tea and lemonade, packages of potato chips, and a container of homemade chocolate chip cookies. God bless Martha. He wouldn't go hungry, that was for sure.

As the sun dropped behind the rim of the mountains, Matt sat at the front window and waited. He'd turned the kitchen light and the front bedroom light on, although he kept the curtains closed. The curtains in those rooms weren't thick enough to prevent light from escaping.

As darkness descended outside, he closed the front curtains and took up watch by the side of the window furthest from the kitchen light. He left a tiny slit open, just enough to peek out and keep watch. It wasn't long before he spotted headlights down the road. Whoever they belonged to didn't come near the driveway. The lights blinked out. Hmm. Just as he'd thought. They were going to approach through the woods.

Matt continued to watch for a few minutes to see if they would come up the road on foot. Nobody showed up. He rushed to the darkened bedroom at the rear where he could see out the side of the cabin. Peering through a slit in the curtains, he waited for a few seconds. Two figures with flashlights headed for the front porch.

They certainly didn't wait long for the sun to go down, but it was dark out there. He couldn't tell anything about the figures. He turned to hurry back to the front door when it crashed open. At the same time, the back door flew open. That wasn't good. He hadn't seen anyone headed toward the back of the cabin. He was woefully outnumbered.

"Come on out here," a male voice called out. "We know

you're here. You can't hide from us."

Maybe he could hide, but glancing around the small bedroom, he realized there was nowhere they wouldn't find him once they began to search. *Lord, help me through this. Whatever this is.*

Matt tucked the gun in the back of his waistband then covered it with his shirttail. They'd likely pat him down, but who knew? Maybe there was a chance.

He inched out of the bedroom and into the kitchen where a young man stood in front of the open back door, a handgun pointed at Matt. "Get out here. Hands up."

Matt put his hands in the air as the guy shoved him toward the living room. There he saw another young man with a handgun and an unarmed older woman—at least she appeared to be unarmed. Both stood in the middle of the living room. The front door stood open, apparently having been kicked in.

"Well, well. We meet at last." The young man waved the gun in his hand as he walked around Matt. "I gotta say, you're hard to kill, buddy."

"Shut up, nephew," the older woman snapped. "That's enough."

The young man, who was dressed in a black leather jacket, slunk behind her, scowling.

She stepped toward Matt. "I may not approve of my nephew's behavior, but I agree with his comment. You and your…friends, for want of a better word, were supposed to die last week, Mr. Scott. You don't die easily." She clasped her hands behind her back and strolled over to turn on the room lights. "Ah, much better. It was simply too dark and dreary in here, don't you think? Now we can conduct business in the light."

Matt stared at the woman before him. He'd seen her before. But…where? "Who are you? Why do you want to kill us?"

The woman, who appeared to be in her fifties, peered

down her nose and sneered at Matt. "It's not your place to ask questions. You've asked far too many, and that's what's gotten you into this place to begin with, hasn't it?"

"Considering you have me at a disadvantage, I think I have a right to know who you are, ma'am. And since your thug here—" Matt glanced at the young man standing behind her holding the gun on him, "—tried to kill me last week, I have a right to know why."

The woman released an ugly laugh. "Since you're going to die anyway, perhaps you're right. My name's Sharon Kent. My husband is Harper Kent. This—" she turned slightly to indicate the young thug, "is my nephew from my mother's side of the family."

She stared at Matt then laughed again. "Ah, now you remember me, don't you?"

Indeed, Matt did. This was the timid woman who had come to Griff Jenkins' trailer and pulled Harper Kent away from their conversation. Timid? Matt didn't think so.

"That's right. I came to Griff's trailer to get my husband. You see, I've had a thing about gambling for, well…let's say, for a long time. There are certain…men who want their money. My husband returned from the war and found I'd accumulated some pretty big gambling debts. When Griff Jenkins started up bootlegging moonshine, my Harper thought it would be a great way to pay off my debts."

Sharon strolled over to the doorway and stared out into the darkness for a few moments as if she stared into the past. "The night Sheriff Baker came looking for Bufford Sawyer was an unfortunate night for the Sheriff. I came down to tell Harper something. I don't even recall what it was now, but I stumbled onto an arrest. I couldn't afford to let the Sheriff arrest my Harper and stop him and Griff Jenkins from continuing their operation."

"So, you shot the sheriff." Matt had lowered his hands during Sharon's tale. Hopefully no one had noticed. If only he could reach behind his back and pull the Colt from his waistband.

Sharon turned suddenly and stared at Matt. "Yes, I did. When no one was watching, I slipped to Griff's car and pulled his handgun from the glovebox. Griff always had it there when he was running moonshine."

"Did you fire the first shot?" If only he could keep Sharon talking.

Her chin came up. "I wanted to give Harper and Griff a chance to get away, so I fired a couple of shots into the air to begin a gunfight. The sheriff and Deputy Harding started firing at who knows what, and then I shot Deputy Harding and then the Sheriff." She lifted a shoulder. "Honestly, I didn't mean to kill the sheriff. I only meant to wing him like I did the deputy." Sharon clasped her fingers together and stared at them. "Once I realized I'd killed him, I dropped the gun and took off for the house. I wasn't sure if Deputy Harding had seen me shoot the sheriff or not, but when he was in the hospital, I paid him a visit. I threatened him. Told him the people who I owed money to for gambling would come after him and kill him if he talked."

"Wow, you must really have been in deep."

Sharon turned an embittered glare on Matt. "You have no idea what kind of people I owe money to, Mr. Scott. I've been in deep with those people for over twenty-seven years."

"So once your husband stopped running moonshine and turned to NASCAR, you hoped your cash cow wouldn't run dry. What will you do if it ever does, Mrs. Kent?"

The woman's face paled. "They'll kill me." Her voice was barely a whisper.

"Perhaps you need help to stop gambling."

She narrowed her eyes. "Perhaps you should shut up." Sharon waved a dismissive hand toward Matt. "Besides, that wasn't all I did. When it was proved that Brodie was innocent of shooting the sheriff, I had to do something about him. After all, he may have seen me shoot the sheriff." Sharon meandered across the living room, picture glass crunching beneath her feet.

"What did you do?" Matt kept his voice low in an attempt to keep her talking.

Sharon stopped and looked down at the broken picture frames on the floor. She bent and lifted one of a family portrait and stared at it. "I visited Brodie when he was alone and told him it might be best if he never told anybody I killed the sheriff. If he did, I'd kill his sweet wife and baby girl. Right after that, he packed up his little family and moved west. I never heard tell where, but all I cared about was that he was gone." She dropped the broken frame to the floor and turned back to Matt. "I'm done with this conversation. It's time for you to take us to wherever you have Miss Simpson and Mrs. Sawyer hidden. I'm ready to rid myself of all of you at the same time."

She turned toward the door just as four men burst through with rifles and shotguns aimed at her and her nephew. At the same time three more men charged through the back door aiming rifles and shotguns at the other young man.

Matt's jaw dropped, but he pulled the Colt .45 from his waistband when he recognized Grandma Etta's brother, Jimmy Miller, leading the charge.

"You okay, Mr. Matt?" Jimmy grinned from behind his cocked 12-gauge shotgun.

Matt blew out a breath then grinned. "I am now. How did you know I needed help?"

"My sister called my niece, Ruthie. She drove out and said Etta wanted to put feet to her prayers." Jimmy chuckled. "Seven pair to be exact. That would be me and my six sons here. We hunkered down in the woods, then we moved in next to the house after these yahoos came inside. And by the by, we heard everything. You got seven witnesses as to who killed Sheriff Baker back in the day."

Matt let out a laugh. "Well, what do you know about that. Thank you, Grandma Etta."

# Epilogue

Skylar stood on tiptoe and reached up to place the Christmas ornament in the empty spot on the Christmas tree. A pair of hands suddenly gripped her waist and lifted her off the floor. She hung the ornament then was lowered down and turned around to face Matt. He drew her into his arms where he held her close.

"Thanks for the lift, kind sir." Skylar giggled then placed a quick kiss on his lips.

Matt heaved a small groan. "Ah, fairest maiden in all of Wyomingland. Can't you show a kind sir your thanks with more than a quick kiss?"

"Let's see if I can." Skylar framed his cheeks with her hands and pulled his head toward her. She kissed him long and sweet and deep.

Matt came up breathing hard, his voice husky when he spoke. "Now that's a kiss. I feel completely and utterly thanked. Is steam coming out of my ears?"

Skylar grinned and wiggled her eyebrows. "No, but would you like it to?"

Matt grabbed her shoulders and set her away from him. "Hang on there, woman. That's about all a man can take and keep his wits about him."

"You two behave yourselves." Grandma Etta chuckled from the couch across the room. "You're supposed to be decorating the Christmas tree. Skylar, your mother and sisters will be here any minute, and Matt, your dad's going to walk in here from the barn soon."

"Yes, ma'am, not to mention my sister's coming from town."

Skylar flashed a cheeky grin at Matt then strode over to sit next to her grandmother. "It's going to be a wonderful Christmas with you here, Grandma Etta. I know the girls and Mom are excited to see you."

"As am I to see them. I can't wait to meet my other granddaughters."

"As for the tree," Skylar cast a critical eye towards it. "That was the last ornament. Isn't the tree beautiful?"

"It's perfect." Grandma Etta patted Skylar's hand. "It's the biggest Christmas tree I've ever seen, but then that's the highest ceiling I've ever seen. This room looks like something out of a decorating magazine."

"Why, thank you, Mrs. Sawyer." A masculine voice approached from the dining room. "My wife and I loved decorating this room when we built the house years ago. After she died, I left it the way it was." Mark Scott strolled into the room and sat in one of the butter-soft cordovan leather armchairs. "Makes it seem like she's near somehow."

Grandma Etta nodded, but before she could reply, Mrs. Holcomb came in carrying a tray of mugs filled with hot apple cider and set it on the coffee table in front of the couch. "I thought you all might enjoy a warm treat."

"That was thoughtful of you, Mrs. H." Matt strode over and retrieved a mug then took a sip. "Mmm, that's good. Thanks."

"You're welcome."

As the others reached for their mugs, the front door bell sounded.

"If you'll excuse me, I'll get that." Mrs. Holcomb hurried away.

"I'm sure that's Mom and the girls." Skylar sipped her

hot cider. "Unless you're expecting someone else."

Mark shook his head. "You've only been home a day, so can't say as anyone would know you're back yet to stop in and say hello."

Mrs. Holcomb stepped back into the room, displeasure stamped on her features. "Miss Harris is here to see…Miss Simpson."

Skylar's heart took a nosedive. Then she turned and met Matt's eyes. He grinned and winked causing her heart to shift back into place. Drawing in a cleansing breath, Skylar smiled and nodded. There was no reason to fret. None whatsoever because this man loved her. In that, she was confident. Since Skylar had found proof of her father's innocence, there was nothing Gina Harris could say or do to cause a problem in her life now. Skylar had most of her family around her, and Mark and Matt would defend her with their dying breath. Any threats this pitiful woman could cast her way would die on the floor.

"Well, well, what do we have here?" Gina strode into the room, her chin in the air as usual. She propped a hand on her hip and glanced around the room. "A cozy gathering, no doubt. It seems the wayward travelers have returned."

Mark stood and strolled toward her. "Seems so. What can I do for you, Gina? We're expecting more family to arrive any minute."

She tipped a finger to her lower lip. "Then, I won't stay long. I just wanted to drop by and see what glad news Skylar was able to find out during her travels." A sneer settled on her features. "You were gone for a while, Skylar. Did you pay someone off to clear your daddy's name? Did you find he was the murderer I told you he was?"

Before Skylar could utter a word or move a muscle, Grandma Etta surged to her feet. "I don't believe we've had the pleasure of meeting, young woman. My name is Etta Sawyer. I'm Brodie Sawyer's mother. Guess I'm closer to the situation in 1945 than anyone in this room. You see, I was there the night Sheriff Baker came to deputize my son, Brodie." Grandma Etta strode slowly toward Gina and stopped a few feet from her. "He never gave my son a weapon. I've talked many times to my other son, Bufford, who was there on the scene at the time Sheriff Baker was killed. Bufford said his brother never had a weapon when he was there that night. The gun that killed the sheriff was dropped by his body by the killer."

Matt set his mug on the coffee table and slipped his hands into his jean's pockets. "We actually caught the killer while we were back in Tennessee, Gina. Pretty remarkable, I know, but it's true. Sharon Kent confessed to me before she thought she was going to kill me, but Grandma Etta's brother and his sons came in and put an end to that."

Gina scoffed. "A woman killed the sheriff in 1945? And after all these years, she tried to kill you? Come on, Matt. That's a likely story."

"It's all true. Grandma Etta's brother, Jimmy Miller, and his six sons were witnesses to the confession. The moonshiners, Griff Jenkins and Harper Kent, were on the scene that night in 1945. Griff Jenkins kept a gun in the glove box of his car that they used to run moonshine. Harper's wife had a gambling problem. Sharon didn't want the sheriff to stop them from running moonshine, so she shot the deputy and the sheriff. She only winged the deputy but killed the sheriff. She dropped the gun and ran away as the moonshiners jumped in their car and sped away.

"That left Brodie and Bufford on the scene. When Brodie checked on the sheriff, he made the mistake of picking up the gun. The state troopers came on the scene at the time and caught him. He was later released after being proven innocent." Matt lowered his brows and eyed Gina. "You spread lies about Skylar's dad and her family without first finding out if there was more to the story. All because you wanted me back. I can tell you right now, that's not happening."

Gina glared first at Matt and Skylar, then she turned her bitter eyes on Grandma Etta. "How do I know you're telling the truth or that you are who you say you are."

Skylar gasped.

"Get out, Gina." Mark strode over to the young woman and pointed toward the door. "I don't have to let you stand here and insult my guests. Get out. Now."

Gina turned toward the door, then whipped around to face the people in the room. "I'll go, but you'll regret this. All of you."

Mark jammed his hands into his rear jean's pockets. "Nope. If you do anything, and I mean anything whatsoever toward me or my family, *you'll* regret it. I'll have words with your father. Don't test me on this. Now get out."

Gina turned on her heel and headed out the door. The front entrance door slammed shut. A couple minutes later, Megan Scott, Matt's half-sister, entered the room from the front entrance, a bemused expression on her features. She carried tote bags filled with Christmas packages.

Matt spotted her first. "Hey, sis. Glad you're here." He gave her a hug. "Come on in and join the fun."

Megan set the totes on the floor and returned Matt's hug. Then she peered around the room. "From the look on Gina's face as she passed me under the portico, I'd say there was anything but fun going on in here. What happened?"

Mark waved a dismissive hand. "Aw, she came here to try and ambush Skylar and Matt after their trip to Tennessee. She hoped they hadn't found information proving Skylar's dad's innocence."

Megan's eyes flew to Skylar's. "And?"

"Oh, we did. We have so much proof." Skylar's smile brightened her face. "But that's for later. Let's put those packages under the tree, and then I'll introduce you to my grandmother."

The doorbell rang again, and things got crazy as Skylar's mom, Shelby, and her three sisters, Holly,

Charlotte, and Becka arrived, all with Christmas presents in tow. More introductions were made as the girls met their Grandma Etta, and Shelby and Grandma Etta grabbed each other in a hug. They hadn't seen each other since 1945 when Brodie moved the family to Wyoming.

No, it hadn't been fun while Gina was present, but after her departure and the whole family arrived, a delightful time ensued. Mrs. Holcomb prepared a wonderful Christmas dinner and even sat down and enjoyed it with the family. A warm fire welcomed everyone to the living room afterward as they enjoyed dessert and coffee and getting to know one another.

In the midst of laughter and camaraderie, Matt leaned close to Skylar and whispered in her ear, "Want to go outside for a bit?"

She gave a nod and allowed him to pull her to her feet. They slipped through the dining room to the back door where they grabbed jackets, gloves, and hats. They made their way through the summer room to the back patio.

"Hey look at this." Skylar surveyed the patio. "Looks like someone's already been here. They started a fire in the firepit and turned on the string lights."

"Hmm, I wonder who that could've been?"

Something in his voice made Skylar turn to eye Matt with a narrowed gaze. "It was you, wasn't it?"

His brows raised. "Who, me?"

"I'll bet you had one of the ranch hands build the fire and keep it going until you could bring me out here." Skylar grabbed Matt's gloved hand and tugged him toward the cushioned patio couch.

He shrugged. "I don't kiss and tell."

"But you haven't kissed me yet."

Matt tugged her close and wrapped her in his arms. "Then let me remedy that oversight." He lowered his head and laid his lips on hers, giving her a tender kiss she wouldn't soon forget.

A few moments later, she stepped back and rested her head on Matt's shoulder. "Now you can say you don't kiss and tell."

"Yes, ma'am."

Skylar felt his heart beating right through his jacket. Could he feel hers? This was right where she wanted to be—in Matt's arms.

He guided her to the couch and pulled her down into his arms. "Is it too cold to sit out here? Will you be okay for a while?" Concern colored his words as he gently lifted her chin with a gloved finger so he could stare into her eyes. He reached to the arm of the couch and grabbed a thick blanket and tucked it around her.

"I'm perfectly fine." Skylar released a soft laugh. "There's so much heat coming off that fire, and wrapped in your arms and this fleece blanket, I could sit out here for hours."

Matt scoffed and shivered. "I don't think I can stay out here that long. I'll be a popsicle."

Skylar chuckled. "Here. I'll share." She tucked the blanket around him.

"Thanks. That's better. The fire's going great, huh?"

"Yes, it is."

They sat snuggling for several moments before Matt asked, "Sky, did your mom or dad ever mention why your family moved to Wyoming?"

"Not really. Other than what Mom told me when she said Dad decided to move us after he was proven innocent from the sheriff's murder."

"It seems your dad had a secret he never told your mom."

Skylar's heart froze. In all this saga, what could Dad have held out from the family? Would it hurt them? Would it hurt Mom to know? How about Grandma Etta and the girls? "Matt, after all we've been through, I'm not sure I want to know."

Matt reached for her hand and gave it a squeeze. "What he did, he did for the safety of your family. Your dad did it because he loved you and your mom."

Skylar gave a brief nod as hot tears gathered behind her eyes. She had to know. The man who was her dad was an amazing man, so whatever he had done would've been done for an important reason. "Okay. Then tell me."

"When Sharon Kent killed Sheriff Baker, she was afraid your dad saw. She feared he knew of her crime and threatened him that if he ever told, she'd kill you and your mom. So, he did the only thing he knew best to do. He moved your family to Wyoming and changed the family name. Your mom told you that part, but you never knew why he did it. Your mom doesn't know either."

"We'll have to tell her, Grandma Etta, and the girls. After Christmas, of course. His secret can wait."

Matt planted a soft kiss on Skylar's temple. "Sure it can. There's plenty of time to tell them later."

The fire snapped and cracked in the firepit, its light dancing softly against the wall of the house. Tendrils of smoke swirled skyward, lifting sparks along with them.

"I received something in the mail a couple of days ago, but I've been waiting until today to share."

"You're simply full of information this evening, aren't you?" Skylar gave a soft laugh. "I hope whatever came in the mail isn't as serious as the last tidbit of info. What did you receive?"

"It's from Griff Jenkins." Matt drew it from inside his jacket pocket and waved it gently. "There's three tickets to the Daytona 500 spring race inside for you, Grandma Etta, and me."

Skylar's eyes widened. "Already? Sweet! How did he get tickets to the spring race?"

Matt shrugged. "He's a race car driver. I suppose he has his ways."

"That's exciting. I've never been to Florida before."

"Neither have I. And we'll drag Grandma Etta if we have to." Matt chuckled.

Skylar cast him a side-eyed grin. "Something tells me we won't have to drag her. I'm sure she'll want to go. She's never been to Florida either."

"There are also hotel reservations in here."

"What?" Skylar's eyes widened. "Seriously?"

"Yup." Matt tucked the envelope back into his jacket pocket. "It'll be a great trip."

"It'll be nice to see Griff and Elizabeth again." Skylar paused. "I've been praying for them to turn to Christ. I hope they will someday."

Matt tugged the blanket up under his chin then pulled Skylar close. "There was some cool news in the letter Griff enclosed with the tickets and reservations. He said that he and Elizabeth thought a lot about what you told them during our visit. Neither of them could get it out of their minds. They talked between themselves and decided to pay a visit to one of those drivers they said was a Christian. Lo and behold, he led them to Christ. What do you think about that?"

Skylar leaned forward to better gaze at Matt. "Are you serious? Did they really accept Christ?"

Matt tilted his head and grinned. He gently pulled her back into his arms. "That's what Griff's letter said. And to think it's because you took the time to share your faith with them. You planted the seed, sweetheart. You may not have actually led them to the Lord, but you played an extremely important part in their coming to salvation. The Holy Spirit watered that seed by convicting them of their need for Christ. That race driver simply harvested their souls by leading them to the Lord. I'm so happy they got saved." He gave her shoulders a gentle squeeze.

Skylar leaned her head on Matt's shoulder. "Me too. The Lord answered our prayers. You just never know what sharing the gospel with someone will do. I can't wait to tell

Grandma Etta."

They sat in silence for a short time enjoying the fire, then Matt cleared his throat. "Um. I have something I would like to ask you, sweetheart. I've been wanting to ask for a long time, but with everything we've been dealing with back east, I didn't want to complicate things. Now that all that's been settled, and we're back home, I…uh, I can ask you." He paused.

Skylar turned from staring at the flames to stare at Matt. "Okay, I'm all ears. What do you want to ask?"

"Yeah, well, you see… I've been wanting to ask if…."

Skylar waited. She didn't want to push him. His hands were moving around beneath the blanket again. What was he doing now?

Matt shoved the top part of the blanket away and held a little black satin box in his gloved hands. He turned slightly toward Skylar. "Sweetheart, it's not a secret that I love you. I've made that plain, but I'm asking you to marry me." He opened the little box, and there nestled in the middle was a large solitaire diamond on a gold band. The diamond sparkled reddish-orange in the light of the dancing flames.

Skylar drew in a gasping breath and held it for several seconds before releasing it on a sigh. "Oh, my goodness! How exquisite." Her eyes flew to Matt's. "I love you, Matt, and I'll never be able to express just how much."

"Then why don't you take from now on to tell me and show me?" He grinned. "And I'll do the same."

Skylar nodded and ran a finger down his cheek, enjoying the feel of the roughness of his evening stubble. "I love that idea. Yes, I'll marry you." She reached up and drew his head down, meeting his lips with hers. The kiss was slow and tender at first, then deepened and grew more urgent and breathtaking. After several moments, Skylar pulled back and rested her forehead against Matt's. "I do love you, Matt Scott."

Matt heaved a satisfied sigh and chuckled. "I love you,

soon-to-be Mrs. Scott. Let's not wait terribly long. Okay?"

"Agreed." Skylar laughed and drew back. "Now how about putting that ring on my finger and seal the deal."

Matt lifted the ring from the little box as Skylar tugged off her left glove. "I'd be more than happy to seal the deal."

Skylar held out her hand as he slid the ring onto her ring finger, then he lifted her hand to his lips and kissed her finger. Matt pulled Skylar back into his arms and laid another kiss on her lips.

"Think we should go back inside and make an announcement?"

Skylar rubbed a soft thumb over his lips. "In a few minutes. We need to practice one more kiss as an engaged couple first. What do you think?"

Matt's eyebrow lifted as the other one dipped. "All you have to do is ask. You can never kiss too much, you know."

With that Matt tugged Skylar close once again and lowered his head to hers. With heartbeats in rhythm, Skylar had no doubt as long as they kept the Lord at the center of their marriage, they could face together whatever trials life tossed at them. They'd already come through difficult times unscathed, and had drawn closer to Christ and to one another. With God's help they would continue to do so. She and Matt had redeemed her father's innocence and had the proof. They had put the past to rest and could move on.

Skylar's heart beat quickened as Matt's kiss deepened. This man was her heart, and she looked forward to what lay in front of them. If his kisses were any example of their life to come, married life promised to be exciting.


The End

Dear Reader,

If you enjoyed reading this book and want to help me to continue writing and publishing more books for your enjoyment, please take a moment to leave a review. They are very important to authors. We depend on them to let other readers know what they think about our books so they in turn will know whether or not to purchase and read them. Should you not care for it, I would appreciate an email to me rather than a negative review. And remember, the author has no control over prices, so please keep that in mind if you're not happy with the cost. You can find me at Amazon, Goodreads and BookBub should you choose to leave a review. Thank you again for reading my story. I hope you enjoyed it.

For His glory,
J. Carol Nemeth

I hope you enjoyed reading Redeeming Brodie: My Father's Secret. Watch for my next book in the *Hearts of the Manhattan Project, The Mathematician*. It'll come out next year. Check out my other books on my website at https://www.jcarolnemeth.com/books.

Here's a sample chapter from *Canyon of Death, Faith in the Parks Book Two*:

# Prologue

"Wow, this trail is treacherous." The tall hiker planted his foot against a large rock to steady himself and surveyed the canyon wall along his left side. "Did you see which way the mountain goat went? I lost sight of him just over there."

"Yeah. He slipped behind that huge boulder." His shorter hiking partner pointed to a large, craggy formation, nearly twice the height of an average man, just below their position. He scratched his goatee-covered chin before yanking off his ball cap and wiping his arm across his forehead. "I wanted to snap his picture but he disappeared. Want to check it out and see if we can catch him back there?"

"Why not? We've gotten some amazing pictures out here. Let's go for it."

Both men edged carefully down to the "boulder" that turned out to be part of the canyon wall. The trail led to the right and away from the wall just before this point creating a divide between the wall and the trail. Scrub vegetation covered the side of the formation.

"Hey, long legs. You jump first then you can catch me," chuckled the shorter of the two hikers.

The taller hiker rolled his eyes and easily jumped across the divide, grabbing hold of the side of the rock formation. Pushing the vegetation aside, he pulled out a flashlight and glanced around the opening before turning back to his hiking partner.

"I don't see any snakes. Go ahead and jump. You'll

make it. I'll give you a hand."

When the second hiker was safely inside the opening of the formation with his partner, they turned to take stock of the situation.

"Are you sure he went this way? Looks like a dead end to me."

"I'm positive he came back here. It has to go somewhere." The short man slid his hands further behind the vegetation, feeling for a fissure in the cliff face.

"Are you sure you want to be doing that? I mean, there still might be snakes and stuff out here, man. Don't get yourself bit. I can't carry your sorry carcass back up that trail." He nodded in the direction they had descended.

His hiking partner turned with a victorious smile as he tugged a clump of vegetation away. Behind it an opening in the rock was large enough for a man to walk through without ducking his head or having to enter sideways.

"Looks almost like it was put there. Intentionally."

"Yeah. Like it was chiseled out. Let's see where it goes." The taller man slipped through as his partner held the vegetation back.

As the hikers slipped into the opening, they realized they were in a small tunnel that ran approximately twenty feet before curving inward along the canyon wall. Light streamed from around the bend lighting the tunnel without the use of their flashlights.

The tunnel walls were dry and smooth, and the floor was scattered with fine rocks and sand. Around the bend, the tunnel opened into an enormous room that hugged the side of the Grand Canyon.

"Oh, my…are you seeing this, man?" The tall hiker gaped at the sight before him.

"I'm seeing it, but I'm not sure what I'm seeing. Do you think the park service knows about this?" His partner's chin dropped in awe. "There's no signs or postings on the rim or anything."

"Or on the trail map."

The mountain goat long forgotten, the hikers carefully explored the brightly lit cavernous room. Cliff dwellings built into the back wall extended several hundred feet in length. Various sized round holes in the floor indicated rooms were likely positioned beneath as well. A large overhang in front of the massive room allowed light in but would hide it from the outside. Lower views of the canyon could be seen but nothing above the overhang. Whoever had lived here hadn't intended to be seen by the outside world.

"I think we better tell someone about this, man. If they already know about it, that's one thing, but if not…"

"Let's snap some pictures. Stand over there by that low wall. That's it."

With pose after pose on their digital camera, the hikers decided to get back and report their find. Who knows? One day they just might be famous.

# Chapter One

"Rock of Ages, cleft for
me,
Let me hide myself in
Thee"

The faint melodic words floated on the morning breeze as Kate Fleming made her way toward Mather Point. She was about to catch her first glimpse of the Grand Canyon and her heart ticked an upbeat in anticipation. She'd waited a long time for this moment.

"Let the water and the
blood,
From Thy wounded side
which flowed,"

The closer Kate got to the south rim of the canyon, the stronger the words grew. Definitely feminine in tone, there was a slight crackle as though she was elderly. It held a quality that indicated the a cappella soloist sang straight from her heart.

People dressed in heavy winter clothing meandered about as they snapped pictures and took selfies with the canyon behind them.

"Be of sin the double
cure,
Save from wrath and
make me pure."

As the Grand Canyon came into view, Kate sucked in the cold morning air in awe, chilling her throat and lungs.

Placing her gloved hands over her nose and mouth, she warmed them up again. The Grand Canyon was the most amazing thing she'd ever seen. Gorgeous earth tones blended with blues, pinks and shadowy purples. With the morning sun still in the eastern sky, long shadows were cast on the western side of ridges and peaks. As a strong, cold breeze blew up from the canyon, Kate zipped up her olive-drab uniform parka and jammed her "Smokey-Bear" hat further down on her head.

> "Could my tears forever
> flow...."

"Shut up, old woman! I don't want to hear you singing."

The angry voice came from Kate's left, drawing her attention from the spectacular view. An elderly woman stood by the chain-link fence which protects visitors from going over the edge of the canyon at the overlook. Her rheumy eyes were focused on the horizon between earth and sky, her thin, arthritic hands raised toward heaven as tears streamed down her wrinkled cheeks. Two young men stood beside her, anger marring their faces.

"Shut up, old woman," one of them yelled. "Stop your screeching!"

Kate quickly approached them to see what the commotion was about. The woman certainly didn't seem to be bothering anyone.

"Excuse me." Kate put as much authority in her voice as she could muster. "What are you two doing here? This lady isn't bothering anyone."

The guys spotted her uniform, belligerence oozing from their expressions. "Well, she's bothering us. I don't want to hear her singing about...God." The last word was spat out with disgust. "She's gotta stop."

Kate laid a kind hand on the woman's arm. "Ma'am, I hate to interrupt you but can I hear your side of this situation?"

The woman's faded blue eyes turned to Kate, tears still wet on her cheeks. "Of course, my dear. I'm eighty-six years old. All my life I've seen pictures of the Grand Canyon, but I've never been here before. Well, now that I'm here, I can't help but be in awe at the wonder of God's creation. He did this." She waved a hand in the direction of the natural wonder spread before them. "It didn't just happen. All I wanted was to praise Him for how marvelous and mighty He is. One look at that view and anyone with half a brain knows God made it."

The two young men sputtered in anger at the pointed remark.

Kate held up her hand. "Fellows, this is a really big canyon. I mean, really big. There's plenty of room for you to see it and for this lady to sing as she desires. Why don't you just move along to another location and enjoy the view. Leave her in peace to enjoy it in her own way."

They cast angry glares in the woman's direction as they shifted their daypacks higher on their backs and left the canyon rim, hopefully to find a spot elsewhere.

"Thank you, miss." The old woman settled a gnarled, arthritic hand on Kate's arm. Gloveless, it felt cold even through Kate's parka sleeve. "I just don't understand how folks can look at that view and not give credit where credit is due. God made it, and He made it for us to enjoy. I just don't think some people want to believe He exists. It's sad really."

"Yes, I think you're right, ma'am." Kate patted the woman's thin shoulder. "And thank you for the reminder. You might want to go inside and warm up though. It's pretty chilly out here. Are you here alone?"

The woman smiled. "No, my son and daughter-in-law are here with me. They went to get coffee, so they'll be back shortly with a cup for me. I just didn't want to leave this view. I want to drink in as much as I can as long as I can."

"I understand," Kate nodded with a smile. "You have a wonderful day, ma'am."

Before Kate realize what she was doing, the woman reached out thin arms and wrapped them around her. Then she stepped back and smiled, contentment written across her wrinkled face.

"Thank you, my dear. These weary eyes have seen a lot of things during my lifetime, but this was the last thing I truly wanted to see before the Lord calls me home. I don't know if that'll be tomorrow or next year or the next, but I'm happy that I got to see this marvel of His handiwork."

Kate started to walked away, then stripping the gloves from her hands, pressed them into the woman's hands and hurried away before she could protest.

As Kate strolled along the canyon rim, she could hear the woman's voice once again lift in praise. She reflected on her words. Kate hadn't given God much credit lately. She believed in Him, had even put her trust in Him, but He'd let her down. Pain sliced through her heart as memories flooded her mind. Nope. She wasn't going to think about all that right now. Whether God put this view here for her to enjoy or not, she could still appreciate the beauty before her. And she wanted to forget. Oh, how she wanted to forget.

Pushing the memories from her mind, she glanced at her watch. She needed to get to the visitor center to meet with Tasha Johnson. Kate had arrived yesterday afternoon. Just long enough to be assigned living quarters and to begin to learn her way around Grand Canyon Village and some of the government offices, but she hadn't yet met Tasha.

With a last long appreciative glance at the canyon, she left it behind and made her way to the visitor center near Mather Point. In spite of the cold wind that swept across the south rim, bundled-up visitors scurried from one overlook to the next, searching for that subtle difference in the scenery. Kate could appreciate that. She was sure she wouldn't get tired of the view any time soon.

Kate slipped inside the visitor center where it was much warmer. Straight ahead was a long information desk with a few park staff members answering questions and passing out park maps. To the right was the entrance to a theater where a video played every few minutes telling about the Grand Canyon National Park and its natural splendor. Exhibits of small wildlife and historical information were arranged to the left. Park visitors meandered about looking at these exhibits and taking in the video in the theater. So, where would she find Tasha Johnson?

"Kate Fleming?"

Kate turned at the soft feminine voice that spoke her name. A young African-American woman met her questioning gaze with a smile. Her flawless ebony skin, black eyes surrounded by long lashes and beautiful white teeth between full lips was striking. Her short, curly black hair set off her beautiful features.

"Yes, I'm Kate Fleming."

The young woman held out her hand. "It's nice to meet you at last, Kate. I'm Tasha Johnson. We've been expecting you."

Kate shook her hand. "It's a pleasure to meet you, Tasha."

"Have you been out to see the canyon yet? That's usually where everyone makes a bee-line to as soon as they arrive." Tasha chuckled. "And no wonder. I've been here three years and still can't get over the view."

"Yes. I just came from Mather Point. It's amazing. I'll be spending a lot of time soaking in the sights." Kate had wanted to work at the Grand Canyon for a long time, and she'd finally made it. But she hadn't planned to come alone. Shoving those painful memories away, she concentrated on Tasha's words.

"Well, I hate to rush you into your job, but I'm going to take you out to the sight and introduce you to the archeologists." Tugging on her parka and her uniform ball cap, Tasha eyed Kate's "Smokey-Bear" hat critically. "If you've got your ball cap, I think you'd better wear it. Much better suited to where we're heading. Good. You're wearing hiking boots. You'll need them."

With a quick trip to Kate's car to exchange hats, the women climbed into Tasha's park SUV.

"As my assistant, your help will be invaluable in keeping an eye on the archaeological team," Tasha explained.

"You're the park liaison, right?" Kate wanted to make sure she had her supervisor's title correct.

"That's right." Tasha flashed a smile. "I have a few projects I'm overseeing, so I need you to keep me informed. You'll be my liaison to the archeological team. My eyes and ears, so to speak. If they have questions you can't answer, bring them to me and we'll get them answered. There are regulations they must follow. I need you to ensure they follow them. If they don't, tell me and I'll deal with it."

"So, what is the team looking for? Anything in particular or just digging until they find something?"

"Oh, no. It's something in particular. A couple of hikers stumbled on a lost Anasazi city a month ago. The park invited the archeological team to investigate."

"What about the hikers? How did they find the site?"

"They were hiking on the Hermit's Trail and followed a mountain goat. It disappeared behind a rock formation and when they went to investigate, they found the city. They snapped a lot of pictures, too, but we confiscated them. No way could we let that out to the public."

"Won't they talk?"

"Probably, although they signed an agreement not to." Tasha stopped the SUV next to a gate with an electronic keypad. She entered a four-digit code and the gate swung upward, allowing them to proceed. "This is Hermit's Road and it's closed to the public except during the winter months. They just closed it last week, so we don't have to worry about competing with tourists anymore. Only park personnel and shuttle buses as well as the Hermit's Rest Gift Shop employees drive out here now. And of course, the archeologists. I'll give you the combination so you'll have access. You'll be driving out here all the time."

They followed the road along the south rim of the canyon to the Hermit's Rest Gift Shop and overlook. Tasha drove a half mile further down a dirt road behind the gift shop and parked beside a building comprised of two mobile construction trailers placed side by side.

"This is the archeologists' office." Tasha climbed out of the SUV. "You might find one or more of the archeologists here but usually they're on-site so it's harder to find them."

"Ok. Good to know." Kate exited the SUV and followed Tasha toward the trailhead. "So, they're not here now?"

Tasha glanced at the dark windows. "Probably not."

Kate's eyes were glued to the view before her. A completely different and amazingly colorful configuration of ridges, peaks and plateaus met her gaze. Tasha's chuckle beside her drew her attention back to her companion.

"Sorry. I'm just in awe of…well…this." Her hand moved in an all-encompassing arc. "It's… gorgeous."

"Yes, it is," Tasha sighed. "I just love it here. But," she pointed at the trailhead, "this is a very treacherous trail to descend. It's not maintained by the park as much as the other trails. So take your time and watch your step. It's going to take some getting used to."

Kate and Craig had hiked a lot of trails in the three years since they'd started dating, and she was confident she was in shape and could tackle it. This did look daunting. What would Craig have said to this bit of adventure? A pang sliced through her heart as it always did when she thought of Craig.

She swallowed hard. Don't go there. It hurt too much.

Tasha eyed Kate closely and laid a hand on her jacketed arm. "Are you ok, girlfriend? Your face is mighty pale. Want to take a minute before we head down? It's not that bad, really."

Kate met Tasha's concerned dark gaze and was touched. The young woman hardly knew her but had read Kate's expression like she'd known her a long time.

Kate flashed a smile in spite of the tears that threatened to spill from her eyes. "No, I'm fine. Really, I am. I just…remembered something…someone. It's okay. I'm ready when you are." She pulled her sunglasses from her jacket pocket and tugged her ball cap lower over her eyes. It probably wouldn't help hide the pain at the memories of Craig, but it was worth a try.

Tasha considered her a moment longer before nodding. "Okay. If you say so. But if you have a problem, just tell me."

Kate understood that she wasn't just talking about the difficulty of the trail. Did she mean she could talk to her about other things too? Would Tasha be a friend she could trust? Time would tell. But some things were just off limits. Totally.

The path down the Hermit's Trail was indeed difficult. In some areas they had to crawl over rocks and boulders while in other places the trail smoothed out for a few feet. Kate concentrated on following Tasha and pushed personal thoughts from her mind.

At a particularly steep and precarious spot on the trail, Tasha stopped and pointed at a large formation on the left of the trail.

"That's the huge boulder the notorious mountain goat disappeared behind. Funny how that goat lost his one claim to fame. We'll never really know what happened to him. But he led the hikers to one very spectacular archeological find." She laughed between gasps for breath. "Come on, girl. We're almost there."

A wide, wooden board had been placed across the divide from the trail to the entrance to the formation, and Kate followed Tasha across to it, waiting for her to disappear behind it. Taking another look at the colorful scenery as she waited, Kate reached up to grab hold of the rock. Her foot slipped and before she knew what was happening, she slid toward the cliff edge several feet below were the trail turned to the right and the canyon wall remained on the left. Her fingers grasped for anything that would hold her, but she continued to slide.

Tasha's voice rang out in fear. "Kate! Grab onto something!"

Kate's heart lodged in her throat even as she slid toward the edge of the cliff. While she scrabbled for a handhold, her mind screamed the words: *Lord, help me!*

Here is the purchase link for *Canyon of Death, Faith in the Parks Book Two.* <u>https://amzn.to/2MC06Q3</u>

Check out the blurb for the first book in the series: *Mountain of Peril, Faith in the Parks Book One*:

When Molly Walker graduated from college, she was thrilled to be hired on as a ranger at Deep Creek Campground in the Great Smoky Mountains National Park. She arrived ready to begin her career and to enjoy all the aspects of her new job, but the one thing she hadn't counted on was the local poachers and their illegal shenanigans. Molly and fellow ranger Jake Stuart try to put a stop to the escalating poaching problem while protecting the animals. In the meantime, Molly finds that the handsome ranger, who is also a local, is a great partner to have on her side. She also finds that she's losing her heart to him when she'd planned to stay focused on her career. Can she give her heart and have a career? She and Jake find themselves in a battle against a group of men with a hidden agenda far more sinister than poaching. Can they be stopped before Molly's life is snuffed out?

Here's the purchase link for *Mountain of Peril, Faith in*

*the Parks Book One*: <u>https://amzn.to/2MBolIF</u>

Here's a sample chapter from *Courage on the Run*:

# Chapter One

"You have the grocery list?" Casey Hartman called to her Aunt Nora as the older woman slipped out the kitchen door heading to her car. Casey suppressed a chuckle at her aunt's disgruntled expression when she reentered the kitchen. Aunt Nora snatched the offending list from the kitchen counter where she'd left it.

"I'll try this again." Aunt Nora grumbled as she headed for the door, her loose auburn bun bobbing on the back of her head.

"You have the check book, right?" Casey tossed over her shoulder as she strolled toward the laundry room at the back of the bed and breakfast she and Aunt Nora ran together.

"Yes, I have the checkbook." Aunt Nora's clipped tones grew fainter as she climbed into her car and drove toward town.

Casey wasn't worried about her aunt's memory. She had done the same thing herself but had actually gotten to the store before realizing it. There was just so much to do in running Belmont Inn. When something slipped, it wasn't surprising. Casey pulled tablecloths and napkins from the dryer and began folding them. Aunt Nora would be gone for a while, and Casey had a list of things to do while she was gone.

The front buzzer rang indicating someone had entered the front door. Casey tossed the unfolded linens back in the dryer and restarted it on tumble. No way would she leave them to wrinkle. Ironing would not be added to her list today.

Casey hurried to the front of the inn and found a tall,

dark-haired young man standing by the counter. She slipped behind it.

"Hi. Can I help you?" She put on her most welcoming smile.

Turning his gaze from the high ceiling and antique furniture to Casey, a grin lifted the corners of his lips. "Hi. I have a reservation for the next few days. I'm Will Kerns."

"Alright. Let me take a look." Casey turned to the laptop beneath the counter and typed in his name. Within seconds she retrieved his information. "Yes, here it is."

She checked him in then reached into a box on the wall and retrieved a key. She walked around the counter. "If you'll follow me, I'll show you to your room, Mr. Kerns."

Casey led him up a wide, straight staircase with a mahogany banister. Thick burgundy carpet on the stair treads silenced their footsteps. Several old portraits graced the walls along the staircase with lighted crystal sconces casting a bright glow.

"Welcome to Belmont Inn, Mr. Kerns." Casey glanced over her shoulder at the young man following her up the stairs. "You may already know that our inn is an original Civil War home, and many of the antiques and portraits you see are from the family who originally lived here. There was a lot of history that took place here and in the town of Belmont."

"That's interesting. Was it your family?"

They reached the landing and Casey stopped and turned to him. "Actually, it was. This home has been in my family since the early 1800s. My great, great, great-grandfather built it."

His eyebrows shot upward. "That's pretty cool. Not many people can say they still live in their ancestral home."

Casey smiled and waved him on. "No, I suppose not."

At the end of the short hallway, she stopped before a tall, wide door, and using the key, unlocked it and swung it open. Stepping back, Casey allowed Mr. Kerns to enter first.

"General Stonewall Jackson, General J.E.B. Stuart, General Ulysses S. Grant, and General Orville Babcock all stayed here. Not all at the same time obviously." Casey released a chuckle. "The town and the house were occupied by both southern and northern armies at various times."

Mr. Kerns dropped his duffle bag on the suitcase stand at the foot of the canopy bed and gazed around the room. "This is quite something."

Casey was proud of the decor in the inn. In this room, the canopy was natural-colored, knotted rope with tassels stretched over the canopy frame. A quilt of the most amazing fall colors covered the bed, while a collection of throw pillows in the same colors were stacked at the head. The burnished oak bed itself was an antique as were the dresser, washstand, and nightstand.

"Don't worry. You won't have to fetch water to use in the washstand." Casey chuckled as she approached a door on a side wall. "Here's a bathroom for your use. Every room has been retrofitted with a bathroom, complete with toilet and shower. Originally, it was the staircase for the servants to access the room."

She stepped over to another tall, wide door and swung it open for his inspection. "Sadly, we don't have regular closets. In the old days they used pegs to hang their clothes on. As you can see, we still do. The closet is long and narrow. There are hangers for you to hang your clothes on the pegs, however, unlike what our ancestors used to do."

"Interesting. I'll make it work."

Casey held out the room key and when he held out his hand, she dropped it in it. "There you go. I hope you enjoy your stay, and if you need anything, don't hesitate to let us know. Breakfast is from 6 a.m. until 8:30 a.m. If you're here for a vacation, I'll be happy to recommend lots of things to see and do in the area. As I mentioned before, we're a historical town so there's lots to check out."

"Thank you. I may take you up on that."

"I lock the doors at 11 p.m. but you have a front door key on your keyring. We understand some guests do stray far from the fold and may come in later. That's why we provide a key. If you come in after hours, please make sure the front door is locked behind you."

"I'll do that." Mr. Kerns held up the keyring and nodded.

~

Casey and Aunt Nora lived at the rear of the inn in a small apartment with two bedrooms, a living room, small kitchen and a bathroom. It was nine o'clock and Aunt Nora was firmly planted before the flat screen TV in the small living room, a bowl of popcorn in her hand.

Casey dropped onto the edge of the overstuffed armchair and shoved her foot into a tennis shoe. "I'm heading out for my evening walk, Aunt Nora."

"Be careful, sweets. I wish you'd walk earlier. It's starting to get cooler these fall evenings. You're going to catch your death, you know." Nora's eyes never left the TV.

"I'd love to, but you know it's hard to do when we have guests. This is when I finally have the time. I'd prefer walking in the morning, but with breakfast prep, that's not going to happen."

"I know."

Casey finished tying her second shoe and stood to her feet. Leaning over the side of Nora's chair, she planted a kiss on her cheek.

Nora's gaze moved to her niece's face. "Love you, kiddo. Be careful. Got your pepper spray?"

Casey held up the palm-sized tube she always carried just in case. "Right here. I'll be back in a while. Love you too."

Casey headed out the front door and across the street where she headed further into town. Of course, in the little town they lived in, everything except a few restaurants were closed. Tugging up the zipper of her jogging jacket against the cool fall air, she power walked past the pre-Civil War era courthouse. She loved the stores and restaurants in Belmont, some of which were built before the Civil War and others which came along in the 1930s when the town expanded a bit. It hadn't changed much since. There were a few other people out walking, and she waved as she passed. Casey never felt fear when she was walking through Belmont. She always felt safe in her town. She carried the pepper spray to please Aunt Nora.

Casey usually took a shortcut down an alley that led to another street where she walked by the old cemetery. There were graves that were dated before the Civil War, and most of her ancestors were buried there as well as her parents. Most people thought she was crazy for walking by there at night, but she wasn't afraid. Yeah, she heard some things that sounded…well, strange. But she didn't go *into* the cemetery. Just along the edge of it. She never saw anything.

Her friend, Jennifer's, Aunt May led a ghost tour in Belmont from May through Halloween and one of the stops led through the cemetery. Supposedly she had lots of stories to tell. Aunt May had been after her for years to come on the tour, but Casey had no desire to creep through the alleyways and the cemetery of Belmont looking for ghosts. It just wasn't her thing.

Casey turned up the alley where her rubber-soled tennis shoes were silent on the concrete pavement. A light shone behind the building on her right at the end of the alley. Strange. There had never been a light on there before. She had always come out at the end of the alley behind the building and into a small empty parking lot onto another street.

Why was there a light on in the parking lot? It wasn't a bright light, but why was it there? Casey crept on silent feet along the side of the building until she got to the end, then she peeked around the corner.

Four men stood with their backs to her a few feet from

where she stood. One man held another man close against him with a knife to his neck, and without warning, slid the knife across the man's neck. Blood spurted even as the man with the knife released him. The man slid to the ground facing in Casey's direction.

Casey released a gasp before she could slap a hand over her mouth. The other three men turned in her direction. Yanking back behind the corner into the shadows, Casey found her feet moving of their own volition as she headed back down the alley.

"Go get her and bring her back here."

The words assaulted Casey's ears even as she rounded the end of the alley and headed down the sidewalk toward Belmont Inn. They would be on her in seconds if she stayed on the sidewalk. She had to find a hiding place until they got past her then she'd wind her way home in the dark evading them. It was the only way to stay alive until she could get back and call the police.

*Lord, help me! Hide me from those evil men. Don't let them find me.*

Casey ducked into Mrs. O'Conner's yard and stuck to the grass where her footsteps were soundless as she headed for the elderly lady's garden shed. Was the backyard protected by a motion sensor light? Casey couldn't remember and sure hoped it wasn't. She made it to the shed in time to drop behind it just as she heard heavy footsteps run past on the sidewalk in front of the house. Casey's heart hammered so hard she hoped she hadn't mistaken it for the footsteps.

Surely the thugs wouldn't start searching through neighborhood yards. Guessing they most likely would, Casey couldn't take that chance. She had to get to the inn fast. After a few minutes, she crept from behind the shed and across the yard toward the next one. Keeping her head on a swivel and ears on alert for any sound, Casey made her way through the next five yards to a street. Two more yards after that and she'd be home.

Casey paused at the edge of the street behind a tree and waited for a car to pass. Heart hammering and breath pumping, she bent at the waist, her hands resting on her knees. Dogs lived at some of the houses where she'd come through the yards, but the Lord had cleared those hurdles. They'd all been inside. *Thank you, Lord.*

Glancing both ways, she stepped out, caution vibrating through every nerve. Here she'd be the most vulnerable as she crossed the street. The thugs could come from nowhere and grab her.

Casey started to step into the street when a hand came around her mouth and she was pulled against a hard chest. Her hands flew to the hand covering her mouth, and she struggled to pull it away.

"Don't scream. I'll pull my hand away, but I just didn't want you to scream. It's okay. Promise you won't scream?"

Casey stilled as she recognized a familiar voice. She nodded and turned as the hand dropped from her mouth.

"Will Kerns? What are you doing out here, and why are you scaring me to death?" Casey's voice was a mere whisper as her hand flew to her chest over her heart.

Will shrugged as he propped his hands on his hips. "I could ask you the same thing. Why are you sculking through your neighbor's backyards?"

Casey glanced over her shoulders and grabbed his hand, pulling him across the street into the next neighbor's backyard. "Ask me again when we get inside the inn. Just help me get there safely."

Here's the purchase link for *Courage on the Run*: https://amzn.to/35ozvjD

Author Bio

A native North Carolinian, Carol always loved reading and making up stories since childhood. She began writing in junior high school. As a young adult, she worked in the National Park Service and served in the US Army where she was stationed in Pisa, Italy. While there she met the love of her live, Mark Nemeth, who also served in the Army. They've lived in various locations including North Yorkshire, England. Now living in West Virginia, in their spare time they enjoy RVing and traveling to research for Carol's books. They have two grown children, Matt and Jennifer, a son-in-law, Flint, a daughter-in-law, Holly, and three amazing grandchildren, Martin, Ava and Gage. They also have two German Shepherd fur babies named Sheba and Cassie who love heading out in the RV.

A multi-published author of multiple books and short stories, Carol is blessed to be an Amazon #1 bestselling author, an ACFW Carol Award Semi-finalist, an American Bookfest finalist, a Selah Award finalist, and an American Legacy Book Award Winner. She's a member of American Christian Fiction Writers and Faith, Hope & Love Christian Writers. She writes romantic suspense, both historical and contemporary. Her goal is to write stories that will be entertaining and enjoyable while at the same time uplifting and faith-building. May Christ always be glorified.

Connect with me on FaceBook

Twitter

Sign up for my newsletter and receive a free short story
www.JCarolNemeth.com

Follow me on Amazon
Goodreads And Bookbub

## Enjoy other books by J. Carol Nemeth

### Faith in the Park Series

Dedication to Love: Prequel to Mountain of Peril
Mountain of Peril, Faith in the Parks Book 1
Canyon of Death, Faith in the Parks Book 2
A Beacon of Love, Prequel to Ocean of Fear
Ocean of Fear, Faith in the Parks Book 3
Glacier of Secrets, Faith in the Parks Book 4
Battlefield of Deceit, Faith in the Parks Book 5

### Christmas

Yorkshire Lass
Parade of Hearts

### Small Town

Death Goes to School
Courage on the Run

### Hearts of the Manhattan Project

The Secretary
The Nurse
The Chemist

## Anthology

<u>The Peaceful Valley Wounded Soldiers Anthology</u>

## Secrets Series
<u>Discovering Elena: My Mother's Secret</u>